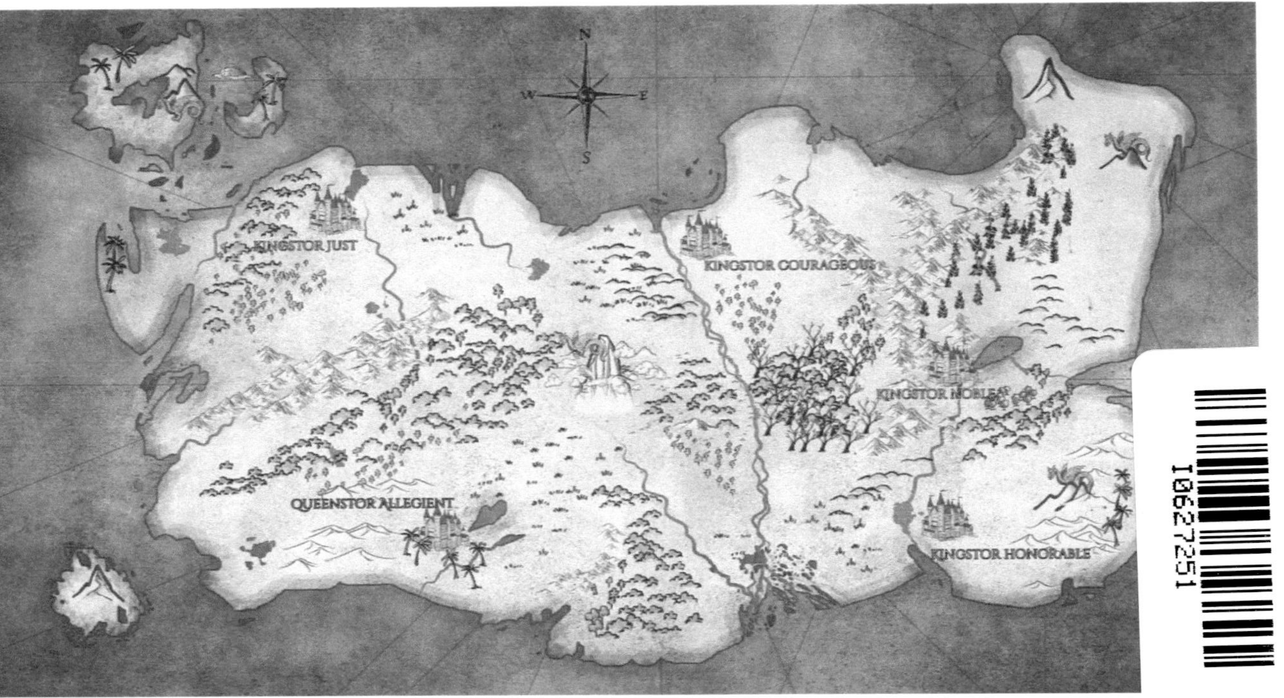
N
W
E
S
KINGSTOR JUST
KINGSTOR COURAGEOUS
KINGSTOR NOBLE
QUEENSTOR ALLEGIENT
KINGSTOR HONORABLE
I0627251

THE CHAMPION OF JUSTICE

<u>Dragons of Avonoa Series</u>
The Gatekeeper of Death (Book One)
The Champion of Justice (Book Two)

Also by author HRB Collotzi:

<u>Avonoa Series</u>
The Secret of Avonoa (Book One)
The Shadow of Avonoa (Book Two)
The Heart of Avonoa (Book Three)
The Traitor of Avonoa (Book Four)
The Krusible of Avonoa (Book Five)

<u>The People of the Storm Series</u>
People of the Storm
People of the Storm 2

THE CHAMPION OF JUSTICE

HRB COLLOTZI

DRAGONS OF AVONOA SERIES BOOK TWO

ISBN: 978-1-962628-15-0
Library of Congress Control Number: 2025903802
Published by HRB Collotzi
Rosemount, Minnesota

www.avonoa.com
www.hrbcollotzi.com

For Jason,

who has always made my dreams come true!

For my kids,

Josh, Ashley and Ryan,

For helping me with brainstorming, beta-reading,

and supporting me every step of the way!

CONTENTS

1

LACKS

A sloppy rhythmic thrum echoed against the compacted mud as the two brown centaurs' hooves beat down the road. Ahead, faint lights blinked from a small town or settlement in the distance, but that wasn't their destination. In fact, any encounter with civilization meant more danger for all parties involved.

"*Why* can't we go home again?" Tyla galloped down the road feeling the shocking reverberations up all four legs with every hoof-fall. With each step her ankles slipped a little more as her muscles threatened to give out completely. She stared into the trees around them with her oversized eyes but struggled to penetrate the dark.

Her twin sister, Eleka, galloped alongside with brown hair and mane flapping like sodden cloth in the rain. "You know why," she said. "If we go to the Centaur Plains, someone might recognize us."

"Yeah," Tyla said, wiping drips of rain mingled with sweat from her forehead. "Centaurs might discover us. But the centaurs aren't the ones chasing us to arrest us."

"Not yet," Eleka said. "But it feels like everyone else is."

"What if we made it home?" Tyla tried again. "Mother would protect us from the goblins, wouldn't she?"

"You must be tired," Eleka said, "because you're not speaking sense. When she finds out what we did—and she probably already knows by now—she'll turn us over to the goblins to rot in the dungeons, and you know it."

Tyla grunted. "Yeah, father would too. But we can't stay out here in the open either."

"I know," Eleka panted next to her. "It would be nice to have some city walls or something to help protect us. But we shouldn't risk it. Remember what happened to Shampy? Emma's parents? Those monsters are going to follow us wherever we go. We can't lead them to someone else's home."

Tyla pulled up short, her legs cramping from the run, but she punched her fists on her hips and used her broad eyes to continue her search into the darkened landscape of thinning trees. The oversized eyes of a centaur would normally be used to distinguish nighttime stars' colors and shapes, but since the skies shrouded with the heavy blanket of the fall-season clouds, the centaur used them now to check for danger.

"What's wrong?" Eleka said, stopping next to her. "Did you see something?"

Tyla shook her head slowly. "Even my eyes can't see anything in this dark. You?"

Eleka narrowed her large eyes at the trees as if attempting to pry out their secrets. "Your eyes have always been better than mine, everyone knows that. You can see the subtlest shift of color in a single star. If you can't see something in the dark, no one can. So why did you stop?"

"I thought I heard something," Tyla said, twitching her pointed ear slightly, attempting to cover her leg pain by holding very still and staring around them. While the trees to the south and east faded from view up into the smaller hills, wide open plains stretched before them to the north and west. The twinkling lights in the distance might indicate a town or city, or they might only be sparkles of rain on the landscape. Straining to make out which they were, her eyes wavered dangerously close to shutting down. The only way they would find out is if they got closer.

"It can't be another one already," Eleka said, drawing closer to Tyla's side. "I could've sworn we left the last one far behind."

"Apparently un-dying monsters move faster than we thought. Or maybe we didn't leave that one far enough behind," Tyla said, taking the weight off one leg to rest it while Eleka looked away.

Tyla felt her sister bump against her side and tap her on the shoulder. "Over here," she said before trotting to the side of the road.

"Where are you going?" Tyla tried to keep the whine out of her voice. Her legs convulsed slightly and threatened not to budge.

"To rest," Eleka said, wading into the grasses on the north side of the road. "We've been running for hours."

"Has it been hours?" Tyla kept her sister in sight but swept the dark and trees and rain with her eyes as well. "It feels more like days."

"It's only been one day," Eleka said, peeking over the tall grass before each step.

At least she's being somewhat cautious, Tyla thought, *for once.*

"One day?" Tyla turned her ankle to shift her weight and rest another leg. "One day since leaving Kirlik?"

"Since *escaping* Kirlik," Eleka clarified. "Yes."

"Wasn't it a whole day after we left Kirlik when those three faerie wraiths surrounded us?" Tyla asked, pointing a thumb over her shoulder as if they were still right behind her.

Eleka shook her head again. "No, that was yesterday, in the middle of the day."

"But we were trying to sleep."

"Yeah, because we'd spent the entire night before running from the two dragons that followed us through the portal *from* Kirlik."

Tyla sighed and closed her eyes. Her forehead relaxed and her eyes closed before she forced them open and blinked against the pattering rain.

"Come on," Eleka waved her over from the grass. "We can't stop in the middle of the road, no matter how much you need a break."

Tyla shrugged. With difficulty, she tilted her hip to turn her hoof from its resting pose, hoping Eleka didn't see the awkward move.

The two centaurs waded through the grass and into the thick bushes to get further away from the beaten road. "We shouldn't stop at all," Tyla said, but she eyed the soft grasses of thick hytocomp through the prickly brambles that snagged on the dragon wrappings around their chests. She pled in her mind for Eleka to lay down first as her own legs began to tremble.

Eleka stepped forward. "I'm tired too," she finally said. Curling up her forelegs, she eased herself onto the hytocomp. "Ahhhh," she sighed in a sing-song voice. "They're soft and squishy." She stretched her arms and rolled onto her lower half's back, kicking her hooves in the air.

"You're always tired," Tyla said critically as she curled up her legs and sat down gingerly on the grass too, making much less display of it than her sister. One of them had to be tough.

"You get tired," Eleka said defensively, righting herself again. "You just won't admit it."

"I told you," Tyla looked back toward the road. "I thought I heard something."

"You did not."

"I did too."

"Did not!"

"Did too!"

"Did n—"

Suddenly a loud ROAR echoed through the mountain pass they had just stumbled through. The twins clamped their mouths and whipped their ears toward the noise. The roar was still some distance away, but they knew better than to make themselves known, at any distance.

"Did!" they agreed in a whisper at the same time.

Eleka guided them to a small copse with tall grasses and a few trees surrounding it. The elevated position offered a decent view of the dark road through the grass, with the city or village lights in the distance and the mountains behind them. To one side, basically directly north of them, their enhanced eyesight showed a blurry view of an open stretch of tumbling low hills and mounds, although a human's view of it would only be a smudge of different shades of gray.

"You don't think we've stumbled onto the Centaur Plains, do you?" Tyla breathed, eyeing the expanse. "Those portals could have spit us out anywhere."

Eleka tilted her head, gazing into the rain. "I know we were all trying to avoid monsters and goblin guards and everything, but I think I found a portal to bring us to the far west side of Avonoa."

Tyla lifted an eyebrow at her sister. "You mean you had time in all that chaos to stop and read the portal banners for direction? In a massive cavern of portals with everyone around us screaming and fighting—and dying?"

"Well, you protected me," Eleka lifted and dropped one shoulder, "like you always do. Thanks to you I had more time than anyone else to estimate which portal would get us to the farthest point away from the actual goblin city."

"Happy to help," Tyla grumbled, rolling her big eyes. "So where do you think we are?"

"I think we're much farther west than the Centaur Plains. Those lights," she waved a hand at the twinkling in the distance, "might be some centaurs on the far west reaches of the plains, but they're more likely coming from a human village. I feel like we're much closer to the Just Kingdom and I can't imagine centaurs would be so far west."

"How can you tell we're so far west?"

Eleka shrugged nonchalantly. "I feel the sea not far to the west and north."

Tyla shook her head at her sister. "You and your sense of direction."

"I have a great sense of direction," Eleka mumbled assuredly to herself, shifting slightly on the grass.

"Exactly," Tyla said, "you can tell how many claw-lengths we are from a stone with the stars out. But what do we do about it?"

Eleka scrunched her face. "Rest for now, then decide how we should keep looking for the keys."

Tyla scoffed. "You mean the dead gatekeeper's keys?"

"Yes."

"The god-touched keys that control the barrier to the World of Souls?"

"Yes."

"The keys that, after the gatekeeper died—"

"—was killed—"

"—was killed, Trivnor blindly scattered across Avonoa to keep the supposedly evil Kelraz from using?"

"Yes."

"The keys that Trivnor made us give our wyrd not to tell anyone about then begged our help to find them?"

"Yes."

"Oh, those keys… Well, I still don't know if we can trust him. Why should we help him with his key problem?"

"For good reason," Eleka huffed, "and you know it."

"We've discussed this," Tyla said pointedly, turning her full body around to glare at her sister. "We've never met this Kelraz guy. Trivnor said that Kelraz killed the gatekeeper to get the keys and the power for himself and Trivnor is trying to keep the keys from him because Kelraz is evil. But how do we know that Kelraz is the evil one and not Trivnor? How do we know we can trust anything he says? He's a faerie!"

"Jassan's a faerie too." Eleka snapped her eyes to Tyla's and waited for a reaction.

"Yeah, but at least he saved us from the dungeons," Tyla mumbled. "You know I don't like faeries—"

"—you didn't like Jassan either, at first."

"—but he proved himself. And Trivnor lied to us."

"About what?"

"About being part dragon," Tyla snapped. "Faerie dragons shouldn't be possible."

Another distinct roar in the distance broke the quiet around them and the twins fell into silence as both of them seethed. Finally, Eleka whispered, "That's the only thing we know that he's lied to us about and I think I know why."

"Oh, really?" Tyla crossed her arms. "Enlighten me."

"I think the Lost Ruck has spells around it," Eleka said.

"The place that Trivnor and Kelraz are from?" Tyla asked.

Eleka jerked her head in a nod as her train of thought took form. "I think there are spells and possibly oaths and stuff that force the Lost Ruck to maintain the secret of its existence and their origin when they leave it. Think about it. When we all showed up at Shampy's, Trivnor told her that he was from the Lost Ruck. She said he risked a lot telling her that, and he said he had risked everything. I think she's from the Lost Ruck too and maybe she got kicked out or chose to live apart or something like that, so she knows what it means to tell someone about the secret."

Tyla blinked at her sister. Realizing that her mouth had popped open, she clapped it shut before grumbling. "I don't think anyone but you can follow that way of thinking."

Eleka sighed. "Anyway, I think he had good reason not to tell us about it. But he was honest about everything else. He tried to get us all home. He did his best to keep us alive and safe. And he let Jassan keep the key."

"Oh, yeah," Tyla said with a grin. "Jassan, the beetle faerie."

Eleka lightly smacked Tyla's arm. "Be nice," she said. "That faerie changing into a beetle with his key, among other things, saved you from the dungeons."

"No," Tyla shook her head, "that faerie saved Trivnor from the dungeon next to ours and Trivnor came back to transport us out with his key."

"Exactly."

Tyla narrowed her eyes at her sister until the emphasis struck her. "Oh. I guess Trivnor did save us."

"And I think we need to trust him and keep hunting for the keys like we promised."

"Alright, alright," Tyla said, rolling into the hytocomp and grasses. "I'll try a little harder to trust him. But if he—ow!"

"What is it?" Eleka asked, her eyes popping open as she lifted her head.

Pulling a hunk of metal from the muck underneath her, Tyla ground her teeth. Using the falling rain to clear away mud, she revealed a torn leather handle, a dented silver pommel and the jagged edge of a broken sword. "Looks like the remnants of a battle," she said, inspecting the metal in her hand.

"Is the blade even sharp?" Eleka asked.

Tyla ran a thumb over the edge of the stunted blade. "No," she said, "but it feels good to have a weapon in my hand again after losing my daggers. No matter how ugly it is."

"You're part dragon," Eleka sneered at her. "Why do you always need a weapon?"

"I don't need anything extra as a dragon," Tyla said, flexing her fingers around the solid handle. "But as a centaur our fingers feel useless without something powerful in them."

"Yeah," Eleka agreed, "but you can't use a broken sword to fight off those things that are following us."

"The wraiths?" Tyla asked. "No, but I can use it against goblins who might want to arrest us for stealing a gem from their palace."

"Wraiths can't die," Eleka pointed at the broken sword, "unless that thing has one of those majikal edges. And without some kind of majik I have a feeling it won't be much use against vengeful goblins either. Their obrucks are too powerful."

"Something is better than nothing," Tyla said, sliding the blunted sword under her dragon wrappings at her back. "I really wish we had never agreed to that summons," she muttered.

"The summons had nothing to do with it," Eleka mumbled back. "You know that."

"I guess," Tyla rubbed her shoulders trying to keep the chill out. "Not doing the summons wouldn't have changed what happened with Trivnor and Kelraz and the keys, only that we wouldn't be involved. We'd be back home with our parents, sleeping in our own beds and helping protect the centaurs too."

"Yeah," Eleka turned her head away, "but that would leave Trivnor on his own to fight Kelraz and find all seven keys in the two weeks before the end of fall, and somehow I just don't think he could do it."

"What are you saying?"

Eleka slowly turned to face Tyla again. "I'm saying, I don't think Trivnor would win without us. I think we were meant to be in that clearing, in that moment, in order to help Trivnor. I think we were meant to help save the world."

"Yeah, well, you think too much," Tyla grumbled. "Let's just try to rest while we can."

Tyla mulled her sister's words after Eleka laid her head on the spongy ground cover and closed her eyes. Eleka lay quietly for a moment while Tyla debated what she'd said. Her heart ached as she remembered her mother dabbing at Tyla's injuries from some sparring match or another and whispering, "This is hard, I know, but you're being prepared for great things and this is part of it."

"Tyla," her sister's voice whispered into the drizzle, disturbing her reverie. "I can't sleep."

"I thought you said you were tired."

"I am," Eleka wrapped her arms around herself, "but I can't sleep."

"You mean you can't relax."

"Can you?"

Instead of answering, Tyla sighed. After another moment of silence while she thought hard, she answered. "What starts with T, ends with T and has tea in it?"

Riddles. Focusing her overactive brain at this moment was the best way Tyla knew to calm her twin and riddles always did the trick. Dragons loved riddles and Eleka more than most. Working her muscles helped Tyla calm her own thoughts and riddles sparked her mind to keep her awake, but exercising her brain was the most soothing thing for her twin.

"Teapot. Too easy."

"But I'd kill for a sip right now."

Eleka snorted and lay with her eyes closed. "Only one color but not one size. Stuck at the bottom, yet easily flies. Present in sun, but not in rain. Doing no harm and feeling no pain."

"That one would be difficult if I wasn't jumping at them," Tyla grinned. "A shadow."

"Fine, you do better then."

"Alright." Tyla thought for moment before she gave her sister a long one. "It can't be seen, can't be felt, can't be heard and can't be smelt. It lies behind stars and under hills. And empty holes it fills. It comes first and follows after, ends life and kills laughter."

"The dark," Eleka said slowly as her voice softened and her breathing evened out. "But let's try to keep things a little more cheery," she mumbled.

"Fine by me," Tyla said, remembering to focus her eyes on the dark around them. "I'm not the one who brought up shadows."

Eleka responded with silence and Tyla thought she might truly be falling asleep. The riddles would have provided the best calming either of them had experienced since they'd been on the run. Finally, Eleka whispered next to her.

"What is it that given one, you'll have either two or none?"

Tyla thought. Scrunching her brows together, she stared into the dark without seeing anything. A plant of some sort that can be propagated? No, you would still have at least one. A feeling? Sorrow? Fear? No, not cheery enough for Eleka right now. Something elemental? Water?

Fire? If given a flame it could light and have two, or not light and have none?

"Fire?" Tyla tried. "Or a drop of water?"

Eleka breathed a light chuckle. "A choice."

Tyla grunted. Of course. Ok, she'll give her sister a hard one too. She remembered a riddle her father had given her a few weeks ago while they were out on a hunting trip together. Although the males, or dans, usually didn't hunt—it was commonly left to the female dragons, or dames—her father was unusually canny when it came to hunting. As they had flown together, it having been a long night, they'd played riddles to keep Tyla alert. Their father was one of the smartest dragons they knew so challenging Tyla was easy for him.

"What can go up and come down without moving?"

"Hmm," Eleka muttered into the sound of the rain.

Tyla waited. Had she actually stumped her smarter sister? She turned to Eleka with a smile but saw her sister's chest rise and fall with long, slow even breaths. Her twin's eyelids twitched and the muscles of her jaw relaxed.

"The temperature," she murmured to her sister's sleeping form, reaching over and pulling up the short cloak Eleka always wore around her shoulders to cover them from the rain. She couldn't imagine how she had held onto it with all the running and fighting. "I'll keep first watch."

2

BRILLIANCE

After a moment longer, making sure her sister was fast asleep, Tyla pulled out the golden circlet with a sparkling blue gem embedded in it that Eleka kept tucked away under her dragon wrappings. As she listened to her sister's deep breathing slowly rise and fall, she scanned the road and sky briefly before placing the circlet on her head, allowing it to adjust against her crown until it sat snugly around her sodden brown hair.

Hello? she said in her mind, pressing the blue gem against her temple. She still wasn't completely comfortable with the idea of the communication gem and the majik involved, but she also craved company, such as it was, from someone other than her sister.

Hello? came the response.

Dasha? Tyla asked, *is that you?*

In the scales! Dasha exclaimed. *Where've you been?*

Tyla held back a snort and focused on pushing the thoughts of her words to Dasha. *Where do you think? Same as yesterday, running from the wraiths. Scrounging for food. Sleeping when we can. We ended up a long way from the goblin city, I hope. I think we're near centaurs now, but Eleka thinks we're headed toward a human village.*

Where? Dasha asked a little cautiously.

Not sure, Tyla answered honestly. *Eleka says we're near the Just Kingdom and you know how exact her directions usually are. We've been seeing a lot of hoof marks and boot prints, so some kind of civilization, anyway.*

Don't think you're safe, Dasha advised. *Remember, Trivnor warned us to stay away from any settlements or villages.*

I know, I know, Tyla said, rubbing her shoulders and arms to push away the cold rain. *But Trivnor can go wherever he wants whenever he wants. For all we know he's sleeping somewhere in a warm bed with a full belly.*

You know that's not true, Dasha said. *Of all of us, if he uses that key, Kelraz will find him immediately and kill him.*

And he has enough wraiths under his control to hunt us all down. Tyla answered. *Ok, I didn't want to ask Eleka. I know there are seven keys, but what do they all do? I can't remember what we're supposed to be looking for.*

We've been trying to remember too, Dasha admitted. *Let's see, Jassan has the Moon Key that lets him change. Trivnor has the Cloud Key that lets him transport. Kelraz, unfortunately, has the Sky Key that lets him corrupt and control souls, turning them into wraiths.*

And the Wind Key is the one that was destroyed, Tyla thought to her.

Right, but we got that gem—

Carefully and with great skill—

Too true, Dasha shot back. *That only leaves three keys, thank Shurka.*

Counting on her fingers as Dasha listed them, Tyla thought quickly of the seven high gods and what their powers might be. *That leaves the Star Key… the Sun Key… and the Air Key. I wonder what they do?*

I'm sure Eleka has it all figured out. Tyla could hear the chiding in Dasha's tone. *Why don't you ask her?*

She's asleep. Tyla tried not to sound perturbed in her mind at the suggestion of Eleka's superior knowledge. *I have first watch tonight. Besides, we can figure this out. My uncle Rylan teaches us about the high gods and how they influence all majik. Let's think, what do the stars do?*

They don't do much, Dasha replied. *They move very slowly across the sky at night and then disappear in the day.*

That's it! Tyla exclaimed. *They disappear. I bet the Star Key can make the person that has it invisible. That's going to be a difficult one to find.*

Ok, let's try to save that one for last, shall we? Dasha said. *How about the others? I bet the Air Key is used for flight. It can probably make things move.*

Most likely, Tyla agreed. *And then the Sun Key. I bet that key can do lots of things. Uncle Rylan says that the goddess of the sun, Shurka, is the most powerful of the gods. Because she reflects the glory of the sun is why dragons love her so much.*

The sun is powerful, yes, Dasha said, *and that power can be used to heal and comfort. Those reasons are why the goblins need to come out from our underground cities. We need the sun again. Without it for thousands of years, we've become grey-skinned. Many of us believe that the sun will change us like it has been changing the dragons.*

But the sun can kill too, Tyla pointed out, reaching behind her back to touch the broken sword like she would her daggers, if she had them. *I bet whoever has the Sun Key is extra powerful. Maybe more powerful than any of those who hold the others. I wouldn't want to go up against anyone with that key. Maybe I'll try to find the Air Key.*

Yeah, Dasha responded with a chuckle. *Look for some human floating around looking confused.*

You'll be the first to know if I spot one. Tyla allowed the corners of her mouth to turn up for the first time in what felt like too long. *I guess it's a good thing you stole these obrucks for us after all.* Absentmindedly, she tapped the circlet on her head.

I knew they would come in handy, Dasha said, her voice lifting in excitement. *Aren't they amazing!*

Ok admit it, you stole them just for the fun of it. Tyla said. *You've always wanted one of these stupid things. Don't deny it.*

I won't, Dasha said, *because they're dead useful like I knew they would be!*

Sure, Tyla agreed before the smile left her face. *Let's just hope they don't make us dead.*

Dasha didn't respond to that, so Tyla took the opportunity to change the subject. *Have you heard from Jassan?*

No, she finally answered. *Nothing from him or the others since…since we all split up.*

Tyla's stomach twisted. *He'd better be ok,* she shot back, *or I'll kill him.*

I bet Emma thinks the same thing, Dasha said. *I think we all do.*

Weird, huh? Tyla squirmed at her own thought as she voiced it in her head to Dasha. *A week ago we were complaining that he was following us around like a pest. We would have given anything to* NOT *know where he was. But now...*

The words in her mind faded away. 'Useless,' she had called him, then he saved her from the dungeons. 'Stupid', then he used the key to quickly change into the most amazing things his mind could imagine. Her eyes brimmed with tears and an obnoxious lump formed in her throat.

She swallowed hard while asking, *What about Trivnor?* Glad she didn't have to use her shaky voice, *Anything from him?*

No, Dasha said.

He gave me the last circlet before he flew through that portal, Tyla reminded her. *I don't think we'll hear from him for a good long while.*

But he has the gem, right? Without waiting for a response she added, *Hopefully he can recreate the Wind Key and we can talk to him again. The wind whispers, right?*

If the goblins don't find him and kill him for stealing it first, yeah, Tyla pointed out. *Do you know what majik will change the gem into a key?* Tyla asked, looking for another reason to keep talking to her friend.

No idea, Dasha answered, her thoughts slowing. *But if Trivnor can complete the majik first, he'll have two keys and leave Kelraz empty handed, right?*

But if the keys draw each other with every use...?

Yes, Dasha sounded resigned, *creating a key will probably pull all the others toward it... powerfully.*

Trivnor and anyone with him will be sitting dutguins while he creates it. Tyla's head snapped up as a screech echoed in the distance. *He'll need protection.*

And from as many of us as possible, but we have no idea where he ended up, Dasha said. *If we find and activate the other keys, or get whoever has them to use them, maybe Kelraz will at least be distracted from Trivnor.*

But would it be enough? Tyla asked, not exactly disagreeing. *I doubt anything we do will put him off for long.*

So what, you, of all of us, aren't going to do whatever it takes to fight back? Dasha thought to Tyla with evident derision.

I didn't say that, Tyla snapped back in her mind. *I just don't know how to do it.* She turned her head to see Eleka's breath still moving deeply and evenly. *Eleka will know what to do.* Her thoughts were still for a moment before she asked Dasha, *So, where are you now, anyway?*

Sandarin, Dasha mumbled. *We got chased into the desert by a wraith. One of the local water farmers took us in. We're sleeping in the barn, but at least we're out of the rain.*

That sounds nice. Tyla glared into the dripping sky above her. *It's been pouring on us all day and night. I don't think it's going to let up any time soon.*

That's good, actually, Dasha said. *When it stops raining fall will be over and the barrier between the World of Souls and us will be gone. For good… we lose.*

Do we really have a chance to win? Tyla finally expressed the thought that had been plaguing her for days. *I know I'm usually the fighter, but shouldn't we all just go home and help fight the wraiths from there? Shouldn't we be protecting our families instead of out here following some mad faerie? Are you certain we're doing the right thing by helping Trivnor? Believing every word he's ever told us?*

Doing everything he tells us to do? As badly as you ever wanted an obruck for yourself, he convinced you to steal these things and get kicked out of the army for doing it.

Yes, Dasha insisted without hesitation. *I know you don't trust him, Tyla, but I do. I never would have stolen anything from the goblins if I didn't believe him. Plus, Trivnor's held to his wyrd. He's protected us as best he could. He's doing everything he can to keep us all safe. As long as we're out here, we have to trust him.*

We've never even spoken to this Kelraz character, Tyla resisted. She remembered her father's words to try to find a peaceful solution to any problem but found it extremely difficult in this moment. Eleka was better at peaceful solutions, but Tyla felt like she had to try the argument now. *We have no idea if we might hear a completely different story from him.*

Dasha was silent. Finally, she whispered, *I trust Trivnor. And I think you should too.*

Tyla woke to a screech in the darkness. The rain had paused for an abnormal length of time and she accidentally fell asleep after talking with Dasha. Snatching the obruck off her head, she sat up. Tyla hoped the sisters' brown torsos and lower bodies still glistening with rain would help them stay camouflaged. Eleka's head also popped up at the new noise.

Thunder rumbled in the distance. A roar and a screech echoed up the pass they had come through. The two centaurs held very still.

Eleka pulled the obruck from Tyla's hand and tucked it under her own wrappings. Tyla only partially noticed the movement as she searched their surroundings. Eleka shifted her short cloak tighter around her shoulders. "I don't like this," she whispered, staring back the way they had come.

"You've said that already. A lot," Tyla said. "What are we supposed to do differently?"

Tyla meant the question as a snide comment, but Eleka answered. "Maybe we should go to that settlement."

"Sure," Tyla snipped, "now that it's your idea, it's a good one?"

Eleka searched around them. "We've obviously landed in the west somewhere on the outskirts of the Centaur Plains," she said softly, more to herself. "Maybe they haven't heard of us or don't know our parents."

"Two daughters of the leader of the warrior centaurs and nieces to the centaur leader," Tyla snorted. "Sure, no one will have heard of us."

Eleka shook her head. "You seem to think that we're royalty or something."

"Close to," Tyla shrugged. A crackle of lightning spilled over the sky, revealing an indistinct shape moving among the trees in the mountains. "I say we stay here," Tyla said, with a sudden desire not to move.

"We're not even sure where *here* is," Eleka mumbled.

Another roar echoed through the pass. She could tell it was getting closer. Lightning popped in little spurts.

"It's better than running head-first into the unknown," Tyla said. "What if someone recognizes us?"

"Really?" Eleka said. "First I say we should stay away from other centaurs and you want to go home to the centaurs. Then I agree and say we should go to a centaur settlement and you say we should stay alone here out in the open? What, you want us to stay here and be the greeting party for that thing?"

"It might just be another dragon," Tyla said.

Another roar sounded that chilled her spine. Even closer.

"If it's just another dragon, then why are they roaring?" Eleka whispered.

"Maybe they saw a wraith too?"

"Then we should either help them or run away. Either way is a huge risk, so which one do you want to take?"

Silence.

The rain pattering around them suddenly poured in an unexpected downburst.

"If we stay low," Tyla said over the noise of the rain, "it'll pass right by us, right?"

"They do seem to attack whoever is closest or within eyesight," Eleka tilted her head in thought. "Jassan and Trivnor led them out as long as the goblins stayed hidden inside their homes. But if Kelraz is in control, all bets are off."

"If Kelraz is in control of this one, we can't predict anything." Bumps having nothing to do with the cold or rain spread over Tyla's arms as she agreed.

"We can't wait here to be attacked," Eleka said. "We have to find some real shelter."

"We won't be attacked if we're not seen," Tyla whispered. "Stay down in the bushes."

"In the rain?"

"It stopped raining." Tyla held out her hand to prove her point, but Eleka was looking toward the road. Tyla followed her eyes. Rain splashed in great puddles on the beaten path. But only the last drops of rain fell from the tips of her ears.

Her breath quickened. Her heart suddenly beat against her ribs. Her fists curled and she began to change into her dark red dragon form before she even looked up.

3

OF MIND

The hulking dragon wraith clung to the branches of the few thin trees above them. In the back of her head Tyla marveled that such a large creature had snuck up on them and now hung silently overhead. Smoky shadow poured from it in waves but blended with the torrents of rain then dissipated when it hit the ground. Scales and hide shriveled tightly against the skeletal body, bringing its claws and double-tails to deadly points. Even some of the human wraiths, normally pretty harmless to dragons in life, could do damage with those sharpened hands. It pulled cracked and indistinct lips back from long, dagger-like fangs in a low snarl as it inched toward them from the tree. Sunken, unblinking black depressions for eyes dissected the twins' every moment. The wraith's bifurcated tail from its past life swung slowly, indicating the creature's readiness to pounce.

Tyla wasn't proud of herself, but she cried aloud together with Eleka as they dashed from the grass. She waited to change completely until they were back on the road, and counted herself fortunate when she saw the wraith's claw scratching at the air where her hind end had been.

Once on the road Tyla fully changed into her dragon form, but she still felt small compared to the colossal black dragon wraith. The dripping shadow billowed from its dragon wings as it launched itself through the air toward them. Lightning writhed across the sky to light the monster's curve of broken wings from behind. The heavy, smoke-like substance rippled in waves behind the wraith as it hurled itself toward the girls. Nightmarish as they were, wraiths were already dead so nothing could hurt them, not fire nor claws. The living retained almost nothing with which to defeat them.

As the wraith flew toward them, Tyla jumped between it and her sister, pushing her twin down the road behind her.

"Go! Go!" she screamed over her shoulder.

With the wraith coming at her, Tyla dodged its first slash of the claws and landed her own across its face. Had the wraith been alive, she might have taken out an eye, but her claws only tore at brittle flesh and the creature simply flinched before turning and advancing again.

Eleka ran down the road behind her, giving Tyla some space. As the wraith advanced, she dodged both swings of the claws and spun to kick it then slap it across the face, with her tail this time. No one had weapons against these types of creatures, and Tyla remembered all too well the black speckled wounds the monsters left on the living. If she had to guess, such wounds would eventually fester, spread and take the victim's life, turning them into a wraith as well. So she stuck with the evade-strong strategy that usually served her.

Again the creature paused, as if confused about what was slowing it.

"Can we pin it down with something until we can get away?" Eleka called while Tyla evaded more strikes. "That worked with the others!"

"No big rocks… or trees," Tyla grunted between gulps of air. "Left those…in the mountains. This one…too big." Having fought many wraiths in the last few days, Tyla knew when to fight and when to run. Every time she hit and confused it, she gained a few steps down the road.

"Tyla," Eleka hollered again. "I see lights!"

"I know," Tyla called back after another sidestep, "head for the village!"

Even as she concentrated on the wraith closing in, Tyla noted that her sister remained in centaur form. Centaurs were superior runners; not even a dragon could outpace a centaur in peak form, but the wraith was already too close to risk trying to change and escape from it on hoof.

"No," Eleka said, "I think they're coming to us!"

Tyla shook her head thinking her sister must be imagining things in her exhaustion-induced haze. "Go!" she yelled, "I'll hold it off!"

Eleka's hooves pounded and splashed ahead on the muddy road. Tyla dodged the wraith again, this time returning a sweep of her tail at the beast's legs, followed by a back claw across the snout. Any living being would have been thrown. The wraith simply stumbled, shook its head and continued toward her.

In the wraith's hesitation, Tyla took a moment to check on her sister's progress. They had fought and fled the monsters together time after time in this way since leaving the goblin city of Kirlik. One of them would impede and distract the beasts in dragon form, the other would hide in centaur form. Then the first—usually Tyla—would fly away, lose the beast in flight or pin it with something and return to the other twin.

Tyla hoped Eleka had had enough time to get away because she didn't have the strength to continue this fight much longer. She felt her muscles weaken with every monster they fought. And they had fought or been forced to escape many. Now, her knees shook and her counters came slower. Too slow.

In a moment of reprieve, she turned as four torches appeared in the darkness. So surprised by them, she turned back to the wraith barely in time to fall to the side before it clawed at her.

On her side in the mud, Tyla threw her back legs against the wraith's chest. She heaved, the same as she had so many times before—a trick she learned from her mother to throw an attacker off her—but she was so weak that she barely pushed the wraith a claw length away.

The wraith lifted a claw over her. Tyla's breath came in ragged gasps. She didn't have any more strength to fight back. She consoled herself with the thought that Eleka would escape and prayed to Shurka that her own newly formed wraith wouldn't hurt her sister.

Suddenly an immense dark shape slammed into the dragon wraith from above Tyla, throwing the creature a good dragon's length away from her. Tyla lifted her head as a brilliant blue dragon landed on her hind legs between Tyla and the wraith. She noticed that the dragon's distinct wing joints ended in claws and no other front claws were evident.

"Go!" the dragon yelled at her over her shoulder. "Run!"

Tyla crawled away and changed into her centaur form once she gained her feet. Her knees shook with every step, but she watched as the torches bounced closer.

She couldn't move as four centaurs hurtled down the road past her, each carrying a torch in one hand, crossbows in the other and ropes strung across their backs and over their shoulders.

The last centaur stopped next to Tyla. "Get to your friend," he jerked his head down the road to where Eleka had disappeared. "We'll take care of this."

He galloped past her, but Tyla froze in place. Unsure whether it was from fear, exhaustion or shock, she couldn't turn away.

The blue dragon fought off the wraith with the same techniques Tyla had been using. She baited it toward her, dodged and countered, but she wasn't trying for killing blows. The dragon knew the wraith wasn't going to die, neither did she expect it to be hurt. She waited for it to recover then struck again. If it got distracted by anything else around it, she would strike at it to goad it toward her again.

While the dragon danced around the wraith, the four centaurs surrounded it. The flames of the torches they had dropped in the mud continued to burn upwards against the falling rain, which could only mean that they burned with dragon fire. The rain continued steadily as the centaurs tied the ropes to their crossbow bolts.

When all the centaurs signaled to the blue dragon that they were ready, she leapt into the air. Grabbing the wraith's head with her back legs, she pumped her wings. While she pulled and yelled, the centaurs lifted and fired their weapons.

Two crossbow bolts landed in the wraith's neck. One landed in its shoulder. The final bolt sliced through the wraith's wing membranes. It nicked the blue dragon's leg and flew toward the centaurs on the other side of her.

The dragon briefly hissed at the centaur, who paid no attention. The centaurs gathered their ropes and with a deafening CRACK, whipped the ends. The ropes crackled with majikal energy, sending the bolts deeper into the wraith.

The wraith screamed and roared, thrashing its head, but it availed the beast nothing. The two bolts in the wraith's neck shot through the monster to the other side. The centaur who hit the beast in the shoulder cracked his rope a few more times and forced it through and out the opposite side near the beast's wing joint.

All four centaurs rushed the monster at once, but they didn't attack. They surged forward and grabbed the crossbow bolt nearest them from the shooter on the opposite side. The centaur retrieved the one that had gone through the wing as well. When all the centaurs gained control of a bolt and the end of a rope at each corner surrounding the wraith, the blue dragon roared. The centaurs pulled the ropes tight. The dragon slammed the wraith to the ground at the same time. Although its legs kicked and flailed, the centaurs controlled the monster from its sides. Wraith shadow spilled across the wet ground as the group cheered and the blue dragon roared in triumph.

"Weren't you told to run?" the blue dragon crawled toward Tyla while the centaurs behind her used their majikal ropes to tie the wraith's legs together. After pinning the creature to the ground, they swept around it, twisting the ropes around its legs and claws.

"I…" Tyla's mouth hung open. Her head felt stuffed with cloth. She gazed in awe as the centaurs bound the wraith's legs and feet together in a matter of seconds. "How did you…?"

"Tyla," Eleka hastened up to her, "what happened? How did you do that?"

Eleka pointed to the dragon wraith bound so tightly it could only twitch on the muddy road.

"Lots of practice," the blue dragon said. "Come on," she pointed a claw down the road. "Let's get you two dry."

Tyla and Eleka followed the blue dragon down the road with the centaurs dragging the grumbling wraith behind them.

"What are you going to do with it?" Eleka asked. "You can't kill it."

Tyla tilted her head at her sister and thought, *Oh, sure, just tell them everything. That will make us sound innocent and not at all involved, right?* She hoped the scathing accusation could be felt without saying it aloud. Eleka bit her lip as if she'd heard it, so Tyla wiped her face of expression in hopes the blue dragon didn't notice the information slip.

"We lock them up," the dragon said matter-of-factly, pointing ahead until Tyla finally saw their destination.

Tall walls loomed in front of them at least three dragon lengths high. The caps of the walls appeared indistinct in the darkness, but on closer inspection Tyla saw bundles of thorns and sticks topping them. Even under the rainy night sky, her sharp centaur sight picked out indistinct centaur profiles walking around the capstone edges.

A timber door spanning three dragons tall and enforced with thick black metal studs and fixtures creaked open, allowing the strange procession inside. It was easily the middle of the night, possibly early morning, so the only movement within the settlement came from guards patrolling. They all stood with staffs, swords and bows at the ready but only aimed at the monster.

"Where will you put it?" Eleka asked.

The dragon pointed in one direction within the settlement. "With the others."

Eleka's eyes brightened with curiosity. "Others?" she asked. "I don't see any place you could restrain these monsters. How many do you have? Why are you keeping them? Can you show us?"

The dragon smirked at the questions. "Yes," she said. "We've restrained plenty of them. And yes, you can come if you want, but stay clear of them and don't get in the way."

"That won't be a problem," Tyla muttered and looked at Eleka.

Eleka pulled Tyla along as the other centaurs dragged the captive. Tyla could tell immediately that they had entered a centaur settlement. The homes were substantial mounds of earth with entrances on one side and smaller openings for windows, covered by slats of wood or heavy waterproof cloth against the seasonal rains. Several cookfires outside the homes had been cleared and, she guessed, moved inside as they usually were for fall. Only a few of the mounds showed smoke drifting from hidden vents in the earthen structures.

Most of the largest settlement structures crowded around the perimeter of the settlement inside tall stone walls. Ascending curved ramps made of wood and stone circled the mounds to give the centaurs access to the tops of the thick walls. Tyla assumed that the structures beneath the ramps were used by the guards, similar to the way her mother set up other walled centaur settlements. The thick walls provided passageways inside that acted like tall, narrow buildings. The walls were wide enough to allow centaurs to patrol the tops of them and use the insides for storage of weapons and food, or protection, if necessary.

The centaurs dragged the restrained monster across the settlement to another considerable set of wooden doors stretching halfway up and set well into the thick boundary wall. Two centaur guards swung the doors wide and the other centaurs pushed the monster through them.

The doors led through the wall into what Tyla could only compare to the inside of a vast cage made of hastily constructed stone and wood with mud floors. The open space crowded with support columns and more wraiths of all shapes and sizes. The entire structure protruded outside the back of the settlement wall, so it was essentially hidden from the centaurs who went about their lives inside the walls, but left unprotected from direct outside attack. Overhead, wood rafters protected the occupants from the heaviest rains, but drips and narrow rivulets fell from several beams and some of the walls pooling on the mud floor.

A variety of wraiths already inside the cage were all bound in similar fashion to the one now being dragged through the doors. Bolts shot through the necks of all the dragons and some of the others. At least two ropes looped from the neck bolts through the bodies of the faerie and human wraiths, and then wrapped around their wraith bodies to finish the restraint. But the few centaur wraiths were spared the worst of the invasive bolts and ropes. They only suffered with ropes wrapped around their bodies. All the wraiths' hands and feet were hobbled and most of them lay moaning and wailing on the cold, wet ground.

"What did that one do?" Eleka said, pointing.

Tyla followed her gaze to the center of the open space where a faerie wraith was tied to a vertical support beam with a cloth tied around its head, covering eyes, nose, mouth and ears.

The blue dragon pulled back her lips to bare her fangs momentarily when she saw the wraith Eleka indicated. "That one…spoke."

Tyla's ears twitched as a tingle ran over her skin. She and Eleka shared a glance.

"What did it say?" Eleka asked with wide eyes before Tyla could stop her.

The dragon closed the door to the wraith prison behind them and turned to the twins. "Does it matter?" she said. "None of the others have spoken. They only screech and wail. The fact that this one spoke is… *unnatural.*" She narrowed her eyes at the girls and Tyla dropped hers away.

"As for you two," the dragon said, "you look like you've been running from that one so long you might just fall over at any moment." As she said it, Tyla promptly felt her knees shake again. "Let's get you somewhere soft so you can do that safely."

4

AND SOUL

She dreamt of the portal cavern in Kirlik. Dark shapes swirled past the even darker yawning openings of the portals themselves. A blur of goblins ran screaming around her, creating a rainbow whirlwind with their small grey faces and contrasting vivid-colored hair. Tyla's eyes fell on one of the goblins, her friend Dasha, with her dazzling purple hair bouncing around her head as she ran. Tyla called out to her, but she stopped and turned in front of a murky portal. Behind Dasha, shadowy, skeletal hands reached through the portal and wrenched her into the depths before she could cry out.

In her dream Tyla's eyes fell on each of her friends in turn. Gizi stood in front of a gigantic portal the perfect size for a dragon. Tremendous dragon wraith claws reached through the portal and sucked the orange dragon into it. Emma was pulled through another. Burk disappeared through another. Lokna, gone. Jassan's pale blue skin grew mottled with black splotches before he was pulled, writhing, into another abyss.

Tyla turned. Eleka stood before her in front of a portal. They called for each other and Eleka reached out to her sister before she too was ripped from behind through the dark entrance. Tyla heard her name called and turned toward Trivnor. He stood in front of the portal next to her and when he threw her an obruck, one of the communication circlets, she caught it and looked back up at the faerie.

"Go," he said.

Suddenly a giant dragon wraith tackled him from the side, shoving Trivnor ahead of him through the portal, just the way it had really happened two days ago.

Tyla spun to follow her sister through the portal where she had disappeared, but found only blank stone walls. She searched the other walls feeling her way along the periphery but unforgiving smooth stone slid along her fingertips as all the other portals faded and winked out of existence.

Exhausted and discouraged, she fell against the wall on her lower half's side, but turned her upper body in time to see wraiths in every form barreling toward her from every side. Clutching the small obruck against her chest, she closed her eyes.

Tyla blinked her eyes open at the earthen walls around her. She might have thought she was at home in her own bed had she not woken shaking with the fresh horror in her mind. Her heart skipped a beat before it pounded an erratic rhythm against her ribs. The dreams came harsh and fast, caught between waking spells when she and her sister found time to hide and sleep.

Usually, she dreamt of the portal cavern, but occasionally her sleeping mind turned to the wraith attack at her friend Emma's castle, where one of the guards died and turned into a wraith himself. Occasionally, the dreams replayed the wraith attack at Shampy's forest home. Sometimes she was in the goblin dungeon and watched her friends being attacked by wraiths in the goblin palace while she remained chained and couldn't break out to help them. Her nightmares on this journey, no matter how brief, always included wraiths.

The dream had been so real and distinct that she still felt the hard metal of the communication obruck in her palm.

Tyla's mind snapped fully awake, and her head bounced off the soft cloth bundles tucked beneath her but she struggled to get her hooves under her. Sensing the sun hovering overhead somewhere in the middle of the sky, she couldn't quite place her surroundings, so she stilled her legs to search the area. She patted her red dragon wrappings around her chest. Empty. The broken sword clung to her back, but no circlet. Where was it? She used it to speak to Dasha, she remembered that much. She was sure she had tucked it under her wrappings. But no, she remembered, she hadn't.

Twisting to look around her bedding spot, Tyla's hand fell on her sister lying next to her. With her breathing still deep and even, Eleka might stay asleep a while longer. Her sister's hand tucked into the fuzzy cloth under and near her head. Following her hand, Tyla's fingertips found the circlet at the end of it, snuggled into the folds of bedding. Heaving a sigh of relief, she pulled her sister's fingers from around the circlet and placed her hands gently next to her face instead. The obruck would be safe for the time being. And hidden, which was even more important.

She finally began to recall that the blue dragon who saved them last night had led them to the farthest edge of the settlement away from the wraith enclosure and into a warm, dry home. It felt so familiar to be in a centaur home again that once the dragon pointed to a pile of soft cloth, they both immediately fell into it and closed their eyes. Now awake, she needed to figure out where they were; if there were goblins nearby to find and arrest them; and then how to locate and rejoin their friends, with or without the keys.

She glanced down at her arms as she used them to push herself back to her feet. Several minor cuts, scrapes and bruises speckled along her shoulders and arms, from ducking into scrub and tumbling against boulders, but most of them had been wiped clean and a creamy salve applied. Most of the surrounding skin was still dirty, but she could tell that the cuts had been attended. She checked her wrappings again. They were still wrapped crisscross over her chest and snugly around her back. As they were majikal in nature, the wrappings didn't retain much dirt, unless faint smudges from clumps of mud. Neither did they tear easily, but with as much abuse as they had taken lately, and no chance to clean or repair them, now they showed nicks and cuts from their fights and flights from the monsters. Seeing smears of mud and tiny thinning spots and tears, she wondered if the majik might be breaking down.

"Good morning," Tyla heard a centaur say as she crept from the sleeping space, still absorbed in and patting her wrappings. "Or I should say, 'good day' considering it's no longer morning?"

A dappled grey centaur with glossy black hair and mane stood in a corner, turned toward his work of stirring a pot over a fire. Not much older than the twins themselves, the broad shoulders of a fighter and sculpted arms flowed from a loose black tunic on his upper body. Around his waist, a belt pinched the tunic together at the bottom with an array of pockets filled with herbs and crystals, indicating a profession. However, Tyla didn't think that profession was the fighter she thought he should be with his build, otherwise those herbs would be knives.

Tyla's stomach fluttered at the sight of him. "Who are you?" she asked, smacking her lips to relieve the cotton feel from her mouth. Suddenly acutely aware of the state of her appearance, she tried to run her hands through her own thick brown hair, but her fingers met so much resistance that she settled for pushing it away from her face and trying to force it to stay at the back of her head by will alone.

"I'm Danyel," he said. "I'm one of the healers around here and I'm guessing some water and food would do you a world of good."

"Did you do this?" Tyla said, indicating the clean scratches along her arm.

Danyel nodded his head but didn't meet her eye. "I couldn't reach all of them without waking you," he said, handing Tyla a bulky flagon from a nearby table.

Tyla shook her head and reached for the flagon. When she brushed his hand, she realized his hands were as soft as a healer's. She mumbled some thanks before guzzling the water.

"Slow down," Danyel warned. "Don't make yourself sick."

Tyla forced herself to pull the mug away from her mouth. "Dragons don't do anything slowly," she said when she caught her breath.

"Ah, yes," Danyel said, leaning over to gently brush aside the hair at her shoulder, exposing the edge of the wing markings on her back. "They told me you were also a dragon." He let her hair fall back in place and pulled a small jar from his pocket. "Can I get to the rest of those cuts now?"

Tyla normally wouldn't have allowed someone to touch her before she first threatened them that they'd likely lose a hand, but the glimmer she caught in Danyel's eye held her speechless for a moment. She simply nodded and turned back to her drink.

Danyel's smooth hands gently rubbed ointment into the remaining cuts. "What's your name, centaur dragon?" he asked as he worked.

Tyla's voice failed her as she breathed in his earthy scent while he hovered inches from her.

"Her name's Tyla," came Eleka's voice behind her, "and I'm Eleka. And if I were you, I wouldn't touch my sister unless you're not very fond of your fingers."

"Tyla," the corners of Danyel's mouth curled up as he repeated her name. "I'll remember to keep my fingers in check."

As he replaced the jar, a flash of an image of Danyel keeping his fingers on her shoulder shot through Tyla's head and blood rushed to her face. She banished the thought and turned away from him.

Danyel gave Eleka a mug of water then turned to collect some bowls from a shelf. "Rest, food and water," he said, filling the bowls with a savory stew from the pot and handing them to each of the twins, "often heal all manner of ails."

Tyla hadn't realized how hungry she was until she tasted the stew. Either it was rich with majik or Danyel was an incredible cook, but either way, the stew disappeared quickly.

"So," Danyel stood nearby, folding his arms while the girls ate, "there's been a lot of commotion about the two of you coming in last night." He nodded at Tyla. "They said you fought off one of those monsters. Is that true?"

Tyla bowed her head further over her stew. She had never been shy about her fighting prowess before. She was very proud of the work she put in with her mother to become a warrior, but for some reason the words to boast about herself now failed her.

"Yes," Eleka answered for her sister. "She saved my life several times. She's gotten pretty good at it."

"Why in the world would you need to get good at fighting those things?" Danyel said. "Don't you have someone to help protect you?"

Tyla tilted her head toward her sister, who shrugged back.

"She's better at fighting than I am and, you know, there's so many of them," Eleka said.

"But what are you doing out there anyway? Without friends or family?" Danyel looked puzzled. "Why would you be wandering alone? Where are you from? Where are you going?"

Danyel's eyes lingered on Tyla as her hand slowly worked at the dregs in her bowl. As much as she wanted to swim in his soothing grey eyes, hers kept sliding away. How much could they say? The best idea was to let Eleka talk. Eleka always knew better what to say…and do, unless it came to fighting.

"We've been running from those things," was the only explanation her sister offered before she bent her head back over her bowl as well.

Danyel nodded, but his eyebrows creased as his mind worked. "Well," he started and paused, "our elders said they wanted to speak with you when you woke."

Tyla and Eleka shared a glance. Danyel's ample eyes bounced between them.

Eleka spoke, holding out her empty bowl. "First, can I have some more, please?"

Danyel nodded and dished up seconds of the stew for each girl. He pulled out a sizable loaf of bread and broke off two pieces for them as well.

"I'll go tell them you're awake," he said as they tucked into the food again. As he stepped past Tyla, his eyes met hers. "Help yourself to more if you like."

Once he'd left the room, Tyla swatted her sister's arm. "What are you doing?" she hissed at her. "'She's gotten pretty good at it'?"

"Well, you weren't doing any better," Eleka hissed back. "You're just standing there silently ogling him."

"Well, he's gorgeous," Tyla snapped back.

"We can't stay here and ogle gorgeous centaurs," Eleka said. "We'll only put him and this settlement in more danger."

"They can obviously take care of themselves here," Tyla said. "Plus, aren't we supposed to be trying to find the keys? Shouldn't we try to get some information before we go?"

"Yes," Eleka agreed, "but we have to be careful. We can't say too much."

"I'll let you ask the questions," Tyla said.

"I don't know, would it be worth the risk? Maybe we should lie low," Eleka considered. "If someone here has a key, I'm guessing we'll hear about it quickly."

"Unless they're trying to hide it," Tyla said, her instinctual suspicious nature coming through. "It wouldn't escape anyone how powerful those keys are. They could even have the one that makes someone invisible."

"How did you…?"

Tyla shrugged. "Just trying to think it through."

"Well, I doubt they could hide that much power for very long," Eleka said. "Besides, what happens if Kelraz discovers us here? We're lucky he didn't discover us last night with all those wraiths."

Tyla silently chewed a crust, imagining the worst of what could happen. Kelraz would commit thousands of wraiths to attack the centaurs until every one of them was dead and turned into a wraith or until he caught one or both of the centaur dragon twins.

"Exactly," Eleka said, reading her twin's mind.

"What are we supposed to tell them?" Tyla mumbled.

"Nothing," Eleka answered her. "We keep our wyrd."

"And leave."

"And leave."

5

KEEPING

"Ah!" A voluminous, cream-colored centaur female burst through the door to the kitchen area where the twins were finishing their food. A dark apron draped over her lower back and a thick linen shirt covered her upper torso and arms. She wore a belt with herbs around her waist similar to Danyel's. "Hello and welcome to my home, girls," she said warmly, embracing each of them in turn while she looked them over with keen eyes as if they were returning long-lost relatives. Tyla felt her spine straighten as her defenses snapped back into place. "I'm May, the healer. And it's so good to see you two up this morning. We were very worried about you last night. You both looked quite sickly."

"Healer?" Tyla asked May. "I thought Danyel was the healer?"

"Apprentice," Danyel said, following May through the doorway, "or assistant, whatever you want to call it."

"Yes," May said, reaching over to ruffle Danyel's dark hair playfully, "but he's as good a healer as any I've known. I can hardly come up with anything more to teach him."

"May," Danyel said, nodding toward the girls while gently tidying the black mess May had created on his head, "this is Eleka and Tyla."

Even though the sisters appeared exactly the same in every aspect of their brown centaur forms, Danyel easily recalled the name of each girl. Tyla glanced down, taking in her own torn and dirty red wrappings, and realized why. Eleka's appearance was obviously cleaner and neater; her long brown hair and mane were less matted and her less-damaged wrappings pulled smoothly around her torso.

"I'm so glad Vanora was able to fetch you girls here safely last night," May said. "Those wretched creatures are plaguing everyone, I hear. I don't know what we're going to do about them."

"So we hear too," Eleka said.

"And have experienced it up close, apparently," Danyel added. "Repeatedly."

"But what happened to you?" May asked, trundling over and lifting Eleka's eyelids with her fingers to peer into her eyes, then turning her head with her hands to inspect her ears. "How did you come to be chased by that beast? How long were you running from it? How far have you come?" She abandoned Eleka and turned to gingerly finger the cuts on Tyla's arms. "You've been through it, I can see that much." The matronly centaur pulled a soft leaf from the belt around her waist without looking at it and began rubbing it over Tyla's arm.

Tyla gave Eleka a sidelong glare, who stared at her hands as she twisted them together nervously. Allowing the ministrations of the healer, Tyla stood still and hoped her sister had come up with a story for their hosts.

In the moment they hesitated, Danyel stepped in. "Perhaps," he interjected, "we should wait to hear the tale when they speak to the elders. I'm sure they would prefer not to have to explain themselves more than once."

"Yes," Eleka nodded, eager to end this scene, "we should be going to see the elders now."

"Oh yes, of course," May said, stopping herself from pulling something else out of her belt pockets. She replaced the soft leaf and considered Tyla's arms a last time. "So sorry to delay you. Right this way, girls."

May led them into a thick, foggy mist outside. As they walked, she explained to Eleka their settlement defenses and talked about the number of centaurs and dragons in their camp. Tyla strained her ears to hear what she was saying, but she wasn't willing to give up her place walking with Danyel behind them to get the information directly. She'd have to get it from Eleka later.

"Sorry about her," Danyel said, lowering his voice and turning his head toward Tyla's as they walked. "She's a lot of personality for others to handle. But it helps her empathize with her patients."

Tyla shrugged. "It's fine," she said. "People often say that about my father too."

"Who's your father?" he asked. "Maybe I know him?"

Tyla pursed her lips to stop herself. What was it about his eyes and gentle tone that made her want to spill her thoughts to him? She and Eleka couldn't tell anyone here who their parents were because the goblins chasing them from Kirlik knew the centaur leaders and would report the girls' misdeeds back to them in no time. They were already at risk of being detained by the goblins quickly and indefinitely if any showed up here asking about them; never mind the trouble they'd be in if their parents found out what they'd done.

"Oh," she hemmed, "he's no one. I'm sure you don't know him."

"Well, that can't be true!" Danyel smiled saying it. "Of all people, your father can't be a 'no one'."

As they walked they both studied the mud ahead of their feet with half-smiles until they reached their destination.

In all centaur settlements, the elders—those who have the most experience in the community—met together in a capacious central structure called the House of Elders. Sometimes, especially in fall, the building was used for councils and other events, celebrations and judgements alike. Like the centaur homes, it was made of mud, wood and stone to shore up the earth around it and topped with a grassy, earthen roof. The central building contained several entrances on each side to symbolize the citizens' open access. The elders' councils and judgements couldn't be held in private or without the rest of the settlement's opinions taken into consideration.

Two large doors on either side of the House of Elders were roomy enough for a dragon to fit through, while the other doors were sized specifically for centaurs. Inside, a few tables leaned against the outer walls and evenly spaced support columns made of dragon-fired stone reached to the ceiling with fires burning in grates beside them. Hytocomp thresholds and a slightly raised wood floor insulated the centaurs from the wet mud underneath. Tyla closed her eyes a moment and pulled in the intoxicating scent of earth and grass. The smell of home. When she opened her eyes, she caught a fleeting glance of Danyel hiding a grin.

When the twins and their escorts entered through one of the centaur entrances, several other centaurs of varying ages already stood together around one of the fires. Beyond the centaurs two dragons sat curled on the ground beside each other: a brown dragon and the brilliant blue dragon who had led the binding of the wraith and the procession here the previous night.

As they made their way through the stone columns, some centaurs pulled away from the group to speak together in low voices, occasionally casting careful glances at the twins. A few more centaurs quietly stepped inside through the other doors and stood off to the side to watch. Everyone seemed curious as to what their visitors had to say.

"Eleka, Tyla," May said as they approached the main group, "might I introduce to you our elders, Filik, Seena, Grays, Noon, Mika, Lem and Saran. The dragon elder is Sylam and you met Vanora last night. Elders, this is Eleka and Tyla," she said, indicating the twins. "Did I get that right?" she added, looking to the girls. "They're twins, after all," she acknowledged, turning back to the elders, "hard to tell apart unless you really know them."

"I can tell the difference," Danyel whispered softly under his breath.

"Yes," Eleka said, nodding her head and stepping forward. "Thank you for taking us in. And thank you, especially, to Vanora and the other centaurs who provided their help when we most needed it last night. We wouldn't be alive without you."

"Don't be modest, girls. As we hear it, you were doing fine on your own," one of the centaur elders replied. She was dark brown, even darker than the twins, but so thin that her ribs jutted out beneath her linen tunic and the drape she wore over her lower half. A silver fur mantle slung across her shoulders and braided black and white hair and mane trickled down her back. "But tell us," she continued, severe lines creasing her face in scrutiny, "how you came to be chased by such a monster at that hour of the night?"

Tyla's eyes slipped to the ground for a moment, but she lifted them quickly in an effort not to appear guilty.

"Yes," another centaur agreed. This centaur was so old that his knobby knees shook and Tyla half expected she would have to catch him when he fell over. She wondered if the effort of standing might be too much for the pale palomino. "Where are you from? Are any more of these monsters coming after you?" he asked in a squeaky voice.

"Peace, Filik," the dark brown centaur said, lifting her hand slightly. Tyla thought May had called the brown centaur Grays when she indicated her during introductions. "We will hear their story first."

Eleka cleared her throat. "Well," she began, trying to put together her strategy, "there's really not much story to tell. We were meeting with our friends… a long way from here. One of those monsters showed up and we all panicked and ran and got separated. My sister and I have been stumbling through the wilderness since then, trying to find our way home."

"And where *is* your home, dear?" Grays asked in a kind tone.

"Uh," Eleka wrung her hands and twisted her fingers but tried not to look nervous. She couldn't say that they belonged to Tor Ekwa, the closest thing the centaurs had to a royal city, because the elders would most certainly send word to have them claimed. Then all manner of wraiths, goblins and centaurs would descend on them at once. They also couldn't name a random settlement nearby for the same reasons. So, while they tried to keep to the truth as much as possible, she and Tyla had already agreed they would have to flat-out lie about where they came from. Now, it was up to Eleka to adapt the truth. "R…Ronvirt," she finally got out. "We belong with Ronvirt."

"Ronvirt?" Danyel muttered the name under his breath.

"I don't know that settlement, dear," Grays said. "This is Zanna. We're near the formerly Just Kingdom, now referred to as Gormirom. Is it nearby?"

Tyla kept herself from snickering when she realized that 'Ronvirt' was simply 'Trivnor' spelled backwards.

Apparently Eleka had decided that in order to hew truth as much as possible, she decided to say that they belonged "with Ronvirt". Or…they belonged with Trivnor.

Eleka blinked, her eyes darting around the room to all the different faces. Her lips twitched and her fingers cavorted together.

"It's near Kanat," Tyla finally stated, unable to bear watching her sister squirm anymore. Eleka usually had all the answers. She wasn't used to making up false ones and certainly wasn't used to forcing others to believe them. Forcing something was Tyla's responsibility. "Is Kanat near here?"

If Eleka's instincts and directions were correct, the settlement would be far away, but it was possible someone here was from Kanat or somewhere near it. The elders also might have a quick means of communication with Kanat centaurs or some other way to contact them. The twins knew it would be a risk to offer any information that might give them away, but Tyla had always been a risk-taker, and she couldn't see any way to avoid it now.

"By Khurta, no!" Grays gasped and Eleka's shoulders dropped in relief. Luckily, it also made her seem disappointed. "That's on the other side of Avonoa! How in the world did you girls get so lost?"

"Um…portals…" Eleka dithered, unable to make full eye contact. Tyla sensed she was losing what little courage she'd first had to stand up to these centaurs.

"It was a mix-up in portals, when the monsters were after us," Tyla said louder. "I'm afraid we were rather shaken in our escape."

"You don't seem shaken now," Vanora sat up behind the centaurs to be seen over their heads. Tyla was relieved to hear that they appeared more unruffled than they felt but now began to wonder if it was a good thing. "In fact, you didn't seem all that shaken when we rescued you last night."

"You know very well that fear does different things to different people," May said gently but firmly, coming to the twins' defense.

"Yes." Vanora stood now and crept closer to Eleka on her clawed wing joints. "However, these two knew that the monsters couldn't be killed. They both looked on the creatures without abhorrence while observing them in the prison. And when I told them that one of them had spoken, instead of being horrified, this one," she nodded toward Eleka, "simply asked me what it had said."

Tyla desperately tried to avoid staring daggers at her sister. For Eleka's part, she kept her head hanging low to avoid exposing her guilt, even though that almost made it worse. She had always been a terrible liar.

"What are you accusing us of?" Tyla blurted before she could stop herself. "Knowing more about wraiths than you?"

Eleka's eyes shot to Tyla before she realized what she'd said. Vanora swung her triangular head toward her and hissed. "No one called them 'wraiths'."

6

LIGHT

"But it makes sense though, doesn't it? That's what we thought they were, anyway," Tyla stammered out to try to cover her mistake while her anger gave way to more guilt. "We only conjectured. We've heard things about them."

"Like that they can't be killed," Eleka added.

"You're suddenly very knowledgeable for not even remembering where your own settlement is." Vanora bit back.

"It doesn't mean we haven't been educated," Tyla snapped. "We're just lost."

A low growl issued from the back of Vanora's throat, but the blue dragon withdrew back to her position behind the centaurs.

"And we feel sorry for you in that," Grays spoke up. "You're very far from home and we're not sure what we can do to help you."

"We won't ask much," Tyla said. "If you could spare some supplies, a little food maybe, then we'll be on our way."

The group of centaur elders shook their heads. Some of them avoided eye contact with both girls. Vanora went so far as to harumph at Tyla's request.

"Well," Tyla could feel the tension in the room climbing and wanted to flee before things got worse. "If you have no food or any more aide to give us then we'll be on our way."

"Wait," Danyel touched Tyla's arm as she and Eleka turned to leave, "no one said we won't help you."

"Yes," May said, "we'll do what we can, but…"

Tyla turned back to May. "But what?"

Grays stepped forward and lifted her chin. "But the elders agree… you can't leave."

"What are you saying?" Eleka asked.

"Are we prisoners now?" Tyla's heart began to beat faster and not because Danyel's hand lingered on her arm. She jerked away from his touch and stepped toward the older centaurs. "What justification do you have to keep us here? Is this what we get for you saving our lives? Do we have to work it off or something?"

"No, of course not. I mean to say that if you insist on leaving, we won't stop you," Grays said, "but we strongly recommend that you stay, and for good reason. Hear us out before you go." She adjusted her mantle around her shoulders. "First, in the beginning, when we sent out our warriors to face these monsters, some of them were killed."

Tyla and Eleka exchanged another glance before they tried to hide it.

"Uh-huh," Grays said, noticing it all the same. "You know more than you say you do. Which means you likely know that the centaur form of those monsters in our prison were once our warriors. No matter how fearsome you think you might be, we did have to save you from that thing last night and stronger warriors than you have fallen victim to them."

Tyla knew it and she knew Eleka knew it too. They saw the change happen with their own eyes when one of the dragons in Kingstor Noble lost their life to one of the monsters while defending the kingdom. The dragon immediately turned to ash and rose from their remains as a horrific wraith right before their eyes.

"If we allowed anyone to leave Zanna now," Grays explained, "especially alone, without an escort or some kind of guard, we would be practically creating one of those creatures ourselves."

"You can't equate the two," Eleka tried to deflect what she was hearing.

"And second," Grays continued, "there is evidence to suggest that centaurs in our area are being hunted specifically."

"Hunted?" Eleka asked. "By who?"

Vanora sat up in the back again. "Our best guess?" The twins looked up at her. "Either the monsters themselves, King Gormin, or some other entity we don't know. Perhaps…centaur dragons…"

"What? Us? How dare you—?" Tyla started, but Eleka cut her off before her anger rose too far.

"Why would anyone hunt centaurs? Even a king?" Eleka said. "That's practically suicide. Especially for a human."

"The king isn't happy about having lost the Just Sword to the goblins," Filik's squeaky voice interjected with more strength than Tyla expected. "That's partly why he renamed the kingdom in his honor."

"But that was seventeen years ago," Eleka pointed out.

"He's never maintained a good relationship with the centaurs in this area," Grays said. "For centuries, we centaurs have been extremely protective of the dragons in the Island Ruck. And that made the centaurs and humans living near each other rather hostile."

"Now," Filik continued on for her, "the king is openly hostile to the centaurs. He suddenly pulled all his protective forces away from our settlements about five days ago…then the disappearances started."

"At the same time the attacks from those monsters started," May added. "It very well could be that he is being just as cautious as we are in defending ourselves from them."

"Or he could be the one sending them to attack us," Grays said, her voice very low.

"We've found hoof prints and boot prints and signs of struggle," Filik said. "I think that's pretty clear. And before you chastise me, Vanora, the hoof prints and boot prints would exempt any part-dragon part-centaurs from suspicion. As far as we know the only dragon prints are from you and Sylam."

Eleka nodded thanks to Filik, but Tyla was too busy thinking to consider it. "Have you followed the tracks?" she asked. "Where were they going? Where did they come from?"

"That's difficult in the rains of fall," Filik reminded her.

Tyla's fighter brain began to strategize and she persisted. "But have you—?"

"Enough!" Vanora cut her off with a roar. "You're not members of this settlement and thus require no more explanations. I would think you would be respectful and grateful for our protection, especially after last night. You'll stay with the healers for now until either we can get a message to your settlement or someone comes for you, or you decide to take your own chances. Until then, help where you can and stay out of trouble. All agreed?"

The rest of the elders nodded in agreement. Even Grays seemed chastised into compliance. Vanora seemed to own more influence in the settlement than anyone else.

"Good," she growled. "I need to hunt. I haven't eaten in days." With a growl, she slipped through the doors and into the foggy sky.

"I guess that explains why she's in such a bad mood." Danyel sounded relieved when the council gathering ended and he, May and the twins left the House of Elders to watch Vanora disappear into the clouds. "She's usually much more friendly."

"She's probably expending a lot more energy fighting these wraiths all the time," Eleka said. "I'm guessing that would make her hungry more often."

"Is that how it works for you?" May asked, turning to Eleka as the four started back across the settlement. "I've always wondered about the differences in digestion rates and ratios when it comes to part-dragon races, but we don't have any changelings in our settlement, so I don't have much experience to draw from."

"You're asking about our digestion?" Tyla asked, wide-eyed.

"Well, yes," May said. "As a healer I must have all the most current information in order to help anyone who needs my aide. Hence, I'm always learning. Digestion is a valuable indicator of health in any creature, so I need to know about not only yours but anyone else's too, for that matter."

"My sister doesn't consider the intricacies of anatomy," Eleka said with a slight air of superiority. Tyla knew it was true, but she threw a nasty face at her sister for saying it in front of Danyel. "Digestion can be different between part-species. A friend of mine says that everything has gone topsy-turvy since changelings began. Sometimes…"

Tyla rolled her eyes, quickly tuning out the onslaught of useless information Eleka and her studious friends overshared with her too often. Instead, she slowed her pace and dropped back, hoping no one would notice. What she really needed to do was figure out the settlement's defenses and how strenuous their hosts would be about "encouraging" them to stay. Plus, she needed time to consider which way they should go if and when they left.

"I hope you're not planning an escape," Danyel slowed from the others to say.

Tyla barely hid her jump at hearing him next to her, but she couldn't tell if her reaction was from surprise or just the sound of his voice. "Why?" she said. "We need to leave."

"But why the urgency?" he asked back. "What's so important that you can't wait for a message to be sent to your home so you'll be safe when you leave?"

She couldn't think of how to reply so she thought it might be best not to answer. Instead, she simply turned her head and continued walking.

"Alright," he said. "If you don't want to tell me, that's fine. Just remember that I'm not the only one who thinks you'll be safer if you stay."

"Safer from what?" she asked. "Yes, the monsters, I know, but we were doing fine hiding from those without anyone's help. What else are we hiding from here?"

"The supposedly Just King," Danyel said. "Do you really want to risk being taken by humans?"

Better than being taken by goblins, she thought to herself. *At least a dragon can easily handle humans.* But, again, she didn't answer Danyel.

"Look," Danyel dropped his effort to persuade her from leaving, "May was right to say that a healer should always be learning. If you have any information about these monsters, can you at least share some of it before you go?"

Tyla pursed her lips, thinking, before she shrugged. "I can try," she said. "But there's not much more I can tell you that you don't already know."

Danyel nodded his head toward the opposite side of the settlement and Tyla trotted after him. "Come with me."

May had no problems letting the two of them go. Danyel called back that they would meet up at her house for the last meal and he and Tyla headed in the other direction. As much as Tyla often wished she didn't have to constantly be with her twin, now she glanced back at her one last time for solace before running off. Eleka, already deep in conversation with May again, didn't notice.

Danyel led Tyla to the edge of the settlement where the wraith prison hid behind closed doors. "So," he said, indicating the two large doors in the wall, "you called the monsters 'wraiths'. What kind of wraiths?"

"Do you know what a wraith is?" Tyla said, trying to stave off mis-answering his questions and giving herself time to think first.

Danyel nodded. "A wraith is a phantom conjured by dark majik, usually for the purpose of serving a master."

Tyla slid her hand along the solid double doors imagining the multiple wraiths on the other side. "Do you know the different kinds of wraiths?"

"Yes," Danyel said, "but I thought I was the one asking the questions here."

Tyla rolled her eyes at him and he grinned. "Humor me," she said. "I have to know what you know first."

Danyel exaggerated her eye roll back at her. "Alright," he said. "There are lots of different wraiths. A wraith is usually born of one or a combination of the base elements, water, air, fire and earth. What I can't figure out is what combinations these could be," he said, nodding his head at the door. "Or why and how any of our people became them."

"None," Tyla said, "I don't think. At least for these. They aren't just simple elemental wraiths anyway. These are soul wraiths. That much I know."

"Soul wraiths?" Danyel said it like the words together tasted bitter in his mouth. "What's a soul wraith?"

"It's a wraith conjured from a soul of the dead. That's why it can't be killed. It's already dead."

Danyel's face went slack. He stared at Tyla without any emotion on his face. Swallowing hard, she turned away from him.

"How do you know this?" Danyel finally asked.

Tyla scuffed her hoof in the mud. She knew how it sounded. Others might think that she had conjured the wraiths or at least that she might be involved in dark majik. She didn't want Danyel thinking either of those things about her.

Danyel turned away from her as the rain began to patter around them. Tyla wrapped her hands around her shoulders, afraid that she'd made him angry or disgusted with her. But over his shoulder he called to her. "Follow me," he said again, this time with very little warmth in his voice.

As the rain pounded and thunder shook the earthen roof, Danyel shunted Tyla into a large, but overly crowded mound building. The guards inside the doors stood ready with ropes looped around their arms, but hadn't bothered with bows, swords or spears. Dozens of centaurs lay behind them either moaning or sleeping. All of the centaurs had copious gashes somewhere on their bodies. Most of the gashes crossed their lower body or chest and arms. One female did lay awake, quiet and still. One slash ran across her pale face, neck and shoulder and a deep cut the length of Tyla's forearm dissected the middle of her white lower body. She stared unblinking at the ceiling of the building with partially lidded eyes. The only indication she was alive was the gentle rise and fall of her chest.

"Hospital?" Tyla whispered reverently.

Danyel nodded.

"And the ropes?" she asked, but she knew the answer.

"In case of new wraiths," Danyel's voice caught as he said it.

When Tyla had taken in everything she could about the unexpected setting, she realized that Eleka and May were also there. Eleka stood next to the wounded centaur female so she stepped over to join her. May steadily made her way through the injured centaurs, applying salves and herbs to their wounds.

When she got closer, Tyla saw the same black speckles in the female centaur's wounds as the ones she remembered from Jassan's injuries. The black spots spilled across the raw flesh.

"Have you seen this before?" Danyel whispered behind the twins.

Tyla glanced briefly at Eleka, who nodded back to her. "Yes, we've seen it," Tyla said. "A friend…"

"'Friend'?" Eleka murmured sidelong to her sister.

"Yes," Tyla said. Seeing the centaur in unimaginable pain, Tyla's heart ached thinking of Jassan in as much pain. That was how they'd left him and hadn't heard anything from him since. "Our friend has the same kind of wound."

"Do you know how we can help them?" Danyel asked.

Eleka caught Tyla's eyes and shook her head. Tyla figured she didn't want her to divulge the fact that Jassan was, in fact, a faerie, therefore any cure for Jassan might not work on centaurs anyway. Besides, they hadn't found anything to help him.

"No," Tyla said. "Our friend is still suffering from it too. At least, as far as we know."

"Have you tried flarote?" Eleka asked Danyel.

"Flarote?" May replied, joining them around the ailing centaur. "We're not animals, no matter what King Gormin thinks."

"But I've seen it help," Eleka said.

"A pure centaur?" May asked.

"Well…no…" Eleka said.

"A part centaur part dragon?" she inquired again.

"Um…no…" Eleka stammered out.

"Has it helped someone with these kinds of wounds?"

"A little," Eleka whispered.

May shook her head. "I've had some little success with the herbs we always use. Sweetgrass mash seems to do the best," she said, "but it's extremely slow-going. Still, I have hope."

"And her?" Tyla looked over at the severely injured female. "Is it helping her?"

May rested her hands on her hips. "I can only assume the blackness is dying tissue," she sighed. "Sweetgrass mash is holding off the infection little by little, but I need to use much more than we have available for now. We're not sure what more to do for her."

"That's what you want from us," Tyla said before she turned to Danyel. "That's why you need to know about the wraiths. So, you can heal her?"

"If there's anything more you can tell us," Danyel begged, "anything at all…"

"I'm sorry," Eleka said. "We can't save any of them."

7

HIDDEN

Danyel accompanied the twins back to the healer's home for a meal and to fully clean themselves. Eleka readily accepted the opportunity, but Tyla tugged at her matted hair and smoothed her dirty wrappings for a minute before she agreed as well.

Taking longer than she normally would have with the bucket of hot water and a rag, she worked at cleaning herself. Time passed quickly as she kept pausing to think about Danyel and his comforting manner toward her, wondering what he might think of her appearance and wanting to make it perfect. Then her thoughts turned to her and Eleka's friends that they'd left behind somewhere. While scrubbing at her hair with May's borrowed comb to untangle the snarls, Dasha's frilly, poofy hair came into her head. Wondering for her friends' safety, her hands slowed. Where were they now? While she and her twin were now safe in someone's cozy home tonight, she had no way of knowing if their friends would be forced to shelter from the rain under the trees, or worse.

She finished cleaning her hair and now tried braiding it away from her face. The hanks of brown hair reminded her of Lokna, their brown dragon friend. Where was he now? If he was safe with Jassan and Burk, why hadn't they tried to contact them with their obruck? Her thoughts about it all got tangled the same way the wet strands of hair did in her fingers.

"You ok in here?" Eleka peeked her head around the curtain.

Tyla dropped her hands from her twisted hair. "Where are they, Eleka? Why haven't they contacted anyone yet?"

Eleka pushed the curtain aside and stepped in to reach over and run her fingers through Tyla's hair. "I'm sure they're ok," she whispered, smoothing the tangles. "We can only worry about ourselves right now. Lokna's a strong dragon. He'll protect Jassan."

Hearing his name, Tyla dropped her gaze. Her breathing caught and her heart trembled.

"I know you want to protect them," Eleka empathized, "but for now, can you focus on protecting yourself?"

"No," Tyla grumbled. "But I *will* worry about protecting you."

"I'll take it," Eleka said.

Feeling her sister's hands slide down her arms, Tyla reached up and discovered that Eleka had quickly and deftly finished a neat, intricate braid that was probably tight enough to stay put and out of her face until she found herself in the World of Souls.

"Uncle Rylan teaching you majik?" she wondered aloud, touching her hair.

Eleka smiled. "It helps me work through problems. I bet if you had yourself a good sparring match with one of the guards out there, you'd feel a lot better too."

Tyla paused to let her worries go for now. "That's true," she agreed before she took a deep breath and swiftly swung toward the door. "And I have just the idea to do it."

"You'll have to do what they say," Danyel instructed as he and Tyla approached the front gates of the settlement in the drizzling rain. Eleka trailed behind them, appearing to carefully take in the buildings and surroundings. Tyla sincerely hoped she might also be searching for a discreet way to get away when the time was right.

"You think I can't do that?" she snapped at him.

"I didn't say that," Danyel said, quickly changing tactics, "you just don't seem like the type that enjoys taking orders. Plus, they still won't let you leave," Danyel pointed out as he escorted Tyla up to the guard post station. As soon as she and Eleka had emerged from tidying themselves, she had specifically requested of Danyel that she be allowed to work with the guards. "They're even making all the farmers check in and out when they go to their own fields now. To start, you'll probably only run messages and errands for them."

"That's fine," Tyla said. "That's what I'm used to. I'm working my way up in the ranks of—" she cut herself off before she could say, "my mother's army". Danyel could not learn that her mother was a high-level warrior, or worse, that she was Ashel, leader of the warrior centaurs and wife of the dragon Trudyn feira Rakgar feira Prakyndar. Instead, she coughed and finished with "—the ranks of the warriors of our settlement."

"Ronvirt?"

"Yes, Ronvirt."

Eleka pursed her lips and threw her an unmistakable look that said, "Careful what you say, worm!" Tyla quickly stuck her tongue out at her sister when Danyel turned his head away. She didn't need that condescending look.

"Watch it!" came a shout from the top of the wall.

"Dragon approaching!" another shout came from a different direction.

The three looked up in time to see Vanora and the other dragon, Sylam, fly over the tall walls without slowing, heading in the direction of the House of Elders. In Vanora's back claws dangled a mess of ropes, wires and hooks.

Tyla galloped ahead of the others, tempted to change into a dragon to beat them there, but she wasn't sure she wanted to display her dark red spotted dragon form in front of Danyel yet. Bursting into one of the centaur doors, she caught Vanora shouting at the other elders.

"They've taken them," she yelled, "all of them! This is proof!"

"Traps," one of the elders hissed as he inspected the ropes. "How did we not see them before?"

"They're designed not to be seen, Lem," Vanora said wryly, stating the obvious. "We were lucky to find this."

"Was anyone hurt?" Danyel asked, coming through the door behind Tyla.

Vanora shook her head. "Wouldn't know, would I? Three more are missing, so they can't tell us."

"Three?!" Filik said, his knobby knees shaking while inspecting the netting over Lem's shoulder.

"That's not good," Grays shook her head, sidling up to Vanora with a falcon on her shoulder. She held up a piece of parchment. "I've received word from Taryn's settlement, Marish."

Vanora looked over the paper as Grays held it in front of her for a moment, then shook her head. "It's still just rumors," she said.

"What rumors?" Danyel asked. His question was echoed by several others still entering the House of Elders.

Grays re-rolled the parchment. "Centaurs in Marish, the settlement south of here where Vanora's sister lives, say that there are rumors of King Gormin hosting some kind of tournament games. Humans are rumored to be taking centaurs and bringing them to Gormitor Castle then they compete in King Gormin's arena. Or, as they're told by the humans, the centaurs are volunteering for the competition. One of their dragons made it back to the settlement and reported that the new king has some kind of champion who fights them. He said that the centaur challenger never wins and the consensus is that the centaurs aren't supposed to make it out alive."

"What about the champion?" Tyla spoke up as everyone around her murmured their dismay. "Is it a human?"

"What else would it be?" one of the other centaurs called out.

"But a single human killing so many centaurs?" Tyla pressed loudly.

"What does it mean?" Danyel shouted, trying to attract attention to Tyla's comments.

"Is the king allowing the centaurs a fair fight?" Tyla asked, directing the question to Grays. "Otherwise, why would he order centaurs be kidnapped and force them to fight in games? It doesn't make sense."

"It doesn't have to make sense," Grays answered her. "The note from Marish says the champion has some kind of majik that makes him stronger than a centaur. Gormin is basically putting them to death."

"Majik," Eleka whispered in Tyla's ear. She pulled her sister away from the others, who continued complaining loudly to each other amidst shouts for action.

"What about it?" Tyla whispered back.

"The key," Eleka said. "This so-called champion could have one of the keys."

The two sisters stared at each other in shared realization.

"We have to get out of here," Tyla finally snapped.

"And do what?" Eleka whispered back. "We can't go barging into a human kingdom and demand they hand over a majikal gem, which they may or may not have, for no reason whatsoever. We can't even get out of this settlement without setting off alarms in everyone's minds."

"Ok, ok, first things first," Tyla said. Her brain began spinning with possible fighting strategies to attain the key, if one existed. If it was anything like Trivnor's or Jassan's keys, it would have specific strengths and weaknesses. Trivnor's key could transport beings, but only two at a time. Jassan's key could transform him into something else, but only if he wasn't touching anyone else. He couldn't even transform if Bubbles, his little adopted pet snake, sat on him. And Trivnor could only transport to a place he had either been before or could see at that moment. She knew if she learned this key's strength she'd be able to figure out some sort of weakness too. Tyla's legs took their first steps before her mind had fully formed its next thought.

"I'll go!" she shouted to the gathered crowd, raising her arm high. Only a few of the others stopped discussing options to rescue the centaurs already in Gormirom.

"What do you mean, you'll go?" Filik demanded. "We made clear to you before, we don't want any centaurs leaving this settlement, least of all you."

Ignoring him, she continued. "We need bait!...And someone to enter these games!" Others began grumbling to talk over her, but she looked at Vanora. "You know I'm right."

"What we need is investigation," Vanora corrected her and many centaurs quieted. "We don't need a young centaur with no experience to be caught floundering around in the wild and need saving. Again."

"I know what majik they're using!" Tyla blurted before she could stop the words.

Everyone heard and silenced themselves.

"And what majik is that?" Vanora pushed past several of the centaur elders to approach the twins.

Tyla clamped her mouth shut. What had she done, how could she be so stupid? She had given her wyrd not to tell anyone about the majik of the Lost Ruck and the gateway to the World of Souls, let alone the secret of the supernatural keys. Those keys were blessed by the gods. How could she possibly explain how she knew about the majik without telling them everything?

"It's a majik goblin stone," Eleka backed up her sister, stepping to her side.

Tyla's head jerked around to her twin. Eleka nodded slightly and Tyla's shoulders relaxed. Of course, her smarter half conjured a clever lie just in time, and close enough to the truth to be believable. Now Tyla just had to agree with everything else her sister said. She had gotten them into this trouble; the least she could do was go along with the one smart enough to get them out.

"Yes," Tyla said. "We've been to the goblins'—"

"We've been to goblin cities."

"We have goblin friends."

"We've seen their majik—"

"And it's powerful—"

"The king is probably using one of their gems." Eleka finished the twins' fully-formed thought.

Vanora shook her head. "Please," she muttered, "can only one of you speak at a time, please?"

Tyla, knowing how the way they expressed themselves together annoyed others, waved to Eleka to speak.

"We have a friend who's a goblin. A goblin dragon, actually," Eleka said. "We've learned how the goblins operate and the powerful gems they use. We're guessing that the gem the king is using is either one of those gems, or very like them."

"Guessing," Vanora said doubtfully, shaking her head again. "We need more than guesses."

"Then let's go out," Tyla insisted. "We can fly out together to hunt down these humans and figure out for ourselves what they're doing. You said yourself that we need more investigation. Let's go out and see if we can catch them using majik or capturing centaurs."

Vanora looked to Grays and shrugged. "It would be easier and safer to fly over the humans as dragons. And Sylam can fly over another area. That will double our search capability."

Grays studied Tyla, who puffed out her chest. "I'm considered a warrior where I come from," Tyla told the older centaur. "I have been trained to fight alongside my brother and sister centaurs."

"Hm." Grays sounded unimpressed but said to Eleka, "And you? Are you a warrior as well?"

"I'm more of a scholar," Eleka answered with a tight smile. "I leave the fighting to my sister."

"I see." Grays's eyes met Vanora's again. "Alright," she said, "take Tyla but Eleka will stay here. Eleka can assist May and Danyel and lend any information about the monsters to them as well."

Vanora turned to Tyla. "Meet me at the gates before the sun meets the horizon," she said.

Tyla nodded and the older blue dragon stalked away.

"What are you doing?" Eleka whispered, shuffling up to her as the elders turned to counsel with each other and the rest of the centaurs dispersed from the structure through the many different doors. Tyla checked to make sure no one was following them and jerked her head to the door.

Outside, the rain poured in sheets, so the sisters ran toward the healer's house.

Once inside, Tyla shook herself to shed most of the rainwater. "We need to get out of here, right?" she answered her sister's earlier question. "Well, what better way to do that than to actually have permission?"

"But I have to stay!" Eleka pointed out. "They're using me as leverage, so you'll come back. Besides, we can't just abandon Zanna to human kidnappings and wraith attacks."

"This is a step in stopping the wraith attacks," Tyla said. "And I'll be helping them discover and hopefully end the kidnappings. Besides, it's not like I wouldn't come back for you anyway."

"Yeah, right. You would go to Gormirom and pick fights and get into trouble and leave me here to pick up the pieces. So just don't forget me," Eleka pouted again, leading her into the kitchen area.

"Ugh," Tyla rolled her eyes. "When will you start trusting my judgement?"

"When you start doing smart things," Eleka said. "And stop making choices just to pick fights."

"Who's picking fights?" Danyel said, coming into the kitchen.

"Tyla," Eleka said. "Always and forever. If there's a fight to be had, she'll be in the beginning, the middle and the end of it."

"I seem to recall that habit saving your life from wraiths all the way here," Tyla sneered.

"And I seem to recall it almost killing you," Eleka bit back. "If we had hidden ourselves better to start with and stayed hidden, we wouldn't be in any of this mess."

"What mess?" Tyla threw her hands up. "It looks to me like we're being fed and sheltered."

"But we can't leave," Eleka said, "to do what we need to do."

"What do you need to do?" Danyel finally jumped in.

Both twins remembered he was there and turned to him. Tyla took a deep breath. Eleka turned back to look at her sister. "Get home," she said, pushing past the other two. "I'm going to lie down for a minute," she grumbled. Before she got past them, she turned her face so Danyel wouldn't see and winked at Tyla then threw her eyes to the ceiling.

Tyla got the message. Maybe from the gestures or maybe from their weird twin mind-reading thing that Eleka claimed they had, but she knew that Eleka wasn't going to rest, she was going to pull out the circlet and try to contact one of their friends to share news. The twins needed to tell Trivnor about the centaur kidnappings and rumors of an unbeatable champion at Gormirom. He could help the twins determine if a key might be in use somewhere near where they were now. They needed to talk to someone, hopefully and especially Trivnor himself.

Danyel pulled out some cheese and bread and handed a chunk of each to Tyla. "I'm sure your family is worried about you," he said.

Tyla shrugged. "Our parents trust us to take care of ourselves."

"But to be gone so long without a word?"

Tyla shook her head. She hesitated, trying not to get herself into the same trouble she had in the House of Elders. "Our parents have …family friends who knew when Eleka and I left. They may be concerned when we don't return immediately, but other parents knew where we were so it could be some time before our parents send someone out to find us."

What she meant was that Dasha's parents knew that the friends had left Kirlik, and when they didn't return in a reasonable period of time, those parents would talk to the twins' parents, Gizi's parents and Lokna's parents and eventually Emma's parents too. Emma's parents, Princess Anna of the Noble Kingdom and Hirowyn of the Rock Clouds would have more resources to hunt everyone down if they needed to. But it was Princess Anna who had given them all permission to leave with Trivnor in the first place. Sure, it was under dire circumstances, and she had no idea how far the friends would have to go or how long they would be gone or the necessity to stage a royal heist. But even knowing none of that, she still gave them permission to leave, and go with a faerie, no less. She would explain all of that to their parents in due time.

It wasn't until Dasha's aunt Shvika caught the friends trying to steal a majikal gem from the goblin's royal palace that they knew several armies might soon be sent out to hunt them down. Once they escaped from the goblin city with the gem, they all had to lay low and keep away from goblins and their homes in order to help Trivnor find the keys to the gateway of the World of Souls and uphold their wyrd.

But Danyel didn't need any of that information. In fact, Tyla reminded herself as she spoke, to be cautious about what she said regarding their history.

"So," Danyel said after a bite of his bread, "what is so urgent that you need to leave now?"

Tyla chewed her cheese slowly. "We just want to go home. That's all." It wasn't a complete lie. They both wanted to put the chaos behind them and get back home as soon as possible. But she was becoming increasingly aware that that would be much later rather than sooner.

"You're not going to run, are you?"

Tyla jumped when a knock sounded on the front door before bursting open. "Danyel!" someone called and a young female centaur stepped into the room. "Danyel! May needs you! She said you're late checking in with Mama."

Danyel dropped his food. "Oops. Come on," he grabbed Tyla's hand and pulled her along to follow the young centaur girl. "You'll like this."

"Wait, you might be confusing me with Eleka—?" she tried to protest but got dragged out into the rain.

"I know who I'm talking to," Danyel said over the thunder outside. "Besides, she's resting."

Tyla smiled to herself hearing that Danyel genuinely recognized her as unique from her twin. Not only her looks, but her energy, her interests and her personality. Tyla occasionally thought about changing her look to see if anyone would notice the twins' differences more easily, but Danyel's recognition gave her confidence that she stood apart.

"What are we doing?" Tyla called breathlessly over the rain. Danyel held her hand tightly as they cantered through muddy puddles. She wasn't opposed to it, even if she had to work to match his gate and pace.

"You'll see," he said, as he slowed in front of another centaur home. The young centaur girl disappeared inside and Danyel pulled Tyla in behind him.

"May?" Danyel called out once they entered. The young girl stood off to the side in a common area to allow them room to enter.

May returned Danyel's greeting from the back of the home and they followed her voice. They passed through first the kitchen, then one living area and another living area before they reached a room at the very back.

The bulk of the room was filled by a single centaur lying on a pallet of blankets and soft hay. Next to her on a similar mound lay two small centaurs, not more than a few days old. The babies' hides were both speckled black and white, like their mother's. Their oversized centaur eyes barely began blinking open and their sloping ears were milky pink in the gentle light around them. Unlike horses, their bony legs were far too slender and frail to support them running around shortly after birth, but their human upper bodies were faster to develop than a normal human's. As one baby rubbed their eyes and stretched, May lifted it from the pile of bedding and offered it a bottle of warm milk.

Danyel quickly scooped up another bottle lying nearby and passed it to Tyla. Tyla took it, assuming she needed to hold it until he was ready for it. The young female who had led them here slipped into the room with a bowl of broth and boiled oat grass for her mother centaur.

Danyel bundled the second baby into his arms with one of the blankets from the bed. Noting the crowded room, he nodded to Tyla, indicating for her to follow him into the living room. She did so and Danyel curled up with the baby against the wall next to the fireplace.

"Well," he said, when Tyla sat next to him.

"Well, what?" Tyla asked. "Oh!" she jumped when he nodded at the bottle in her hands.

She held it out for him, but he shook his head. "My hands are a little full," he said. "Can you feed her?"

"Ok, I guess," she said a little uncertainly. Tyla tipped the bulbous end toward the baby, who sucked it into her mouth and didn't let go. One of the child's hands also caught hold of Tyla's finger and curled around it so tight, Tyla thought the tip of her finger might explode. "She's strong!" she said. "You're going to be a little fighter, aren't you?" she muttered to the baby. The baby stopped sucking long enough to smile up at her, with the tip of the bottle dangling on the edge of her lips.

Danyel pulled the blanket further up the new centaur's legs and covered her lower half. "She might need to be," he said quietly.

Tyla met his eyes when she heard his tone. "What do you mean?"

"Her father," Danyel said, keeping his eyes trained on the baby, "he disappeared. He was one of the first ones. He's been gone three days."

"What's his name?" Tyla whispered, also not able to take her eyes from the child.

"Her father's name is Myles," Danyel answered.

"And what's her name?" she asked, nodding down at the little newborn.

"Her mother is thinking of naming her Kira."

"Well, Kira," Tyla said stroking the baby's hand with her free thumb, "I'm going to bring your father home." She finally swept her eyes up to Danyel and saw the smile on his face, but it didn't begin to reflect her determination. "I'm going to bring them all home."

8

THE PREDECESSOR

Although it couldn't be seen through the clouds, Tyla sensed the sun at the borders of the horizon as she trotted up to the gates. She eyed the sentries posted on the wall above her and some of them watched her closely inside the settlement walls as others stared outside.

"Wasn't sure you would actually come," Vanora said, sidling up to Tyla from behind and moving to the side of the gates.

"Why wouldn't I?" Tyla said. "I'm the one who actually wants to get out of here, remember?"

Vanora nodded. "Yes, that's why I thought you might leave without permission before I got here."

Tyla rolled her eyes. "I do have some honor, you know."

The older dragon shrugged before she nodded to the guards. "Follow me," she said as they pulled the gates open.

The rain had eased to a steady drizzle, but most centaurs still kept to their homes anyway. The drizzle began to irritate her hide, so Tyla did a quick scan around them.

"What are you looking for?" Vanora asked, eyeing her.

"Nothing," Tyla shook off the question.

"Are you going to change into a dragon, or did you expect me to carry you? Because I'm not carrying you," Vanora stood still, her gaze locked.

Tyla ground her teeth and allowed the fire in her belly to burn bright and strong in order to change into her dark red dragon form.

"Was that so hard?" Vanora growled, marching through the opening.

"Not hard, no," Tyla bit back, following the blue dragon past the centaurs watching from the wall and the two at the gates. She glared at them openly to discourage any reactions to her spots. When they didn't offer any, she turned back to Vanora.

"You don't like others to see your dragon form, is that it?" Vanora asked.

Tyla ground her teeth more and shrugged her shoulders. "I'm not keen on the spots," she said.

"Have others ever teased you about them?"

Tyla raised her top lip in a snarl. "They wouldn't dare."

"Or maybe they don't care, have you ever thought of that?" Vanora said, turning toward the sky. "Perhaps you're the only one who is truly worried about them."

Tyla shook her head. She'd heard it all before from her mother, Eleka, even her father, and she was sick of arguing about it. Her spots looked ridiculous, they just weren't what an intimidating dragon should look like, and no one could convince her otherwise. So she decided to change the subject.

"Why do you use the gates?" Tyla asked. "Can't you just fly over the wall to go in and out?"

"I could," Vanora answered. "But I don't, out of courtesy if not safety. If the guards see a dragon flying over, they know it's not one of us who lives here and sends for us right away."

The two dragons launched into the sky and Tyla's heart lifted. She hadn't realized how restrained she'd felt not being able to change and fly whenever the notion took her. Her parents never restricted her flying and changing. In fact, they traded turns taking her out as often as possible. So the past few days of being forced to stay on the ground wore on her patience. But as she ascended closer to the clouds she shied away from flying too high, remembering Trivnor's caution that the boundary to the World of Souls hovered somewhere not very far above them.

She spread her wings in the dying light, not worrying about who saw her spots for a moment. After spiraling through the rain briefly, she glanced at Vanora, who inspected her.

"What?" she said. "Am I already doing something wrong?"

Vanora shook her head. "You seem very happy to be flying."

"It's not good to restrain a dragon," Tyla said. "You should know that better than any of those centaurs."

"I'll keep it in mind," she said. "But it's still not safe for two young centaur dragons to be traveling by themselves in this area right now."

Tyla nodded. She didn't want to admit that the older dragon was right about that, but she and her sister must eventually get on their way and help find the other keys. Trusting Trivnor's story or not, they couldn't allow a human who would attack and kidnap centaurs to retain such power. "We can't stay here forever," she told her. "We'll have to either earn your trust or find some other means of compromise. Because we will leave, eventually."

Vanora nodded as they flew together. "Perhaps this will help with both of those issues."

"I'm guessing we're not searching over the plains," Tyla said as they flew closer to Gormirom, and the king's city of Gormitor, keeping the plains to their right.

Vanora grunted. "The centaurs who have disappeared have all gone either through the pass from the settlement or into the forest between us and the humans. In the beginning, some of the centaurs were simply traveling to Gormitor to trade. Since the disappearances started, the centaurs have been searching the trees and forests. But they can't travel as fast as I can search flying over them and have risked getting caught by humans on the ground."

"They can't travel as fast as *we* can," Tyla amended her statement.

Tyla thought she caught the beginning of an eyeroll from the big dragon. "Yes," Vanora said. "We need to search the forest for humans and see if our centaurs might be with them. We have to catch them in the act if we are to provide any proof beyond the note from Marish to the elders."

"What will you do?" Tyla asked. "If we find proof? What do you think the elders will do if we find anything?"

"I'm not sure," Vanora said, swinging in the sky. "I hope they'll be riled to action. Perhaps request troops from Tor Ekwa and march on Gormitor itself. Anything to get our kin back."

Tyla flinched slightly when Vanora mentioned her home. If her uncle Joss learned of centaur kidnappings, he would swiftly send her mother and their armies out to confront the human king about it. She and Eleka could be caught. However, if she became aware of any messages sent to their home about the troubles here, she and Eleka could be well away before any troops arrived.

Tyla followed Vanora through the darkening sky, but while Vanora scanned the landscape around them, Tyla scanned not only the ground but the sky as well. She viewed from the air what she and Eleka had missed when scurrying like roaches through the farthest mountain pass onto the plains. The settlement stretched to the north with the centaur fields and orchards tucked in a small valley further north and east of the settlement. The earthen mounds of the centaur homes protected the fields from storm and wind. A river created a gorge that wriggled further north to spill into the ocean much farther away and unseen ahead even to Tyla's eyes and Eleka's senses.

"Are there any human villages between here and Zanna?" Tyla asked. "Could those humans be involved in any of the disappearances? Or even be trying to help the centaurs?"

Vanora shook her head. "The humans we know were the first ones we asked, but the only centaur settlements or human villages between here and the king's city of Gormitor, have dragons in them as well, and those dragons would never allow such behavior. The dragons' loyalties go back centuries and I'm certain they would help the centaurs, but even they haven't seen any centaurs in days."

"And what's beyond Gormitor?" Tyla had never been this far west. She'd never had the same urges to explore Avonoa like Eleka did, so she had to familiarize herself with some of the distant reaches now.

"A few small human villages are to the north between the ocean and Gormitor," Vanora said, pointing her head in the direction. "Then south of Gormitor and spreading west to the ocean are so many human villages that most centaurs and dragons don't even go out that way."

"It's all so close to the Island Ruck," Tyla said, gazing into the distance. Although she couldn't see through the clouds to the Island Ruck out at sea, she squinted into the rain and imagined how close she really was.

"It's farther than you might think, but yes, it does feel tightly condensed as you fly over, especially on a clear day," Vanora said. "I remember back when this was the

Just Kingdom. Their human laws were very strict regarding engaging with centaurs and dragons. The authorities upheld those laws and the humans were very answerable. They didn't instigate much, if any, interaction with other species and when they did interact, they behaved with decorum. Since losing the Just Sword, their laws and adherence to them have dwindled to almost nothing."

Instead of going over the fields and plains leading deeper into centaur territories, Vanora led Tyla over the forested hills separating the human kingdom from the centaurs. The looming mountains to the south of the settlement were well behind them now and they slowly seemed to diminish beneath the rocky hills and tall trees they skirted. A beaten road led from the mountains behind them where the goblin portals hid, past the centaur settlement they'd left, then ahead of them to slip between the hills and trees to the human kingdom beyond. Vanora and Tyla flew low over the treetops in silence. Tyla's eyes constantly scanned the ground for humans or centaurs but also the clouds and rain, for any black creature that might drop from above.

"What are you looking for?" Vanora whispered after they swept deeper above the trees turning toward the kingdom of Gormirom's territory.

"I'm looking for humans," Tyla said. "Isn't that what you wanted me to do?"

"Yes," Vanora peered at her through narrowed eyes. "But you keep looking into the sky as well. Last I knew, humans can't fly."

Tyla shook her head, but grinned when she remembered the conversation with Dasha about flying humans. "We don't want any surprises from above."

"Like what?"

"Like anything." Tyla tried to be as vague as possible. She'd already put her claw in her mouth about too many things and she didn't want to buckle about the World of Souls under Vanora's questioning. She couldn't let on that she knew much more and she couldn't be sure of Vanora's knowledge, either. If she shared too much, Vanora was certainly smart enough to put pieces together. She knew it was best to avoid sensitive conversations and was reminded again when her heart quickened at the memory of wraiths literally dripping from the clouds around the Inner Mountain as their group waited in the stone bowl of the Krusible.

"Mm-hm," Vanora growled in the back of her throat. "You won't include us in your counsel and yet you expect us to trust you?"

She made it sound like a question, but Tyla felt like it was more of an accusation. "I want you to trust me, yes," she answered. "I just can't figure out how to accomplish that and be true to my wyrd at the same time."

Tyla realized her slip about giving her wyrd, but breathed again when Vanora's eyes locked onto something in the distance and she didn't press the subject. "Maybe start by helping me deal with *that*," she muttered so low that Tyla barely heard her.

When Tyla met Vanora's eyes, the blue dragon nodded her head toward the ground and Tyla turned to inspect what she indicated.

In the forest a long way from Zanna, small brown tents tucked together under the tree canopy. A whisper of smoke rose from a covered fire, but no other movement was immediately visible.

Tyla turned to Vanora to ask her about it, but Vanora shook her head at her. "Not here," she hissed so low that Tyla wasn't sure she'd heard it.

Once they'd flown far past the little camp, Vanora finally nodded. "I prefer not to speak around humans," she said. "Call it old prejudice, but I don't want them to hear me." As they flew on, she pointed to the ground several times. "There. And over there. These are the places where centaurs were last seen. Many of them show signs of struggle."

Tyla searched the areas. "They're all places well within reach of that camp."

Vanora nodded. "And the camp is situated almost directly between Gormitor and Zanna."

"It seems the most likely placement the humans would use if they needed easy access to roaming centaurs," Tyla said. "Maybe we should go back and look closer?"

"Not yet," Vanora swung her wings around to go further north. "We have to catch them in the act, remember? Let's circle a bit more and see what we can come up with."

"Where are we going?" Tyla asked.

"We're going to search the area between Zanna and the other villages to the north," Vanora said. "If we can catch the humans trapping, attacking or transporting captured centaurs, we'll have the proof we need to retaliate and return their attack in full force. But if we see something, you will only do as I tell you. Do you understand? Or else I'll take you straight back to Zanna right now."

"I understand," Tyla said, riling a little at the threat, as if she was a child. "I can follow orders. But shouldn't we be searching directly between the humans' camp and maybe even closer to Gormitor?"

"Maybe," Vanora said, "and we'll get there. But first I want to make sure I can trust you to do as you're told."

They flew in silence using the dying light and their altitude as cover.

"Can I ask you something?" Tyla finally spoke. When Vanora nodded, she continued. "Why do you live with the centaurs? I've only seen two dragons in Zanna and if you're both treated as elders, that means you've been there a long time. Why?"

Vanora tilted her head in thought and looked as if she was inspecting the trees. Finally, she spoke. "Sylam came in his own travels from the Rock Cloud Ruck and has his own reasons for being in Zanna. As for me, I fell in love with a centaur a long time ago. And you're right, I have been here for several years. He and I were both hoping one or both of us would change, but before that could happen…he died."

"I'm sorry," Tyla said.

Vanora nodded in thanks and said, "It's been a few years since he died, but by that time this was my home, so I never left."

"And your sister in Marish?" Tyla said.

"Oh," Vanora grinned, "same reason. She fell in love with a centaur and she's been living with the centaurs ever since, but her mate is still alive. She changed pretty quickly and they have four centaur dragons now."

"Good for her," Tyla said.

"Yes," Vanora agreed. "Although I'm starting to ascertain how complicated it is for her to deal with raising part-centaur part-dragons. Especially when they're young."

"We're not that bad, are we?" Tyla asked.

"That depends on one's behavior. Like telling the whole truth about where you come from," Vanora said pointedly.

Tyla looked ahead, wondering if she could or should tell Vanora their story. Perhaps the older dragon would be willing to help them. Might there be a way to tell her the truth without breaking her wyrd? Eleka could figure it out. She would have to ask her when they got back.

She realized that they had naturally swung around for another pass at the humans' camp and while avoiding Vanora's inquiring gaze, her eyes fell upon a light and smoke in the distance. "I see a light and there's more smoke," she said, desperate to change the subject.

"Can you?" Vanora asked. "I suppose a centaur dragon *would* have the best vision."

"We should definitely check it out," Tyla said and tilted her wings to circle around the side of the camp and head toward the new smoke.

Before she got very far, Vanora shot in front of her. "Where do you think you're going, fledgling?"

Tyla pulled up short. "We need to go see what it is," she said, trying to hide her indignance. "There was nothing to the north. That's the only thing we've seen and it looks like there's more activity now than when we saw it before."

"I gave you no such order," Vanora growled.

"But you're not certain what it is either," Tyla argued. "Let's get there and fly over quickly, just to see. It's dark enough now that we could probably even land and no one would see us."

As the two dragons beat their wings to hover a moment, Vanora's eyes bounced between Tyla and the smoke in the distance. Finally, she snorted. "Alright," she conceded. "Curiosity wins. But you'll stay hidden, airborne and silent unless I say otherwise."

Tyla jerked her head in a nod and Vanora led the way toward the smoke. As they flew closer, Tyla noticed the first signs of movement. She could see now that more than one fire burned in the clearing, hidden among the branches below them. She inched closer to whisper to Vanora. "I can find out more if I land as a centaur. I can get close enough to hear conversations. It's well dark. They'll never see me."

"You can also be caught," Vanora bit back.

"I can fight my way out as a dragon and you can back me up."

Vanora didn't answer, her eyes bouncing between Tyla, the camp below them and the directions of Gormitor and Zanna.

They circled high over the campsite and beyond the firelight. A handful of humans sheltered together beneath trees next to one of the small fires. A few tents huddled under the thickest of canopies around the edge of the clearing, but on one side a break in the trees yawned without any shelter. In the space, a corral packed horses together near the humans. All the horses pressed against a far wall of the corral. Neighs of worry and fear drifted up through the trees.

Tyla looked to Vanora, assuming the older dragon would want them to avoid a confrontation and leave. She opened her mouth, ready to protest again, but the words caught in her throat when Vanora's lip pulled back to bare her fangs. She wondered if she was mad because Tyla had pressed the matter of landing, but Vanora's eyes hadn't left the campsite.

Veering closer, she followed Vanora's dangerously narrowing eyes. She swung up and over Vanora to peer between the trees where the blue dragon still stared down below. Rounding some trees, the branches broke apart and Tyla caught a clearer view of the corral. When she saw the creatures inside huddled together, shaking heads and bumping against each other in agitation, the realization hit her. They weren't all horses.

9

NEEDS

"Follow me," Vanora growled low.

Tyla flew behind as Vanora swept over the tall trees next to the open area. Vanora landed as silent as a shadow and Tyla mirrored her action, floating down next to her, then landing in her centaur form. Vanora showed no sign of disapproval and nodded at her.

The two stepped carefully toward the corral where five centaurs stood hobbled in the cold fall rain. The centaurs huddled together, Tyla assumed to keep each other warm, alongside eight horses on one side of the corral.

"Keep watch," Vanora whispered, holding out her claw to indicate that Tyla should stay back.

Dropping behind, Tyla surveyed the area. The humans kept to the opposite side of the encampment. A quick search of the trees around them told her that they hadn't posted any sentries on this side, which seemed odd. The cover of dark and rain would make it easy for any outsider to sneak in and open the corral and free the centaurs. So why weren't the humans concerned about it?

Are these humans really that stupid? she wondered. *Or do they think the centaurs are that cowed?*

Tyla's eyebrows scrunched together. Humans were bold even if they didn't really have the right mind for strategy, but this seemed extraordinarily lacking in security. A twig creaked short of a complete snap somewhere through the trees. Was that fog slipping over the muddy forest floor?

"Wait, something's wrong," Tyla whispered as Vanora crept away from her.

Vanora stopped and swung her long neck to face Tyla. "What is it?" she whispered back. "Did you see something?"

Tyla shook her head. Her skin prickled. "Something doesn't feel right."

Vanora paused for a moment, then shook her head, ready for action. "We have to free them."

She turned back to creep closer to the enclosure. Just as Vanora used her claws to cut the bindings on the corral fence to gain access, Tyla caught sight of movement in the trees. Silently stepping closer to make sure it wasn't a human, she tilted her head and the movement revealed itself as only another tree with branches shaking in the wind.

The rain eased enough for Tyla to keep Vanora in sight so she searched the forest around them with her back to Vanora. No sign of movement except the trembling naked branches. Silently, the horizontal fence posts fell into Vanora's waiting claws and she lay them on the soft ground. The hobbled centaurs had taken note of Vanora so she signaled them to keep quiet. Meanwhile, Tyla continued sweeping her large eyes around the corral and behind them.

This is too easy, she thought. *Even humans aren't this ignorant. Why don't they have sentries on this side?*

Stilling her eyes and ears, she glimpsed it again. Something black and tangled slunk behind a tree on the opposite side of the corral where Vanora busily cut the hobbles from the centaurs' hooves. Tyla cautiously stepped closer, sinking her hooves in soft mud.

Suddenly a black shape sprang from the trees in front of Tyla. A massive centaur, dripping shadow from stretched, striated muscular hands darted toward her. Tyla's eyes widened on his bearded face just before his hands, the size of her head, seized her throat and he screamed a guttural bellow alerting everyone in the camp to their presence. Luckily, Tyla's training kicked in from muscle memory before she could even think about it. She threw her head forward and down and twisted out from under his grip before it fully tightened.

The centaur wraith bellowed and raged, grasping at air as he tried to grab Tyla again. Tyla glanced over at the others, making sure the centaurs' escape was unimpeded. Just as Vanora cut the last hobble, pain blossomed suddenly against Tyla's shoulder and chest. She flew—not of her own will—into the fence of the corral when the centaur wraith rose up and kicked her with both front hooves. The thick wooden beams of the corral burst apart against Tyla's back and shoulder as she slammed to the ground beyond them. Her breath knocked out of her, she lay for a moment on the soggy ground.

"Tyla!" Vanora yelled.

Blackness briefly danced with stars at the edges of Tyla's vision. Vanora tromped up behind her as she blinked the darkness away.

Looking up at Vanora, Tyla watched the older dragon's eyes drift to the centaur wraith.

"Killian?" Vanora whispered.

"Stop them!" the humans finally screamed from the encampment.

The humans converged with black-tipped swords, but Vanora didn't seem able to tear her eyes off the wraith.

Tyla turned as the centaur prisoners stumbled out of the corral and into the woods. One woman supported a man to help him trot into the dark trees. Another man slowed and turned to Tyla with a questioning look on his face. His eyes bounced between her and the oncoming humans.

Tyla waved at him, pain slashing at her back. "Go!" she yelled and pain flared in her side too.

She pushed herself from the ground as Vanora took a step closer to the centaur wraith, whispering her long gone love's name.

The wraith roared and snatched at the empty air but didn't advance.

Why isn't it attacking us? Tyla wondered.

"Vanora," she said aloud. "We have to go."

She reached up to pull on the dragon the best she could while in her centaur form as the dragon began to weep. "Killian," she mumbled. Inspecting the centaur wraith's hooves through the rain and mud and swirling misty shadow, Tyla could barely make out the hobble attached to a chain keeping him secured to a substantial tree. It was the only thing keeping Tyla and Vanora alive.

"That's not your Killian," Tyla said to Vanora. "Come on!"

The first human was almost upon them.

"No!" Vanora cried. Before she could even see the human, she swept her heavy tail into a man, throwing him into the wraith.

The human screamed and the wraith attacked. The wraith scratched, clawed and pounded at the man. The human lost his sword in the first blow from Vanora's tail and now punch after punch hammered at him unhindered. He quickly went still. The centaur wraith of Killian flung the human's body to the side, but the shadow of the human's wraith quickly formed and rose in front of them. The dripping black shadow of a man with shriveled black skin, clawlike fingers and sunken holes for eyes stood and turned toward the oncomers.

The other humans held back and attempted to surround the growing number of enemies. They glanced between the centaur wraith, hobbled and limited, the newly formed human wraith, unfettered, the dragon and the injured centaur.

"Need some rope!" one of the men yelled, pointing to the new human wraith. "And get that one under control," he yelled again, pointing to the centaur wraith who was at one time Vanora's Killian.

"Come on!" Tyla yelled at Vanora, who stood with her jaw agape and tears forming at the edges of her eyes.

With the humans starting to creep around them, Tyla changed back into her dragon form. After a brief jolt of pain in her back, she blew fire at the humans and tugged on Vanora, who finally snapped out of her shock and grief and began to move, but painstakingly slowly.

Tyla grabbed Vanora's face with her claws and turned it toward her, forcing the blue dragon's eyes to meet hers. "That's not your Killian," she said again firmly. "We have to go."

Vanora nodded wordlessly and Tyla released her. Blowing fire at the humans to keep them away, the two females ran after the escaping centaurs.

They followed the centaurs galloping directly toward Zanna, no matter the terrain. Vanora didn't dare let them out of her sight and would scout ahead in flight or follow on claw as she saw fit. However, she didn't say much to Tyla. Tyla flew overhead, slowly circling and on the alert.

As the rain softened to a drizzle, Tyla sensed the moons overhead. After a much longer night than either she or Vanora had planned, the group finally caught sight of the settlement walls. Vanora happened to be silently flying next to Tyla when they saw the settlement with the gates standing wide open.

"Now what?" Vanora grumbled, more to herself than anyone else.

The two dragons hung back, hovering outside the settlement walls to wait as the former centaur captives limped through the open gates. As soon as they were all through, Tyla and Vanora landed on the ground and loped through after them.

"What's going on?" Vanora demanded of the centaur sentries standing beside the gates. "Why are the gates open like this?"

The gate guards began closing it behind her. "Sorry," one of the guards said. "We saw you coming and decided to keep it open for you."

"*Keep* it open?" Vanora asked. "Why did you have it open in the first place?"

"Some goblins arrived just before you and the others," the guard said. "They've been taken to the House of Elders and we've sent for the other elders."

Tyla's heart jumped. Goblins. As soon as she heard the word she knew exactly why they were there. She knew they must have been sent by Shvika or maybe even have Shvika herself in the party. Her stomach dropped and her heart picked up its pace immediately.

As Vanora left to join the goblins and the elders, Tyla turned toward the healers' house. "Aren't you coming?" Vanora called to her. "I thought you might want to help me report what happened. And see the goblins."

"Um, no, you can tell them about it. I figure I've caused enough trouble for one day," Tyla said shuffling backward. "I could use some sleep. And a healer."

Without waiting to hear Vanora's response, Tyla lumbered away. If she stayed and fell under the older dragon's scrutiny, Vanora would unravel the reasons for her anxiety. Tyla waited until she was outside the healers' house before changing back into her centaur form and exploding through the doors.

Tyla burst into the kitchen looking for Eleka and found Danyel and her sister standing together there, casually chatting and laughing. She wished that the blood she could feel rising in her cheeks wasn't so obvious. The pair might not have seen her flushed face had she stayed as a dragon. She could only hope they wouldn't know the real reason.

"Goblins!" she blurted as soon as she saw them. Was Eleka touching his hand? *No*, she must have been imagining it.

"Where've you been?" Danyel said. "I thought you would be back long ago."

"Goblins?" Eleka cut him off, the smile draining from her face.

"Yes," Tyla said, choosing to ignore Danyel's pointless question—he knew she had left with Vanora. *Why are you up so late?* she wanted to ask. "They arrived just before we got back." Her emotions were heightened already and she couldn't help but glare accusingly at her sister.

"We hardly ever receive goblins around here," Danyel said. "I wonder what they could want. Let's go find out."

Danyel stepped over to Tyla and offered his hand, but Tyla yanked hers away, leaving his empty. "Maybe later," she said, still boring her eyes into Eleka's.

"What happened to your back?" Danyel said, skirting around her to inspect the injury when it caught his eye.

"It's nothing," she replied curtly. "I'm fine."

"This doesn't look fine," he said. "I should probably apply some—"

"I said I'm fine." Tyla couldn't hide her irritation and shrugged away from him. "I need to talk to my sister."

Danyel's hands dropped to his side. Tyla's face burned more, but she ignored it. In silence, Danyel trotted out the door.

"What do we do?" Tyla said once the door closed behind Danyel. "They're here for us."

"You don't know that," Eleka said.

"Why else would they be here?" Tyla snapped.

"I don't know!" Eleka snapped back loudly, throwing her hands in the air. "It could be anything. Maybe they're checking on settlements and offering help with the wraiths."

"Not likely. They're not exactly known for going out of their way to help others." Tyla slipped to a nearby window and peeked around the curtain. "They probably sent goblins through each of the portals we disappeared through and now they're hunting us all down. That's what I would do."

"Or…they need help defending themselves," Eleka said, crossing her arms. Tyla couldn't understand why Eleka couldn't see the obvious. "Maybe they got attacked the same as everyone else and they need a safe haven. There could be any number of reasons they're here."

"No!" Tyla shouted to shut her up. "Finding the thieves of a priceless majikal gem taken from the depths of the royal palace! *That* would be their first priority." She seethed trying to get through to her sister. "We have to leave! Now!"

"And go where?" Eleka shouted back.

Tyla shook her head, her jaw hanging open, not believing her sister couldn't see it. "I don't know," she said after a moment, "you're the smart one, you figure it out. Anywhere but here!"

"Look," Eleka said, trying to calm her sister down, "I talked to Dasha."

Tyla stopped and spun on her. "And?"

"And," she tugged at her hair, "everyone else is in the same predicament as we are. Whether they're here for us or not, the goblins have enough to deal with tracking down all nine of us. We don't know if they have enough forces to follow all of us. They might be prioritizing all of us and only going after certain culprits first. No one has spoken to any of the boys, not Trivnor, Lokna, Burk, or Jassan. The goblins may have already found them. But I think chasing a faerie they'd discovered deep in the palace might be their first priority, rather than pursuing a couple of young centaurs."

Tyla shivered. She had never liked any faeries before Jassan. Ever. They were too quiet and reserved to be trustworthy. She could only imagine the same prejudices lingered in the goblins' minds.

But Jassan had seemed just as scared and vulnerable as she was, yet he still risked his life to save her and her sister from the dungeons. He saved each of them and barely escaped with his life. He had even gone so far in his compassion for others as to coax dozens of wraiths away from the goblin city of Kirlik to save the goblins who were still, at this moment, trying to hunt them all down. He had only behaved with complete trustworthiness.

"They never saw his face," Tyla said. "But they've seen ours."

"And Trivnor's," Eleka muttered. "I think he would be their priority."

Tyla sighed. Her hands shook so she balled them into fists at her side then relaxed the muscles in her arm. "I guess you could be right," she mumbled back."

"Look," Eleka said again, "it's late. You're probably exhausted."

Tyla nodded. She should be tired, but her mind was still hyper-alert. "More hungry," she said.

Eleka shook her head. "Of course you are." She pulled some bread and butter and apples out of the cabinet. Before she could finish spreading the butter on the bread, Tyla grabbed an apple and poured her emotion into devouring it. The injury on her back pinched a little, but dulled enough that she could ignore it.

"Dasha and I agreed," Eleka said, "that for now, no news will have to be good news."

Tyla took the buttered bread but paused before stuffing it in her mouth to ask, "How do you mean?"

Eleka shook her head again and picked up another piece to butter. "We think Kelraz would be gloating if he'd found Jassan or Trivnor or anyone else. He certainly would be if he got Trivnor's or Jassan's keys. Or any key. The keys would make him much more dangerous and he would make sure we all knew it. We would have heard by now if anything serious had happened to him."

Tyla swallowed. "That's true," she said. "Maybe Kelraz hasn't found him after all. He might be safe and hiding somewhere."

Eleka nodded. "I think he got away," she said. "Lokna and Burk are there to help him. I think they all got away."

Somehow, instead of discussing the entire group of boys, or Trivnor who was supposed to be guiding them, the conversation only focused on the one person, really. Jassan. And Tyla didn't even mind.

Tyla nodded, staring out the window at the rain splattering the mud. "They did. They had to."

10

TO FIND

Once her stomach calmed with food, Tyla took Eleka's advice to lie down. After both twins tried to use the communication circlet and reached no one, they finally both fell into a fitful rest.

This time she dreamed of Dasha being attacked in the forest outside of Marrack, where they first met for the summons. A wraith jumped up onto a tree and crashed down on top of Dasha in her dragon form. She shrank down to her goblin form, but both she and the wraith spun their heads to stare at Tyla.

Tyla tried to run to Dasha's aide, but her feet stuck fast in soft mud. She tried shifting from dragon to centaur and back again, but nothing helped and she couldn't get closer to helping her friend as she screamed and begged Tyla to save her.

Unable to run, Tyla glanced down at her legs to see hobbles, the same ones the captured centaurs at the camp had been wearing. She tried to bend down and unclasp them, but Eleka grabbed her shoulders to stop her.

"Tyla!" she yelled in her face. "Why aren't you helping? Tyla!"

"Tyla!" Dasha screamed.

"Tyla!" Eleka whispered.

Tyla's eyes blinked open rapidly to clear the dream out of her mind. Someone was still shaking her arm and she whirled on Danyel's voice.

"Come with me," he said, once she blinked fully awake, "both of you."

All too early in the morning for either of them, possibly only a few hours after falling asleep, Tyla looked over to see that Eleka was awake and looking as confused as she was, but without a word they both stood.

"Danyel," Tyla started, "what—"

"No," he said. He held up a hand to stop her from speaking but didn't meet her eyes. "Stay quiet."

Eleka pursed her lips at the warning and Tyla grit her teeth. He had discovered something. They would just have to wait to find out what it was.

He led the twins through the other rooms and out the back door of the little healers' house. He led them behind the mound of one building to another mound. When he came to the space between the two homes, he stopped and held a hand out to halt the twins. After checking around the corner, he waved for them to follow him behind the next home.

"Where are we going?" Eleka whispered.

"Quiet," Danyel whispered back. "You can't be seen."

Tyla glimpsed Eleka's wide eyes mirroring her reaction. He had said '*you*' can't be seen…not 'we'.

The day was unseasonably clear, meaning only a light mist and heavy, low clouds in the sky, which made it more difficult to dodge the growing crowd of centaurs cantering excitedly in the good weather. Eventually, Danyel led the twins to a bigger dwelling, one made of hard-packed clay and dragon-fired stone walls. The back door was large enough for a dragon to enter.

Each one pushing aside the heavy drapery as they entered, Tyla knew who to expect. Vanora sat curled against the wall. Alone.

Danyel gave Tyla a fleeting glance before stepping over to stand beside Vanora.

"Who *are* you?" Vanora asked with suspicion in her measured tone.

"We told you who we are," Tyla said.

"What's this all about?" Eleka asked.

"You know why the goblins are here," Vanora said, "don't you?"

"Shopping for frogs' eyes for a stew?" Tyla quipped.

Vanora growled and bared her fangs. Rising slowly, she stayed low enough to assume an attack posture. "This is no joking matter, young one."

"They're looking for you," Danyel prompted the twins, without judgement, "aren't they?"

"What makes you say that?" Eleka stepped bravely between Vanora and Tyla.

"You saved my life last night," Vanora said, glaring at Tyla. "And I saved yours—by keeping the fact that you're here in the settlement from the goblins."

Both of the twins' eyes met Vanora's. The dragon nodded knowingly. "When I didn't offer them the information they asked for, the rest of the elders followed my lead. So they haven't been made aware of your presence. Yet."

"They're looking for twins," Danyel said. "Twin, brown centaur dragons. Female… young."

His eyes met Tyla's then fell.

"And?" Tyla said, whipping her head back to Vanora.

"And," Vanora crept closer, "now you need to tell us what you are doing here, where you are going, and maybe most important, why? And anything else that might be pertinent for us to know about the situation before we turn you over to the goblins."

"Please," Eleka begged. "Please, what we're doing is important."

"Which is what?" Vanora barked. "Stealing priceless gems from the goblin's royal palace?"

Tyla swallowed. Her eyes fell to the floor and she watched Eleka's hoof shuffling.

"We don't have it," Eleka finally answered.

"Oh," Vanora said, "but you know who does."

They hadn't heard a question, so neither of them responded.

Vanora drew in a breath, puffing out her chest and pulling up her posture over them. "Look," she said, "let me be clear. I don't trust goblins. They're too arrogant for my taste. But your trustworthiness is still in question as well. Even more so now that the goblins have made their case. If you can't explain yourselves now, I'll have to—"

"We gave our wyrd," Tyla blurted.

Eleka looked at her sister, but for once she didn't have an accusatory glare. "We gave our wyrd," Eleka echoed.

"We can't tell you what we're doing—"

"—or where we're going."

"We can only promise that we're not common thieves—"

"—and that what we're doing is of the utmost importance."

"That's it?" Vanora rumbled. "That's all you can give me?"

Eleka shrugged, but Tyla stepped forward. "No, it isn't," she said. "I can tell you this. We can help Killian."

Vanora's maw popped open hearing her beloved's name.

"Tyla," Eleka chided.

"He was dead long before these attacks started," Vanora said. "You can't bring him back."

"No," Tyla said. "But we *can* help him."

Vanora sniffed and stared at the ceiling of her home for what seemed an eternity. Finally, she pinched her eyes shut and muttered, "I'll get you over the wall."

Danyel hugged his shoulders, his head hanging. "Where will you go?"

"Gormitor," Tyla said.

The three centaurs stood atop the wall around the settlement, hiding behind a covered ramp at the side. Vanora had informed the guards that the girls would be leaving over the wall and not to sound any alarm or hinder them in any way. Before she went back to the House of Elders she told Tyle and Eleka that she would blow a flame into the sky when the goblins were contained and wouldn't discover their flight.

"Why Gormitor?" Danyel said. The twins shared a glance and Danyel threw up his hands. "I know, I know. You can't tell me."

Tyla shook her head, patting her red wrappings. The three of them had gone back to the healers' home under the twins' guise of retaining Eleka's shoulder cloak and maybe a weapon for their journey, but while her twin retrieved the circlet and knife from the bed's folds, Tyla distracted Danyel. When Eleka came back out, she handed Tyla the broken sword purposefully and threw the little cloak over her shoulders.

Tyla checked that the stunted sword was tucked under her wrappings. "Saying anything would only put you in more danger and break our wyrd," she said.

"What if I come with you?" he pressed. "I could give you my wyrd as well. Whatever your secret is, I'll keep it too."

"May would never let you go," Tyla said.

"Or Vanora," Eleka put in.

Danyel grunted. "Well," he mumbled, "if you ever come back this way…"

"Hopefully not with monsters and goblins chasing us?" Tyla smirked.

"Yeah," he said. "Maybe not that. But I wouldn't mind seeing you again."

"Yeah," Tyla shrugged nonchalantly, trying not to look too happy that he'd voiced it and also hyper-aware that Eleka stood nearby listening, "maybe."

Fire erupted into the misty sky from the direction of the House of Elders.

"Tyla," Eleka said, gently "we have to go."

Tyla nodded and stepped toward the edge of the wall as Danyel stepped toward her. He stopped and she took another step. Before she could think of what else to say or do, she had taken her red dragon form and was in the air. Danyel shrank away from her, standing on the wall, staring into the drizzle with one hand raised in farewell.

Once Danyel and Vanora and Zanna were dozens of dragon lengths behind them, Eleka snorted. "What do we do now?" she said, her scaly dragon brows pinched together and her eyes darting between the trees below them.

"How should I know?" Tyla grumbled. "You're the smart one. You're supposed to point me in the direction of heads that need bashing." A vision of Killian's wraith doing just that came into Tyla's head. She shivered and shook the image away.

"I'm serious," Eleka repeated, "what are we supposed to do?"

"Come on, you're the brains," Tyla insisted. "You figure it out. I've said all along that we should go home. But the key is in Gormitor, so that's where we have to go, right?"

"We're actually not positive about that," Eleka said.

Tyla shot her a glare. "What are you talking about?"

"Think about it," Eleka said. "All we really know is that humans are kidnapping centaurs, but we've only heard rumors about a competition and some super-strong champion. That's it. That's all we have. I'm not sure what we can do about the key if we don't find out what's really going on first."

"Ok, let's see," Tyla said, "we get to Gormitor." For direction, she pointed her claw toward the far side of the forest of trees with the plains behind them. "Next, we find out if there *is* such a competition and who this so-called champion is. Then, I challenge the champion. Winner gets the key. Easy."

"Right," Eleka scoffed. "Easy. Unless the champion is much larger and stronger than you."

"Are you saying I can't beat a human?!"

"Maybe," Eleka shrugged. "But you have no idea what they're capable of."

"All the more reason to get there and find out."

"But how do we do that without getting into more trouble? Or getting captured ourselves?"

"Look," Tyla rolled her eyes, "Maybe you should—"

With a sudden roar, an immense black shadow rose straight up from the trees in front of the twins. Its wingspan stretched across the sky, blocking the soggy horizon in front of them. Dark shadow roiled from the scales of the enormous dragon wraith. It roared and clawed at the girls in the air.

Tyla reacted without thinking. She grabbed the dragon's front claws and used the momentum they had together to swing them into opposite positions before letting go.

"Into the trees!" Eleka yelled. "Maybe it won't follow us!"

"Dive!" Tyla yelled.

Without looking back, the twins dove into the trees and changed back to centaur form, hitting the ground mid-gallop. Hurtling through the trees, they jumped over bushes and fallen logs until the roar of the dragon wraith faded behind them.

Tyla turned to see how much time they had. "It's not following us," she said as she slowed her pace. "Why isn't it following us?"

Another roar echoed from their left in the trees. Dark shadow drifted through the trunks, shifting the mist that lay against the ground.

"Doesn't matter," Eleka whispered. "Come on."

Tyla didn't need urging. She couldn't see how many wraiths whispered through the forest beside them, so her brain conjured dozens. Turning, she galloped after her sister.

"We need to find a break in the trees and get back into the air," Tyla said.

"No," Eleka nodded in the direction of the wraith they had seen, "we can't fly or that one will see us again.

Besides, we've been pushing our luck flying anyways. Remember what Trivnor said about the World of Souls in the clouds?"

"No," Tyla lied, "but I do remember the Rock Clouds dripping with wraiths." Her sister was right about flying. They fell to a canter before Eleka threw her arm out in front of her sister.

"Whoa!" she yelled over the sound of a raging river.

Tyla stopped next to her to peer over a sharp cliff. The trees growing out of the cliff face disguised the sudden drop. A torrential flooded river churned beneath them. Even Tyla knew better than to brave a full river in the fall season. The constant rain filled rivers, lakes and oceans with unknown depths and fatal currents. She wasn't sure even the mad dragons of the Island Ruck would brave such treacherous waters.

"We go around," Eleka said.

"We could easily fly over," Tyla bit back. "And there's a break in the trees on the other side and even a couple boulders. If we could—"

"We go around," Eleka snapped each word, then turned and took off through the forest that ran along the clifftop.

They soon had to slow, unable to keep up such a demanding pace in their centaur forms. Tyla remembered her mother's constant nagging at home that she go out running to build up her stamina. But Tyla was only interested in combat training. She figured she could always change into her dragon form and cover more ground flying farther and longer, if not faster.

"Gormitor isn't very far," Eleka said. "We should probably find somewhere to rest and come up with a plan."

"I told you my plan," Tyla said. "Challenge champion. Bash heads. Take key."

"You realize that you might have to kill someone to take the key, don't you?"

"Of course," Tyla said. "It's not like I haven't killed before."

"You've killed animals, not humans," Eleka said. "It's not the same."

"It's close enough."

"Plus, killing one would turn them into a wraith."

"And I've never had to fend off one of those either, right."

Eleka spread her hands between them. "I hope you know what you're getting into."

"You really don't think I'm capable of doing anything without you, do you?" Tyla growled.

"That's not true," Eleka said. "You're perfectly capable of getting yourself into trouble."

"'at makes two o' you," a raspy voice sneered from the dark trees.

11

BALANCE

"Snag 'em!" a man's gravelly voice yelled.

Tyla stopped and glared into the trees, where the voice seemed to have come from. She could make out the fuzzy outline of a human man leaning against a boulder. He smiled a crooked smile at Tyla before four other men jumped out from the trees on either side of and behind the girls with more men waiting behind them in the dark.

"Oh, now you've done it!" Tyla said. Although she wasn't sure if she was madder at the man with the ugly sneer or her sister for distracting her from watching for danger. Either way, she spun to face the oncoming humans. Unfortunately, the men weren't alone.

The humans spread out enough to allow space for the wraiths that followed them out of the trees. Four centaur wraiths with chains around their necks like dogs approached the girls, their faces twisted and snarling, their hands shaped like claws with human fingertips that looked as sharp as any dragon's. Using long majikal ropes, like the ones they'd seen used in Zanna, attached to the chains on the wraiths, the men used the monsters to herd the twins close together.

Tyla roared, changing to her dragon form. Unfortunately, the thick tree canopy overhead impeded her lift. They'd have to claw their way up the trunks to the sky while also fighting the wraiths and the humans.

Shadow dripped from the nearest wraith as it inched closer to Tyla. Eleka changed almost immediately after Tyla and now her tail bumped against her back, red scales scraping against her sister.

"Now what?" Eleka said, her voice trembling.

"Follow me," Tyla growled.

She launched herself at the nearest human, a skinny man with thick arms holding two chains attached to wraiths on either side of him. She figured that if his hands were busy, she might be able to kill him quickly and escape. Running at him, she raised her front claw, but got slammed in the side, knocking her away from the man and into the base of a tree sitting atop a rock. Tyla looked up from the ground as a wraith raised its hooves to pummel her.

She swung her tail and knocked the monster off its hind legs. With a screech the wraith flew into the man holding the chain. This time, the wraith took the closest prey. Tyla turned away when the screaming started.

But she didn't have time to rejoice. She jumped to her feet again and saw another centaur wraith galloping toward her. Kicking her back leg out before it reached her, she swung her front claw at the nearest human, catching him across the face and neck. It should have been a good blow, but he jumped backward and was only scratched. It wasn't the killing blow she needed. However, when he fell to the ground howling in pain, he unintentionally released the chain restraining the wraith.

The wraith paused a moment, glancing between the injured man and its original victim. Tyla didn't wait for it to make up its mind. Planting her front legs, she swung the back of her body around to use the momentum of both her back legs to push the wraith into the injured man. The centaur wraith attacked the human with its strong front hooves and after a few moments another human wraith drifted from the ground, hovering over the mutilated human body.

Tyla sagged. She couldn't win this fight. Anyone she killed would only come back, but stronger. All she could do now was escape. She spun to urge her twin to follow her and her stomach dropped.

"Eleka!" Tyla bellowed.

Her sister lay on the forest floor in her streaked red dragon form, a net of woven majikal chains thrown over her. One of the human men grasped his bloody leg and leaned against a tree. Another man tried to control a wraith by whipping the majikal rope, either urging it to attack Tyla again or stop it from attacking him, Tyla couldn't be sure.

"I can' believe 'at dragon monster trick worked," the ugly man said, standing over Eleka.

Tyla saw red on the edges of her vision while focusing singularly on her twin. She shoved her feet into the dirt, but the strong hands of a wraith clamped onto her tail. She flicked him off, but another wraith grabbed at her back claw as she lifted it from the mud and threw it to the side.

Unblinking, her eyes locked on Eleka, lying still under the glimmering net. Something beat across her back, but she didn't take her eyes from her sister. Chills shuddered through her wing joint, but she pressed toward Eleka, crying her name.

A hard thud resounded against her side. A sharp coldness sliced across her back where she had landed against the fence while freeing the centaurs. In the back of her mind, she wondered if the wraiths would do additional damage to the injury although she hadn't had time to check what damage had already been done.

She couldn't move her limbs the way she wanted to, it felt like she was trying to slog through a sand pit in the desert. Shaking her body to excise the beasts so she could move seemed to work for a moment, but one remained stubbornly attached to her front leg. Lifting that leg into the air, she shook it, hoping to fling the monster far into the trees, however she underestimated the strength of the creature clinging to her. A reverberating crack shook her limb. Pain blossomed in her middle joint. But she ignored it and shook her entire body again. This time, the pressure from her back eased and she assumed she'd shaken off someone or something else.

She took a breath to scream Eleka's name again, but her sister's eyes fluttered open.

"Ty…" Eleka whimpered.

"Eleka!" Tyla shrieked and turned to the human. "What did you do to her?"

The ugly man smiled again. In that moment, Tyla hated the fact that centaur dragons could see better than any other creature when she easily distinguished his thin, stubbly lips peel back to reveal dirty, crooked teeth.

Tyla turned to use her fangs to release her from the monsters bearing down on her, but her eyes fell on all the men and wraiths converging. She whipped her tail and knocked over two wraiths. She kicked out with her legs and threw two men against the same boulder she'd just been thrown into.

"Tyla," Eleka whispered. Her eyes didn't seem able to focus on her sister. "Go." She blinked and her head rolled slowly to the side to rest in the mud.

"NO!" Tyla screamed again, her entire body thrumming with heat and energy.

"Don' you worry," the ugly man said. "We'll take good care o' you girls. Righ' until the momen' you're scheduled t' die."

Tyla bellowed. Fire blazed from her maw and she swept it in an arc to catch human, wraith and forest alike. The ugly man covered his face with his long cloak before the fire hit him. When she stopped, his cloak fell away, unsinged, and his grin remained. The other men had dodged it, but the trees around them had been taken. Dragon fire burned longer in the rain than normal fire, but the rain would put it out eventually. The fire didn't have any effect on the wraiths.

Tyla kicked and clawed and scratched at every attempt of the wraiths or humans to close in. If she killed these humans, she would have even more wraiths to deal with. She had to go. She had to listen to her sister. If nothing else, she must listen to her sister.

"Recoil, return," that's how her mother had trained her. Whenever Tyla continued to push herself against another centaur or her trainers or other dragons until the point of exhaustion, her mother, Ashel, would step in. "Recoil in an unwinnable fight—to yourself, your camp, your home—so you can return to battle or war and fight stronger the next time. You won't win every fight immediately or even the first time through," she would say. "Sometimes you'll have to save yourself and your body to continue the fight later. Recoil, then return."

Tyla kicked the nearest wraith, grabbed a human, and threw him into the next wraith. Spinning, she spewed fire in a circle.

But her mother's advice couldn't always be right, could it? What if she was fighting for her life? Would 'recoil' always be the right move? What if it took too long in the moment? What if doing it meant she would die? What if recoiling meant Eleka would die?

Is she? The sound of her mother's voice penetrated her memory. *Are you?*

No, she realized. *I'm outnumbered, but Eleka isn't dying now, she's only captured. They won't kill her. Will they? No, right now, they won't.*

She grasped the nearest tree, now burning through the trunk with dragon fire, and jerked on it, snapping it at the weakened charred point. Once free, Tyla threw the heavy trunk into the wraiths trying to untangle themselves while the others attacked the men.

Seeing a break in the canopy, Tyla jumped onto the broken tree trunk, then threw herself at the next tree higher up.

"Don' you dare le' tha' whelp escape!" the ugly man bellowed, but the remainder of his men were busy fighting off the wraiths of the others.

Clinging to the side of a tree, Tyla turned a steely glare on the ugly man with the crooked teeth. "You should fear for yourself," she hissed. "I'll make sure you suffer." She gave her sister one last glance, lying still behind the human, before throwing herself into the sky above the trees.

She cried the entire way back. She couldn't help it. She had done it again. Her leg throbbed, but she ignored it.

Why can't you listen to your smarter half? she berated herself. *If I hadn't insisted we go straight to Gormitor immediately, this never would have happened.*

Tyla knew that Eleka had the communication circlet tucked under the back of her dragon wrappings. With any luck, her captors wouldn't find it, or know what it was if they did. But their luck hadn't exactly been spectacular for some time now. The tears came again when Tyla imagined the ugly man searching her sister and pulling out the precious majikal item.

Without the obruck, Tyla couldn't speak with anyone else. She couldn't call for help from Trivnor or Jassan because no one knew where they were. Besides, she figured they must not have functional obrucks or someone would have heard from them by now. There was really only one place she could go for help and was already on her way there.

Heading for Danyel's settlement, she gawked at a familiar dragon wraith bobbing in the sky and this time noticed the chain holding it to the tree below. She growled and berated herself for falling for such a simple, stupid trap. It should never have worked. Certainly not on her.

When the lights of Zanna winked in the distance she began wondering what she might say to Danyel. Could she slip into the settlement without the goblins noticing? Had they already discovered Vanora's lies that helped her and Eleka escape? What could she possibly say to Vanora to beg her help getting Eleka back?

This was the first moment she realized that she had no idea what they would do with Eleka. She couldn't even be certain where they would take her. And she had no way of getting any of that information. Unless…

Tyla shot over the wall of the settlement and the heads of the centaurs guarding it. Shouts and yells chased her, but she didn't stop. She flew straight to the vast double doors with centaur guards on either side. She didn't bother to demand they be opened, she grabbed at the doors with her dragon claws. Her claws didn't fit through the handles so she sank them into the wooden frames. Her right claw screamed so she placed her left claw over it to lend the strength she needed to break through the wood. She pulled and ripped a hole where the handles should have been and used it to free the doors from their hinges as well.

He'll know! her mind screamed. *Kelraz will know!*

The yelling increased behind her, but she continued to ignore it. She entered the wraith cage and glanced around at all the smoky, dripping monsters. Normally, she assumed they would be wailing and thrashing in their bonds. Not this time.

He's here.

Every wraith in the enclosure sat silently. She didn't pause to look at them. The yelling and bellyaching from outside calmed as the centaurs observed how passively the wraiths reacted to Tyla's presence, but she stepped further into the enclosure, tripping slightly when pain lanced up her front leg. She kicked aside a couple of faerie wraiths who hissed at her. Shouldering aside another centaur wraith who wriggled to right himself, she found the one she wanted. She pushed past all of them until she settled in front of the faerie wraith tied to a pole at the center of the enclosure.

She ripped the bindings from the wraith's head and face with her good claw. Once it was free, she wrapped her good claw around the faerie wraith's throat and lifted it up in the air. Slamming it against the column, she screamed, "Where is she?!"

The faerie wraith dripped shadow as it turned its face up to look at her. A taut smile twisted its expression. Its hollow pits for eyes glared at her. "Where…is…who?" The voice scraped inside her ears like claws on slate.

"You know who!" she yelled, punching the faerie wraith against the column again. Tyla felt the eyes of the settlement on her from the door, but no one entered or tried to stop her.

The wraith hissed a wicked laugh. Shadow dripped from it and pooled around Tyla's claws before disappearing into the soggy ground.

Another centaur wraith lay on its side nearby with its legs bound in chains and its hands in ropes behind its back. "And you know where," it grumbled up to her.

Tyla growled at the centaur wraith on the ground. "Gormitor."

A faerie wraith to her left with a majikal rope twisted through its stomach and wrapping around its neck and arms cackled, "The castle!"

Another centaur wraith whispered, "Bring your friend."

The one next to it whispered, "Jassan," and the name echoed through the enclosure from many phantom mouths.

"Maybe we can trade," the voices trailed off and ended.

Tyla froze and icy chills scampered down her spine that had nothing to do with the pain in her leg. She realized what they meant—he wanted Jassan. Kelraz was still looking for him. He must still be alive.

Suddenly, imagining Jassan's blue freckled face in the creature she held in her claw, Tyla released the faerie wraith in horror. She turned toward the doors not seeing anything as her thoughts swirled. When she blinked and cleared her vision, a small grey creature stood by her claws.

"Nice to meet you, Tyla," the goblin said. He reached out his hand and touched her claw. When they connected, a paralyzing shock jolted her whole body. Tyla's vision went dark as the ground thudded against her face.

12

SHACKLED

"Was that really necessary?"

"You tell me. You're the one who said she wasn't here."

Tyla woke to arguing voices bouncing over her. She remembered the painful shock that had knocked her out. The shock had passed, but the remnants of it prickled her scales. She opened her eyes and wriggled.

"Easy," a gruff voice said to her. "No sudden movements."

Tyla opened her eyes fully to take in her surroundings. She lay on her side inside the House of Elders. Several of the centaur elders and a few others from the settlement stood over her, talking and casting furtive glances in her direction.

"What's going on?" she whispered, a metallic flavor on her tongue. The same taste she always got when she went to the Rock Clouds to visit Lokna and Gizi.

Trying to stand, her legs twitched but wouldn't obey and an icy coldness tore through her front leg at the ankle. Inspecting them, she found her front and rear legs hobbled, each hobble chained to a different support beam in the House of Elders.

"What's going on? What are you doing to me?" Panic rose in her voice. "I have to save my sister!" Ignoring the stabbing lancing up her front leg, she shook at her chains and found them extremely secure.

"Oh, ho, you *do* have a sister, do you?" the gruff voice returned.

Tyla swung her head around to the voice. A goblin sat on a box nearby. The goblin was small by goblin standards. Even Dasha might have been taller though at least ten years younger.

"Who are you?" Tyla asked.

"My name is Trykirt," the goblin said. A yellow sash with green goblinish writing on it, and a short silver sword the size of Tyla's centaur forearm strapped to his lower back, marked him as a goblin guard. Tyla had never learned to read or write goblinish. Goblins usually labeled the portals they created in both goblinish and the common language. The faerie portals often got labeled with faerie tongue as well. Tyla had only learned the common language as that was what the centaurs used so she had no idea what the sash labeled him as.

The goblin adjusted his belt as he stood to talk with her, swinging his sword around to his hip. The circlet he wore didn't entirely hold back his long, thick blue hair. He pushed curls out of his eyes and said, "The goblin king is looking for you and your friends. You'll be coming with me. You have much to answer for."

"I don't care what you do with me," Tyla growled, "as long as someone helps my sister."

"What happened to your sister?" Grays moved away from the other centaurs toward Tyla. "Where is she?"

"She was taken," Tyla's lip trembled as she thought of what happened, "by the humans."

"By humans?" Grays said.

Tyla nodded.

Grays turned to the other elders. "This has gone on long enough," she said. "Something will have to be done about it." She turned back to Tyla. "Could you show us where?"

Hope bubbled inside her and Tyla nodded again, but Trykirt jumped between them and waved his hands. "Now, hold on," he said. "This centaur dragon isn't going anywhere with you. She's coming to the goblin city to answer for her crimes."

Grays stepped toward the goblin, close enough that she had to crane her neck to look down at him. "Is that so?"

Trykirt looked up at the towering centaur. Tyla admired the fact that Trykirt showed no evidence of intimidation or fear. "She's an enemy of the crown and nation of goblins," he said. "She'll come with us back to Kirlik to stand trial in front of the king for her crimes."

"How can you be sure this is the centaur you are looking for?" Grays asked.

Trykirt tapped his circlet. "The blue gem connects the minds of the wearers," he said. "We were sent here with an accurate description and *image* of the thieves."

Grays glanced at Tyla, who couldn't meet the older centaur's eyes. She knew she was guilty of the crime they sought her for. Eleka had been the one to actually take the gem they needed. The goblins might not have even known whether it was her or Tyla since they were identical, but they had both been in the same area deep within the palace, inside the armory and the jeweler's vaults. Tyla hadn't made it inside the vault where Eleka worked to find the gem using Trivnor's exacting instructions; she had only been inside the armory where the goblins' finished obrucks hung in racks. But she and Trivnor were caught there, subdued and dragged off to the dungeon. Eleka had taken the biggest risk by continuing the heist undiscovered while Tyla and Trivnor led the goblins away from the jeweler's area. But in the end she got caught too and it had been Jassan who freed them all.

"You told us earlier," Grays said to the goblin, "that the thieves stole a priceless gem from the royal palace, but you've refused to tell us what the gem looks like or what it was for."

Trykirt began to look uncomfortable for the first time. "Yes?"

"Did you find the gem on Tyla?" Grays asked.

"No," he grunted. "But she has eight other accomplices, any one of whom she could have handed it off to."

"Eight!" Grays exclaimed. "We have only seen Tyla and her sister. They were alone when those monsters attacked them at our doors. No one accompanied them."

"They split up by then," Trykirt explained slowly. "Criminals do that occasionally."

"Criminals?" Grays huffed in exasperation. "We didn't see criminals when we saved them. We only saw two tired and scared young centaur dragons on their own with nowhere to turn."

"Is that why you lied when you told me they weren't here?" Trykirt growled.

"We didn't lie," Grays said. "They weren't here when you asked. Tyla came back when you saw her."

"You didn't offer any information that they had been here at all," Trykirt said.

"Well," Grays shrugged gracefully in her furry mantle, "I didn't think it was any of your business who we allow into our walls. And it still isn't."

"Any of our business?!" Trykirt shouted. "They stole from the goblin palace!"

"Which you still can't prove," Grays said coolly. "Unless you're willing to pass me that obruck of yours so I can see the image of the culprits myself."

"Hardly," Trykirt ground out through clenched teeth. He punched his fists on his hips and searched the area as if searching for answers. "The obruck," he started quietly before pointing up at the centaur towering over him and raising his voice. "They would have a circlet with them, like mine," he pointed to the golden obruck with multiple embedded gems atop his blue hair. "The culprits at the palace stole a gem and three circlets like mine, each one had a single blue gem. Did this centaur dragon or her sister have something like that? At any point when they were here?"

Tyla almost smiled, but contained her relief. She remembered Eleka's careful protection of the obruck. She blessed her sister's name that Eleka insisted she stuff the circlet in her dragon wrappings on her back to keep it safe and out of anyone else's sight.

Tyla looked at the little goblin. "I have nothing of the sort," she snapped at him. "You can search me."

"And no one here has seen anything like it either," Grays supported her.

Trykirt's grin faded. He pursed his lips. "Fine," he said. "If she's not the right centaur dragon, that will be discovered by the king's inquiry. She can come with us to Kirlik to clear her name."

"And who said," Grays said slowly with narrowed eyes, "that we would allow you to take one of our citizens?"

The other elders stepped up behind Grays's flanks with crossed arms and narrowed eyes. Even Tyla in her dragon form trembled at the assembled ferocity.

"What are you saying?" Trykirt murmured low.

"I'm saying," Grays said, standing to her full height, "that goblins can't walk into our settlement and demand we turn over one of our own. You have not earned that authority here. You goblins seem to think that you are the ultimate authority of justice in Avonoa. But we centaurs will *all* die before we allow you to assert your will over us, our people, our loved ones and, yes, our allies. We wouldn't allow such brazen action by the faeries in the Days of Silence and we certainly won't allow it now."

Trykirt's face turned several different colors throughout Grays's speech. Tyla didn't even have names for that many colors. His lips pursed, then parted, then pursed again. His jaw worked as if he wanted to say something but kept it closed. Finally, he seemed to decide which approach he needed to take. "I'm going to consult with my leaders," he said through gritted teeth. "I'll be back and she—" he pointed to Tyla, "—had better still be here."

With a last scathing glare at first the elders, then Tyla, Trykirt turned and stormed out of the door, the blue gem in his obruck already glowing.

Once he was gone, the other elders wandered away and spoke in hushed tones to each other. Grays came to stand next to Tyla.

The older centaur paused to take a long, deep breath before she spoke. "I don't know if you've done the things he claims," she said quietly, "but right now, I don't care. We need you to show us where the humans attacked you. Their camp seems to move with every new event and we need to find them before they can move again."

"I can't show you anything," Tyla said, kicking her back legs to rattle the chains.

"I'm aware of that," Grays said. "I am also *un*aware of a certain young healer that may be on his way to help you. But I *am* aware that Vanora is outside the walls searching for the humans right now. And she's not very far. Close enough for a certain young healer to find her."

Tyla locked eyes with the wise elder.

"I'm sorry about your sister," Grays said reverently. "You've done a great service to our settlement in freeing those centaurs. In the unlikely event that you miraculously escape these bonds, if you are innocent of these crimes, I would encourage you to come back and we will help you clear your name. We owe you several lives."

Tyla stared at the older centaur. The severe lines on her face that Tyla had mistaken for anger, she now understood reflected her wisdom and experience. The older woman knew the good, better and best ways to help a desperate young centaur.

Gentle clops ambled through one of the doorways on the opposite side of the large hall. Danyel entered with a heavy cloak over his shoulders and a couple of bags hanging over his lower back. He nodded wordlessly to Grays, who nodded back. Tyla heard the wise centaur mutter under her breath as she trotted over to join him. "You don't have much time." Then she clopped loudly over to the other elders and the entire group congregated in front of the door the goblin had used to exit. Their movement hid the goblin's door from Tyla's view and left a clear space for a sprint to the door on the far side of the building. The elders had all turned their backs to her and muttered together quietly.

Danyel moved in front of Tyla, taking no notice of her dark red dragon spots. "I've got something for those," he said, nodding instead toward the hobbles and chains and turning to rummage through his bags.

"I have that piece of broken sword," she whispered to him, fleetingly thinking in the back of her mind of her self-consciousness about her spots. It seemed childish now. "It's on my back under my wrappings."

Danyel shook his head before she finished. "It won't work," he said. "These are majikal bindings. You can't cut them with an ordinary sword."

"Maybe I can slip out of them," she said, thinking she could change into her centaur form and easily escape the too-large bonds when she did. She tried to cool the fire in her belly to shrink her body and change, but her fire only grew hotter. When she tried again, she felt her fire burn up her belly into her chest and curve toward her obviously broken front leg. "Oh spit," she muttered, then shook her chains at Danyel, wincing when the icy pain fought with the burning spreading down her leg. "Get me out of these things. I'll take care of the rest."

Danyel looked at her sternly, holding a round bottle in his fist. "You'll take me with you this time, right?" he said, shaking the sloshing green liquid. "No leaving me behind and escaping by yourself?"

She rolled her eyes. "Yes, of course," she said. "I don't think I have a choice."

"I know," he nodded. Leaning over her bonds, Danyel unstopped the bottle and tilted the green liquid over the chains.

"Ack!" Tyla tried to squelch her yelp as it washed over the manacle around her leg and spilled onto her ankle. It hissed at the metal and dripped freezing ice onto her red scales. "Why?" she shot at Danyel.

"I'm sorry!" He apologized fervently but continued working. "It's the best I had on short notice." He leaned over and splashed more green liquid on both sets of chains.

The liquid sizzled until it burned through the hobbles and manacles. A scuffling commotion outside made her heart pound against her chest. By the time she heard Trykirt's voice outside the door, she had shaken her dragon legs and watched the chains fall away.

Trykirt pushed aside the door to enter, but was slowed when it bumped against the elders. "I beg your pardon," he snapped at them, trying to push the gathering aside. "What do you think you're doing?!" he cried out, finding himself smothered by their centaur hides. He finally managed to push through the elders as Tyla and Danyel tumbled across the room to the far side.

"Where are you going?" Grays sounded curious but unperturbed and didn't raise her voice as she watched Tyla and Danyel make it to the far door.

"Come back here!" Trykirt yelled, his face turning colors again.

Danyel ducked out the door ahead of Tyla. Her back legs pushed her through after him, but Trykirt was impossibly fast and almost made it to her tail by the time it slipped through the door. Tyla slid to the side, avoiding the reach of Trykirt's fingers. She instantly recalled the lightning pain shooting through her and jerked her tail away just in time. Danyel ran toward the settlement wall in front of them and she sprang toward him with her front legs outstretched. Grabbing the centaur around his lower belly, she snapped her wings out, pushed off the ground with her back legs and yanked her tail to the side again to avoid the goblin's lightning touch. Pressing her wings hard against the pounding rain, she yelled to Danyel, "Hold onto my arm!" She twisted her head around to see the goblin staring at them, his bright, now clearly purple-colored face practically pulsing with rage.

13

TRUTHS

"What happened to your wrist?" Danyel shouted over the sound of goblins and centaurs yelling below them and the deluge they now flew through.

"Maybe later?!" Tyla called back as she flew over the walls of Danyel's settlement. Unable to grip Danyel without pain stabbing up her arm from her injured claw, he kept slipping precariously as he tried to inspect it and avoid hurting it at the same time.

An arrow came whistling through the rain falling around them as Tyla met the tops of the trees. The goblins ran to the top of the settlement wall and nocked their bows for a second volley, Trykirt pointing his little sword in their direction, while the centaur guards atop the walls jumped between the fleeing prisoner and the goblins, some even nocked their own bows and slowly swayed their tips toward the goblins.

"They're not very happy," Tyla said with a satisfied smile. As she pivoted back in the direction of the gorge and where Eleka had been captured, she glanced down at Danyel in her claw.

He glared up at her. "Put me down!" he finally barked.

Tyla circled low before she dove into the trees. Landing with a thump, she awkwardly dropped Danyel in the process. He scrambled to his hooves, wiping off mud, but the tumble wasn't what he focused on.

"What did you do to your wrist?" he demanded, pointing to the offending limb.

Tyla shrugged, limping on her other three legs. She turned back into a centaur to take the weight off her injured arm, but when her front dragon legs separated into centaur arms and front legs in the process, she cried out. Her right arm dangled at an unnatural angle as if it had another joint.

"I think it's broken," Danyel said matter-of-factly.

Tyla breathlessly cradled her arm to her chest. "You're the most observant healer I've met," she forced out wryly.

Danyel's mouth twitched in a half-grin. "What happened?"

"We were surrounded by wraiths," Tyla hissed as Danyel took her arm and rolled it over carefully. "At least I escaped."

"But Eleka didn't," he said softly.

Tyla dropped her chin so Danyel wouldn't see the pain in her eyes. "There was nothing I could do," she muttered. "I tried to save her, but... I..."

Danyel put his arm around her shoulders. "It's alright," he said tenderly. "You did everything you could, I know that. So does Eleka."

"But I didn't," she said, pushing him away with her good hand. "I didn't do everything. I should have died trying to save her. Instead, I ran away. I abandoned her."

"I'm guessing she told you to go," Danyel said. "Didn't she?"

Tyla nodded, fighting back the tears. She rued the fact that they always came easier in her centaur form.

"Well, then," Danyel said, "you listened to her. You finally did exactly what she wanted. Which means you probably did the right thing."

Tyla shrugged, but she couldn't force herself to answer. Right or wrong, did it really matter anymore? She would hate herself for her action for the rest of her life…and Eleka's life.

Danyel nodded toward the trees and motioned for Tyla to follow him. "I think this is the way we'll find Vanora," he said. "And along the way I'm going to look at that wrist, even if you kill me for trying."

"The goblins can travel faster than anyone expects," Tyla said, trotting alongside. "We can't slow down or they'll catch up."

"Even though you already flew this far?"

"It's not very far, and, yes, they're that fast," she said, picking up a decent pace and pulling ahead.

Danyel took a moment to catch up and grumbled, "I would really love to hear how you came to know all of this."

"Keep up," was all Tyla could answer.

They trotted closely together in the direction Danyel had indicated while he touched her arm and turned her wrist over in his hands. In her centaur form without her dark dragon scales blocking the light to her skin, Tyla contemplated the blotchy color swathing her wrist.

"I could bind it," Danyel said, "and give you a poultice to help with healing. But flying and allowing it to heal in your dragon form might be more helpful. Your dragon leg acts as a splint when your centaur arm and front leg are conjoined."

"Eleka says that a dragon's innate majikal healing power works better than any potions," Tyla said, slowing to stop them and look at Danyel. "She's always right and I hate it."

Danyel's hand slid up Tyla's arm to her shoulder. A chill continued up her neck into her head when it stayed there. "If she's always right," he said gently, "then she must have been right to tell you to leave."

"Who left?" Another voice joined theirs from behind. Tyla jumped, but glimpsed the brilliant blue of Vanora through the trees. Danyel had led them directly to her.

"Tyla," Danyel answered.

"The humans took Eleka," Tyla clarified, remembering the event and trying unsuccessfully to keep the growl of anger from her voice. "And I had to leave to save myself."

"So you could live to save Eleka later," Vanora said. "Yes, that makes sense. But we need to leave here and save ourselves now. The goblins are headed this way. Tyla, are you good to fly?"

Tyla nodded with a glance at the sky. She looked past the raindrops trickling over her face and imagined each one turning black and coalescing into a wraith—so many, large and small. Could she tell Vanora and Danyel what she knew of the World of Souls leaking into the living world? Should she? She opted instead for a simple question, "Is it safe?"

Vanora squinted at her. "Why wouldn't it be?"

"Those things," Tyla tried to hide her anxiety about sharing the skies with wraiths, or worse, being sucked into the World of Souls. "I've seen them drop from the sky."

"Really?" Danyel asked. "I haven't seen that. Vanora?"

Vanora shook her head. "You sure they didn't fly up at you within thick clouds?"

"Maybe," Tyla said, but she knew perfectly well that they had come *down* out of the clouds above her. She knew the three of them had to move fast but she had to discourage flight. Pointing at Danyel, she asked, "What will Danyel do? I swore I wouldn't leave him behind again." Which earned another half-grin from Danyel.

"I'll carry him," Vanora said. "I'm bigger and stronger and uninjured."

Vanora had won the run-or-fly debate. "Sorry," Tyla apologized to Danyel as Vanora wrapped her claws around his middle.

"I'll live," Danyel said good-naturedly, shrugging his shoulders. "At least you're not leaving me again. But stay close."

Tyla changed into her dragon form and the two dragons lifted into the air with Danyel in tow as the sky thickened and thunder rumbled.

"There," Tyla said, pointing with her good claw. The gorge ahead of them split the trees apart. Remembering the trap she'd fallen for, she explained, "They used a dragon wraith to lure us to where they wanted us to land. We encountered it here…"

As she spoke, a roar assailed them from below. Tyla recognized the same colossal wraith lifting into the air in front of her again, but she made sure to lead the others in a wide arc well outside its reach.

"I know it can't reach us," Danyel said, as the wraith struggled against its bonds, "but let's get away from it. Just to be certain."

"Agreed," both dragons said at once.

"We'll go to the far side," Vanora indicated with a nod of her head.

Tyla guessed that Vanora didn't want any possibility of nearby humans to hear or see exactly where they were going to land. They found the area where the two girls had been attacked and circled it from above, carefully using a wide arc to search the ground and especially the trees carefully before they settled on the far side of the gorge and rushing water.

Tyla stared out from a rocky ledge with the river raging below them.

"I don't see anything," Danyel said beside her.

"Nor should you," Vanora explained. "This spot has been used and discovered, so the humans would have left and taken Eleka away by now. They'll either hand her off to someone else or take her back to Gormitor themselves."

"Would they go back with only one captive?" Danyel asked. "You two freed all the other prisoners in this area. Wouldn't they wait until they have more? Perhaps we can rescue her sooner if we find where they've been camping?"

Tyla grinned remembering the centaurs being liberated and galloping away from their captors into the forest.

"Not sure," Vanora said. "We might have to search for a second site before we move on to the king's city."

"No," Tyla shook her head remembering her conversation with the faerie wraith in Zanna's prison. "No, the humans took her back to Gormitor. They won't delay and keep her out here nor will they wait until they catch more centaurs. They will take her directly to the castle themselves."

"Themselves?" Danyel asked. "They wouldn't pass her along to someone else and wait out here for more?"

"No," Tyla said, staring distractedly into the distance, only seeing Eleka's limp form trapped under the silver net. "She's too valuable to him. He won't want to risk losing her."

"Valuable to whom?" Danyel asked.

"He has to be here," Tyla murmured to herself. "What else would he be doing? How else would he know?"

Tyla found herself staring toward the castle. *What is he doing? If the king is using the wraiths to bait and trap and imprison centaurs, Kelraz must be involved.* Shivers ran up her spine as she considered the possibilities, but she also realized that she could be wrong. The humans kept the wraiths on chains and leashes, like the dragon trap in the forest, which was definitely gruesome and horrible, but did they require Kelraz for any of that?

Maybe I was too quick to assume Kelraz was inhabiting the wraiths, she thought. Visible shivers rattled her. *It's possible the wraiths might have simply killed me if the centaurs hadn't had them restrained, or possibly just overwhelmed me with sheer numbers in that prison. Eleka would have stopped me from going in there.*

But Kelraz had unmistakably answered her through the faerie wraith. He obviously knew her location and where Eleka had been taken. But was he physically present in Gormitor or just his wraiths? She knew he would lie about making a trade for Jassan, but would he actually be there in the flesh? Or would he send a wraith to do his dirty work?

"It doesn't matter," she answered herself out loud, but still low. Staring into the distance, she imagined a dragon wraith with its claws around Eleka's neck, pointing to Tyla and demanding Jassan in return. "She would still be alive."

"Tyla," Danyel said, shaking her a little when she didn't answer. "Who would find your sister so valuable to capture?"

Tyla blinked rainwater from her eyelashes. At least she hoped it was rainwater. "Someone dangerous," was all she could spit out.

Vanora met her eyes. "You know this from the faerie wraith?" she asked.

Tyla nodded. She glanced at Vanora but cast her eyes away as quickly as possible. The older dragon most likely knew of her conversation with the faerie wraith in the prison. Vanora had probably even guessed that more complications were at play between the twins and all the wraiths, not just the faerie wraith. Tyla couldn't fully hold the other dragon's eye for fear that Vanora might read straight into her mind and discover all their secrets.

"What about the dragon wraith?" Danyel asked. "The one back there. If they're using it to trap anyone, would they just leave it?"

"Probably," Tyla said. "They can always come back to it. It would be difficult to drag it along with them anyway."

"How did the humans catch either of you?" Vanora asked. "Sure, the dragon wraith would get you where they wanted you, but that couldn't be all they did. You're both smarter than that. And stronger."

"They controlled more wraiths on chains," Tyla said, her voice low and icy. "They must be using them to lure other centaurs into traps as well. The humans used the wraiths to force us where they wanted us. We couldn't fly because we were in the trees. While we fought with them, they threw some majikal net over Eleka. She seemed dazed, then she fell unconscious."

"You were in your dragon forms, I'm guessing?" Danyel watched Tyla intently.

"I don't know about the net, but I think I know what they used to subdue her. Sleep dust," Vanora growled. "I'd bet my life on it."

"Sleep dust?" Tyla narrowed her eyes at Vanora. "What's 'sleep dust'?"

"Long ago the faeries concocted a type of powder that when blown into the face of a dragon and inhaled by the dragon, the dust would render them unconscious," Vanora answered. "But it can be used on any creature: dragon, human, faerie or even…"

"Centaurs," Danyel said.

Tyla would have paled if she'd been in her centaur form. "I've heard of something like that," she managed to say. "My friend's father had it used on him a long time ago, before the start of the dragon war."

"And the dragon war ended its production," Vanora said. "Along with dragon poison, it has been outlawed and the remnants of the ingredients and the spell process to make it have been scrubbed from memories everywhere. With great prejudice."

She lifted her lip in a small snarl and Tyla wondered if the older dragon might have been among those who helped wipe the product from the land. Or perhaps she had seen it in use.

"To have and be using something of that nature now could mean a number of things," Danyel whispered. "None of them good."

The three fell silent. Danyel stared into the distance and absentmindedly touched the bags slung over his back. His eyes twitched back and forth and Tyla wondered if he was going over in his head the herbs and medicines in his bag and hoping he might have something to counter the treacherous potion. Hearing about the types of dark majik the humans were willing to use, Tyla's mind began numbering the things these humans could be subjecting Eleka to at that moment.

"Look," Vanora said, breaking the silence, "we're going to do whatever we need to do to get your sister back and save whoever we can from the humans, but before we start..." she swung her eyes up to Tyla's, "one way or another, we're going to have to prove that you can be trusted." Before Tyla could protest, Vanora lifted her front claw wing joint to stop her. "I'm aware that you've given your wyrd. But you're going to have to give us something too, Tyla. We're trusting you rather blindly. Our entire centaur settlement has defied the goblins and possibly started a war on your behalf. We've proven that we're willing to help you, so you need to benefit us with some answers to our questions. True answers. Whole answers."

Tyla crossed her arms in front of her, trying to calculate what she could and couldn't say. "We did it," she murmured. "Eleka and I. We helped... someone... steal the gem from the goblin palace."

"Why?" Vanora growled.

She met the blue dragon's eyes and shook her head. "All I can tell you is..." she hemmed for a moment until some powerful emotion punched a hole through her heart. "All I can tell you is that it was the right thing to do. Given the choice... I would do it again."

Vanora nodded slowly in acceptance. "Alright then. Do you have the gem?"

Tyla shook her head.

"Does Eleka have the gem? Is that why you need to save her?"

"No," Tyla said. "I need to save her because she's my sister. But we also stole three obrucks with communication gems in them. Eleka has the one we've been using to keep in contact with the rest of our friends."

"So you *do* have the circlet Trykirt suspected you had," Vanora said.

"Yes."

"No one in the settlement ever saw it," Danyel added.

"We're a little smarter than that. Especially Eleka," Tyla said.

"I'm guessing you don't have it now," Vanora stated. "Or you would be contacting these friends of yours."

Tyla shook her head. "Eleka had it on her when she was captured. There's no way to know if the humans found it and took it from her or not."

"So," Vanora tilted her head in the direction of the king's castle, "it's possible that she may be contacting your friends as we speak."

"The same friends who have the gem," Danyel clarified.

Tyla nodded. "But the obrucks we have are broken and unreliable. And we don't know where the gem is, I swear. We haven't even heard from some of our friends." Her eyes fell thinking of Trivnor's and all of the boys' lack of communication. Now with Eleka imprisoned Tyla had lost communication with everyone. Who knew what

Kelraz's plans might be for them? She had no way of knowing if anyone was even alive or dead.

"Are *they* trustworthy?" Danyel asked, idly twisting a string on the edge of the bag holding his herbs. "These friends of yours? The person who has the gem? Do you trust them?"

Tyla met his eyes. "With my life." She thought of the majikal sword that Jassan held that could kill a wraith and wipe their soul from existence and added, "And my death."

"And the wraiths?" Vanora asked. "What is your knowledge of them?"

"I know what they are," Tyla said, "how they are created, and who controls them. I know what he wants… and how to stop him."

"And can you tell us any of that?"

Tyla thought for a moment. She had already told them that the wraiths came from souls in the World of Souls. But she couldn't tell them that Kelraz conjured them with the Sky Key he retained. She couldn't tell them that he wanted all the keys and the power of the gods. She couldn't tell them that he wanted to destroy the world of the living and rule over both the living and the dead as if he were a god himself. And she couldn't tell them that the only way to stop him was to find all the other keys before he did. So, she settled with a small shake of her head.

"Well," Vanora grunted and stared into the pouring sky. "That isn't much, but I sense there are valid reasons for your hesitation and I think I can surmise some of them. If someone is controlling these wraiths, they are probably working in league with the supposedly Just King and helping him use the wraiths to kidnap centaurs. Which means that particular someone is no friend of mine. I'll get you as close to Gormitor as I can, but then I'll have to leave and keep the goblins off your trail. The rest will be up to you."

"And me," Danyel said.

Tyla nodded at him. "Us."

14

ASSISTANCE

"Through there," Tyla pointed ahead to a group of low buildings. "It has to be one of those."

In her centaur form again, she and Danyel hiked through some of the more difficult parts of the forests outside Gormitor so they could approach the small area Vanora had described.

The three had flown a little further together, avoiding goblins, watching for wraiths and allowing Vanora to explain where to find a friend of hers who lived in a small village outside the king's city. They hoped that her friend would help the young centaurs but couldn't be certain of it. Vanora then left them and returned to Zanna to head off the goblins.

Tyla and Danyel trotted down the hill overlooking the sprawling farmlands next to the massive city of Gormitor inside the Kingdom of Gormirom, which was once called the Just Kingdom by everyone in Avonoa. She couldn't help but compare what she saw before them to Kingstor Noble, where Emma and Burk lived. The formerly Just Kingdom boasted a spacious castle inside Gormitor city, with a lower city inside the walls and farms and small villages outside, the same as Kingstor Noble. But the similarities between the two kingdoms stopped there.

Back before the dragon war, the merlons atop the battlements of Kingstor Noble had been curved like claws to deter dragons from landing on the walls of the castle. Since the end of the war brought peace between dragons and humans, several dragons now lived peacefully within the kingdom walls. As a gesture of peace, the Noble king, Emma's uncle, had ordered the curved and pointed tips be cut off to make the top of the castle walls flat and easily accessible for dragons. It had been a gesture of peace.

The authorities in the Kingdom of Justice, however, had not followed Noble's lead. The tops of the towers still retained a bulbous, rounded roof coming to a point at the very top. Around that top, fixtures of stone and shingle splayed out and ended in several points, as if a giant rain droplet had frozen just as it exploded from the collision with the roof. The rooftops still sparkled with dragon scales. Dragon scales that had been shed were easy to gather as many of them didn't crumble to ash when they fell off a dragon's body the way a dragon did when they died. A dragon would find landing on the Just Kingdom rooftops extremely slippery and difficult to find purchase, and possibly dangerous. The rooftops had been designed that way before the humans learned that dragons were intelligent and could be reasoned with, but the king hadn't seen any value in altering them in the seventeen years since the end of the war.

Furthering the garish, and somewhat belligerent, architecture, each merlon displayed matching stone eruptions at the top. They lined up over the heads of the men walking the tops of the battlements like the hefty fronded trees lining the streets in the city. The castle windows were shaped like flowers with curved edges and the wooden doors displayed intricately carved panoramic details. The entire castle and the walls surrounding both the king's ostentatious home and the huge city gave Tyla the impression that everything was exploding all at once, like a majikal light shower display.

"I thought the human kingdoms changed all their structures to prove to dragons that they were welcome in the kingdoms," Tyla said, pointing to the sloped roofs and sharp battlements.

Danyel followed her sightline. "King Grisivere before and now Gormin haven't changed a thing other than King Gormin giving the kingdom his name, Gormirom. If you ask me, I'm not sure they exactly welcome anyone but humans."

"Well," Tyla said, tugging on her crisscrossed dragon wrappings, "I guess I won't be flying in."

"Or out," Danyel added.

"I don't know," Tyla countered as they trudged across a field of slushy mud. "I couldn't land on top of those rooftops if my life depended on it. I don't think any dragon could. Going in I would have to fly straight to a space somewhere on the inside of the city."

"If you don't get shot out of the sky first," Danyel added.

"True," Tyla agreed. "But if I found a nice open space while I was *in* the city, I might be able to push my wings hard enough to get over the walls if I need to."

Danyel pointed at the battlements around the top. "The whole place is set up for the guards to watch anyone inside as much as outside. Any way you look at it, those points are facing in all directions."

Tyla pursed her lips in thought. "We'll have to get closer to figure it out," she said.

"How close?" Danyel murmured. When she didn't answer he repeated, "How close are you thinking, Tyla?"

"Too close," Tyla finally answered. She didn't want to explain everything she was plotting yet. She didn't want Danyel trying to stop her or following her, but she couldn't come up with any alternatives other than dragging him along.

"Look," Tyla pointed to a building on the other side of the field in front of them. "That looks big enough to house a dragon or even several. Maybe we'll find Vanora's friend there."

The two centaurs walked through the mud toward the dwelling. As they got closer to it, they gaped at the tall, sprawling structure extended out in the opposite direction of their approach. It stretched the length of several of the smaller houses around them and wrapped toward the back of the city walls further on. They crept past a few of the houses on the outskirts by the farming fields to silently slip toward the building.

"Don't you think you should change back to your dragon form?" Danyel whispered loudly over the patter of rain. "We might be safer approaching people if they know you're a dragon."

"I don't think so," Tyla said. "Welcome or not, dragons can be very intimidating."

"Especially you," Danyel chuckled.

Tyla wanted to smile, but didn't quite know what to make of the comment so she shrugged it off. "Well, I don't want to scare anyone away, do I?"

"So what do we do?" he asked. "Knock at the door?"

"I guess so," Tyla said. "I'm sick of being wet already."

Tyla pushed moisture from her face and approached the yawning doorway of the vast structure. Only a heavy cloth hung over the opening, so Tyla thumped her good fist against the lintel of the doorway and shouted, "Hello! Is anyone home?"

A moment later a bulky male grey dragon poked his head out of the opening. He looked over the pair for only a second before asking in a gruff voice, "What are you doing out there? A couple of centaurs out in the open? Kruh's scruffy beard, you must have a death wish!"

"We're looking for—" Tyla started, but the older grey dragon cut her off.

"Doesn't matter, doesn't matter," he pushed aside the cloth and waved for them to enter. "Come inside before you're taken away too."

Danyel's brow creased with worry, but Tyla stepped quickly ahead of him into the large building.

Upon entering, Tyla felt herself thaw in the warmth immediately. She breathed a sigh of relief and shook the water from her hind quarters. Despite Danyel's assertions that she was intimidating as a dragon, she still hesitated to change in front of him unless absolutely necessary. This grey male was wide and brawny; she doubted he would find her intimidating anyway.

Danyel entered behind her and shook off the rain in like fashion while Tyla stared around them in wonder. The massive structure looked like the perfect place to house dozens of dragons. Unlike the waystation still under construction in the Noble Kingdom, this structure was in full use. A long tunnel led along one side through which Tyla could see several partitioned spaces with a heavy cloth hanging in front of each. Opposite the entrance, another wide tunnel ran deeper into the earth down broad stone steps.

To the right of where they entered, two other dragons lay against the stone wall. One was a female of brilliant green but her tail and back claws were bright white, as if they'd been dipped in paint. She had the same distinction of being from the Island Ruck as Vanora, with her front claws attached to her wings at the wing joint in place of front legs. The third dragon alongside her was a young male. He was much younger than Tyla and Danyel, possibly only five or six winters. Like his father who had greeted them, the little dragon had four claws and a double tail and short ridges down his head. His grey head popped off the ground as soon as the visitors entered.

"Who are you?" the little dragon chirped almost as soon as they appeared. He bounced across the space to plant himself in front of them.

"I'm Tyla," she said. "This is my friend Danyel."

"Centaurs!" he squeaked. "I've only seen centaurs in the games! What are you doing here?"

"Yes, indeed," the colorful female said, lifting her head up as well. "What are you doing here?"

"We're looking for a dragon named Sharot," Tyla said, as the little dragon bounced up and down on the tips of his claws. "We were sent by Vanora."

"Vanora?" the female stood fully. "Is she alright?"

"She's fine," Tyla said quickly, hoping not to invite more trouble. "At least, she was when she left us. It's really us who need help and Vanora thought Sharot might give it."

The dame nodded her green head in acknowledgement. "And so I shall."

"Makus," Sharot said. "Why don't you and Narsun find something for our guests to eat? Tyla, Danyel, join me here."

As Tyla watched little Narsun bouncing along in his dan's wake with question after question about 'what centaurs eat' and 'would the centaurs be here long' and 'could he play with them', she was reminded of the little newborn, Kira, back at Zanna.

"So," Sharot said, folding her bright green self against the wall again, "what brings you to our little edge of the world? It's very dangerous around here for centaurs to wander. Don't tell me you've come to volunteer for the games." It sounded more like a warning than a question.

"Games?" Danyel said. "What games?"

"The new king, Gormin, has introduced games with his champion at the head," Sharot said. "They're calling him the Champion of Justice, although I'm not sure how much justice the city still retains. But centaurs are supposedly coming from all over to compete."

"Compete for what?" Danyel asked before Tyla could stop him.

"It's never discussed in the open, so I can't be sure," Sharot said. "Pride, riches, something of that nature is usually what most conversations center around, although I don't believe it. All I've seen is that the centaurs who have gone into the games to compete haven't come back out."

"That's why we're here," Tyla responded, having heard plenty. "Not to compete, but because centaurs from Zanna and other settlements have been disappearing."

Sharot's eyes widened slightly, but she nodded as if unsurprised. "Do you have any ideas as to what is happening?"

"More than ideas," Danyel said.

Sharot lifted a scaly eyebrow.

"We found kidnapped centaurs between Zanna and here and we freed them," Tyla said. "The humans are kidnapping them and holding them in pens."

Sharot's brows creased and the white tip of her tail flicked. "I knew it," she growled. "I knew something was going on. Centaurs have been showing up in the arena out of nowhere, presumably to fight, but they always lose, then disappear into the castle. No one has seen them coming or going. Once they lose, and they always lose, they're taken directly into the castle and are supposedly taken to the plush rooms the king has given them. Either that, or they leave the kingdom in the middle of the night, but whether they've left dead or alive is the question."

"Do they all disappear?" Danyel asked. "Do they fight just one match then they're not seen again?"

Sharot shook her head. "No," she said. "Sometimes they come back and fight again. I'm not sure what their motivation is for being here, but people are saying that the king's faerie is actually—"

"King's faerie?!" Tyla cried out, almost jumping up in shock. "What faerie?"

"Not sure who he is," Sharot said, noticing her reaction and providing more detail. "He showed up one day sitting in the king's box with him. He watches from under his hood, usually, and comments occasionally to the king."

"What does he look like?" Tyla asked, thinking of Trivnor's purple skin and black hair.

"Green," Sharot said. "Black and silver hair. People suspect he's running some sort of majikal experiment. Either that or he wants the champion's stone."

Tyla had been pondering Kelraz's potential nearby presence, but those thoughts vanished and she shook her head to clear it. "Stone?" she asked. "What stone?"

"You're telling them about the sun stone without me?" young Narsun's voice echoed up the tunnel passageway behind them. "Let me tell them! I want to tell them!"

Sharot nodded and closed her mouth tight, waving a claw for Narsun to proceed. While he explained, his father Makus placed plates of fruit and vegetables at Tyla's and Danyel's feet. Tyla ignored the proffered food, too anxious to hear what Narsun had to say.

"Ok," Narsun said, prancing through the room. "One day, the champion found his stone. It's bright yellow and shines like the sun." He splayed his claws to imitate the sun shining in the sky. "The stone gives him the power of the sun. No one knows for sure where he got it or how. He showed up one day and the sun stone was stuck to his chest." The little dragon sat up and held both front claws to the right side of his chest. "If he takes off his tunic, you might be in trouble, because he can blast you with it. BOOM!" He slammed both front claws against the hard packed earth then tumbled to the ground giggling.

Tyla whipped her head toward Danyel, expecting to see her sister's eyes lighting up and yelling, "That's it! That's what we came for! We have to get it!"

"Are you alright, Tyla?" Sharot asked. "You look like you've been pushed off a cliff and forgotten how to fly."

15

PROTECTION

"Why centaurs?" Danyel asked.

It was late and the rain pounded against the earthen roof of the massive dwelling. Sharot had insisted Narsun get off to bed with promises that she would take him into town to see the games in the morning. Apparently, it was the only promise that could coerce the little fledgling to bed down. Makus minded the young dragon before returning to Sharot, Danyel and Tyla.

Tyla stood apart, munching on some of the apples Makus gave them in order to avoid answering questions. Listening to the conversation, she chewed on her next steps in her mind.

"Not sure," Sharot answered Danyel. "Ever since old king Grisivere died a few years ago, his son, Gormin, has, for some reason, not been happy with the centaurs, or even the dragons for that matter. We are but a few dragons who still live in the area and that's only because we run this waystation for traveling dragons and well…others."

"So do centaurs travel through here too?" Danyel asked.

"Not for years," Sharot answered. "King Gormin is young and he's made many mistakes but he almost seems proud of them. He began to levy a heavy tax on any village that allowed centaurs to stay or even just visit. He drove away the centaurs and their sympathizers quickly and they've never returned. But he didn't dare provoke dragons the same way. The people wouldn't allow it and the dragons certainly wouldn't stand for it either. Already there are many human dragons here. The king can't afford to make them his enemies too. The centaurs, however…" Her voice trailed away with the unspoken threat.

"So," Danyel summed up, "the king drives the centaurs out. The champion gains his stone. The champion makes an exhibition of fighting and beating centaurs. Why? What for? What's the king's goal?"

"Goal?" Sharot said. "I'm not sure he has a goal. The supposedly Just Kingdom has always held regular championship tournaments. Men from around the kingdom come to compete in sport against each other to be the king's champion, but for the winner it was always simply a title and a point of pride. The champion would collect riches of some sort, be welcomed at the castle, that kind of thing. They've never really had any duties of any sort."

Sharot went on. "Leman lost the most recent tournament; that was two weeks ago now. Then he came back a week ago and challenged the reigning champion to fight one-on-one, which is possible at any time, but extremely rare. Some people say Leman changed how he fought at that challenge, but since it was outside of the regular tournament there weren't many witnesses for it. So Leman won his challenge and was taken into the king's confidence as the new champion. These new 'games' with Leman fighting the centaurs started the very next day."

She continued. "A couple of centaurs were seen within the Gormitor walls the day the games started last week; no one knew why they were even here. Some people say the king offered them a chance to become the champion of his new games and they took up the challenge, confident that they could win. Others say the king offered the centaurs no choice and they were forced to fight his unbeatable champion in the arena. Either way, those centaurs have never been seen leaving Gormitor. The faerie showed up a day or two later and he and the king have presided over these 'games' every day for almost a week now."

"And the centaurs?" Danyel asked. "You have no idea where they are?"

"No," Sharot shook her head. "The arena butts up against the rear of the castle, where it's said that the king provides the competitors' extravagant rooms in which to recover. In any case, the centaurs go straight back into the castle through the stable after they fight. The guards claim they need time to rest and heal first before they decide if they want to fight again."

"But the centaurs aren't killed?" Danyel asked doubtfully.

"No," Sharot said. "The king hasn't had anyone killed in the arena. The centaurs are allowed to concede the fight and go back into the castle to rest and heal. But no one has been allowed to visit them. At least, not that I've heard about, anyway."

"Challengers can concede?" Danyel said. "And no one has died?"

"Of course not," Tyla grumbled, throwing aside her apple core, "they would just change into a wraith."

"A wraith?" Sharot rumbled and looked sternly at each centaur. "What dark majik are you two dealing with?"

Tyla shook her head. She could have kicked herself for spitting out the wrong thing again. She was so used to Eleka taking the lead in conversations that required appropriate questions and tact.

"The monsters," Tyla corrected herself.

"What monsters?" Sharot asked, and it was Tyla's and Danyel's turn to stare at her dumbfounded.

"The dark monsters," Tyla said, "the ones attacking everyone they can see? Dripping shadow? Black skin and bone? Many resembling someone you once knew?"

"You haven't seen them?" Danyel asked, incredulously.

"I haven't seen anything like that," Sharot said breathlessly, her eyes wide with surprise and fear.

"They're everywhere," Danyel said. "The monsters roam the forest near our settlement and have killed some of our warriors who went out to fight them. A new monster rose from each of the dead centaur warriors' bodies," Danyel clarified. "We've been able to capture some and have them locked up to protect ourselves. Our majishuns have been able to ascertain that they are, indeed, wraiths."

"I don't know about wraiths," Sharot said. "We've been informed that something threatening is out in the wilderness, but we've been assured protection if we avoid the forests. We haven't seen anything that horrible around here."

"How is that possible?" Tyla uttered under her breath.

Danyel turned to Tyla. "If the people avoid the forests, that would make it easier to kidnap centaurs and not accidentally stumble upon other humans."

"King Gormin claims he is protecting Gormirom's borders," Sharot said. "He may be keeping his word… for once."

"You've heard nothing about these monsters, though?" Tyla squinted at her, still in disbelief. "None of them have attacked your village or other villages around the kingdom?"

Sharot shook her head, horror still evident in her eye. "What have you brought to our home?"

Tyla thought of little Narsun snuggled in his earthen cave below them. Happy and blissfully unaware that evil people like Kelraz existed in Avonoa. Unaware that souls of the dead roamed Avonoa looking for all manner of living species to kill. Unaware that honorable centaurs like Kira's father were being kidnapped from their homes and most likely forced to fight—'til close to death—against a supernaturally-strong, unbeatable champion. Oblivious that evil majik crept closer to his home every moment.

"Evil majik," Tyla repeated her thought in disgust. "Evil, dangerous, dark majik that we have no business involving you in. If you could show us to a room for tonight, we'll leave immediately in the morning."

She stood and stepped toward the tunnel with the sleeping rooms, angling her face away from the others as her eyes swam with tears. She knew what she had to do, but no idea how to do it. If Eleka were here, she would know. All Tyla knew was that evil followed her wherever she went and she needed to stop putting kind people and dragons and centaurs who would help them at risk. She needed Eleka. She didn't need anyone else.

"Of course," Sharot said, standing and leading them down the hall to the second opening. "The first two are open if you'd like separate rooms. They can be kind of roomy and chilly for one, though. Even with the rock floors heated by dragon fire underneath."

"That's why it's so warm in here," Danyel said with a grin.

"Oh, yes," Sharot said, "I apologize. A centaur may not find the warmth as comfortable."

"I'll be fine," he answered her, waving off the suggestion. "It actually feels quite nice given the season."

"Yes," she said, "the rainy season of fall can be difficult for many. But those of us from the Island Ruck thrive with the volume of constant water in the air. It's what we're used to."

With her thoughts never very far from Eleka, Tyla thought of a question that Eleka would probably be dying to ask Sharot. Not knowing if she'd gotten the opportunity to ask Vanora, Tyla asked Sharot now in her stead. "Do Island Ruck dragons really swim in the ocean?" she blurted before looking up at two questioning faces.

"Yes," Sharot answered with a chuckle. "Yes, we swim. That's how we hunt for most of our food."

"You're fishermen," Danyel said. "Or fisher-dragons?"

Sharot smiled. "We call ourselves 'ocean hunters'. But yes, we hunt fish, among other things."

Tyla nodded, barely able to hide her sadness that she couldn't turn to Eleka and watch her eyes light up with new questions, so she slipped into the first room past Sharot. Danyel bid goodnight to Sharot before sidling in behind her and dropping the heavy cloth.

"Do you mind?" he asked shyly. "These rooms are enormous. I'll sit quietly in the corner if you like. Besides, I have a feeling you might try to leave me behind again if we get separated. Don't deny it."

Tyla shook her head. She hadn't fully formed any plan yet, but he did bring up an option that she thought would only make her feel worse. "I'll take the company too," she said. "Although I might have to sleep as a dragon to let my wrist heal."

"Good idea." Danyel pulled the bags from his back and the belt from his waist. He began rummaging through them. "I should put something on it," he mumbled, pointing to her aching hand and arm.

"Didn't you say it would heal itself if I stay in my dragon form?"

"Yes," he confirmed, "it will, but I have a few things that will be beneficial while you're a dragon too."

"What all do you have in that bag?" Tyla asked. "It looks like it would be too heavy for even my dragon back to carry."

Danyel grinned. "I like to be prepared. I've got all kinds of herbs, some edible, some not." He pulled out several cloth packets with sprigs and leaves jutting from the edges. "I've got some food, and…" he eyed her mischievously, "I also have a few things that might be prohibited in some circles." He pulled out a handful of small waterproof bladders with stoppers in the tops. Each of them sloshed with liquid inside.

"Prohibited?" Tyla asked, wondering if they might be arrested for something other than simply being centaurs. "Like what?"

Danyel shrugged. "Like flarote," he said, picking up a little bladder the size of his fist.

"That's only illegal for faeries."

"I said 'some circles'."

"But for my break?" Tyla said, holding up her ruined arm. The splotches of color on her skin began to brighten like ink splashed over parchment.

"No," Danyel shook his head. "I think the flarote might be better for the scratch on your back, but I'm not sure. No, I wanted to try this type of seaweed that Vanora said they use in the Island Ruck." He peeled back the layers of a wax-covered packet to exhibit a lump of fluorescent green that didn't resemble any plants Tyla had heard of. "She says it works really well to heal stuff. Especially for dragons."

Tyla wrinkled her nose. "Seaweed? Gross."

"Come on," Danyel pled. "I've never been able to try it on a dragon before."

"I'm no one's experiment," Tyla said, shaking her head emphatically.

"Fine," Danyel replaced the packet, "I'll go with tried and true. But I warn you, since this works best on centaurs, I can't be certain how well it will work when you're in your dragon form for healing and sleeping."

"I'm sure it will manage to heal, either way," Tyla said, wriggling a little further from him to give herself room to change. She found that her efforts weren't enough when she changed into her spotted red dragon form and her front leg brushed the side of his dappled grey belly.

Danyel seemed unconcerned, so Tyla left her leg where it had fallen. It needed to be close enough for him to reach with his healing potions anyway. After a few minutes of grinding together herbs and oils, Danyel spread a thick pink paste across the lower joint of her leg in front of him. The mixture tingled slightly before it warmed up.

"I think it's working," Tyla said. "I can feel something."

"Good," Danyel grinned as he packed his ingredients back into his bag. "Shurka knows you're going to go into Gormitor swinging, so we need you fighting fit."

Tyla nodded, not trusting her voice. Her mind snapped back to Eleka's face, half-conscious and lying under a silver net. *Go*, she whispered in her memory.

Tyla didn't dare move her leg for fear of undoing all of Danyel's work, so she settled with laying her head on the ground next to her treated leg and tucking the other one under her. Luckily, salty tears were easier to keep away from her eyes in her dragon form. She could barely swallow for the lump in her throat before forcing out through her fangs, "We have to rescue her, Danyel. We have to."

She pinched her eyes shut as he maneuvered himself to lie down next to her and gently slung his arm over her long neck before whispering, "We will."

16

GORMITOR

"You can't go!" Tyla insisted, raising her voice. "It's not safe!"

"Will you be safer without me?" Danyel responded loudly to meet her tone. "I can go anywhere I choose, and I choose to go with you!"

They fell asleep quickly and easily the night before. Feeling safe and comfortable with Danyel's arm over her, Tyla drifted off with strategies swirling in her head about how to infiltrate the castle and free Eleka. Envisioning her success allowed her to drift off.

However, upon waking, she realized two conflicting things in quick succession. One, thankfully, that her wrist was much better, and two, with trepidation, that in order to be successful at infiltrating an evil human kingdom and rescuing her sister, she had to go alone. Danyel could not be there with her. She would be overly concerned for his safety and worrying about him would distract her from the things she needed to do—namely, walk straight into danger. She put weight on her wrist to test it first as a dragon, and then again when she changed back into her centaur form. Fortunately, her centaur wrist stayed straight and felt strong and the discoloration faded to almost imperceptible. Seeing how well he had healed her, she knew Danyel would be needed in an different capacity and told him the moment he woke.

To avoid having to explain herself and invite further confrontation, Tyla pushed aside the heavy cloth to join the others, who were already beginning their morning. She found Narsun busily running around the main area and Sharot bidding farewell to two dragon guests. When Danyel joined Tyla, the visiting dragons allowed their eyes to briefly scan the two centaurs, but they quickly slipped out the front door without saying a word.

Narsun had his mother's attention now and started bouncing around, begging her to leave for the games.

"Go see if your dromdan is ready to go as well," Sharot said to the hyperactive little dragon. "Ah, you two are up!" she greeted Tyla and Danyel. "As you can see, Narsun is well ready to head into the city."

"I'm ready too," Danyel said, slinging his bags over his lower back. "When do we leave?"

"You're not going," Tyla grumbled to him. "Let me go in as a dragon and I'll come back and tell you everything."

"You won't though, will you?" he looked down and shook his head before meeting her eyes. "And what will I do if you don't come back?"

"It will be dangerous," Sharot agreed in a low tone, turning her head from Narsun's whereabouts, "for any centaurs to be in Gormitor city, even more than simply being found within Gormirom borders."

"You heard her," Tyla emphasized. "It's too dangerous for a centaur to be in the city."

"If I stay here and Sharot is found to have hidden me, she may be forced to pay a price as well," Danyel countered.

"That would be better than you being arrested in the city and forced to fight in those ridiculous games."

"If you had your way," Danyel said, reading her mind, "you would be doing all of this yourself, wouldn't you?"

"If you would let me, yes," she said. "One thing is for certain, we shouldn't be dragging Sharot and her family into any of this."

Narsun came bouncing up the stairs at that moment and her words caught in her throat. "Mother," he chirped, "Father says he's ready to go too."

Sharot had been watching the two young centaurs bicker and now looked at each of them sternly. "And you?" she said to Tyla. "Will you be going as a dragon or a centaur?"

She looked down at her wrist. It looked better, but she knew she couldn't put all her dragon weight on it yet.

"You can't go as a dragon," Danyel said gently, seeing her hesitation. "You won't be able to walk."

"And if you go as a centaur, you'll be walking into trouble," Sharot added.

"Yes," Tyla said, speaking mostly to Danyel, "but if anything goes horribly wrong I can change. You can't."

"Then I'll have to trust you to help me," Danyel said with a sly grin.

Tyla sighed. "And I will, but I'm not much help to anyone right now. I can't let you put yourself in danger knowing I won't be able to help you."

"Here," Makus appeared at the top of the stairs and threw two long cloaks at Tyla. "Wear these."

Tyla took one and handed the other to Danyel. The cloaks were simple—brown and long, much longer than the short cloak around Danyel's shoulders. The cloaks that centaurs usually wore stopped at the middle or bottom of their upper half, but these were long enough to cover their lower half as well and part of their tail. "How will wearing these help?"

Makus shrugged. "They might not," he said. "But you may pass as human riders on horseback if no one looks directly at you. At least you might blend in a little more with the crowd."

"In your dragon form you'll stand out and draw more attention to Danyel. So, stay as a centaur and keep between us," Sharot said. "Perhaps with the cloaks you'll both go largely unnoticed."

"Doubtful," Tyla muttered, but she donned the brown cloak over her shoulders.

Danyel's bags hung over his back, so the cloak on top of them almost helped conceal his shape. But Tyla had no such luck; she carried nothing, so her back was bare and the cloak sculpted her lower equine body.

Sharot frowned. "Like I said, stay between us."

The little dragon family and the centaurs slipped out the door into the rain. "We shouldn't have involved you at all," Tyla told Vanora's friend. "What we're doing is dangerous to anyone around us."

"What *are* you doing, anyway?" Sharot asked, her bright green scales glistening under the light rain. "You're here to investigate the centaur kidnappings, but I don't think I've gotten the whole story yet." Narsun eagerly ran ahead and Sharot kept her eye on him while Makus closed the gap and pulled Danyel closer, trying to keep him hidden. Narsun began pointing out all the wonderful things in their town and calling back to the centaurs with his parents.

Tyla opened her mouth to answer but stopped when Eleka came into her mind.

What would Eleka say? she thought to herself. *How much can I tell her?*

"My sister was taken," she finally answered. "I want to find her and make sure she's alright."

Sharot wheeled her long neck to look at Tyla with concern before she returned her gaze to where Narsun was pointing out the orchards to Danyel and calling out every flavor of apple grown.

"I can't say I blame you," Sharot said. "If it was my family, I would do everything I could as well. Are you sure she's here?"

"Very," Tyla answered, shivering with the thought of Kelraz's wraiths hissing at her.

"Then perhaps," Sharot offered, "we can stroll around Gormitor and make some subtle inquiries about the centaur challengers."

Tyla nodded. "On one condition," she said. "At any sign of trouble, you and your family leave us behind and pretend you never met us."

Sharot lifted a scaly brow at Tyla again, but grinned. "You're in no position to make conditions."

"Aren't these games a somewhat barbaric display?" Tyla asked as they made their way toward the towering walls of Gormitor.

"Hardly," Sharot scoffed. "Don't dragons fight for fun? Don't we pit ourselves against other worthy challengers in games of speed or agility or likewise? Don't centaurs train by fighting each other? Leman doesn't kill or permanently maim his challengers—so far, anyway. At least, they say he tries not to. He's a very talented fighter and he appears to be quite respectful of skill. He knows how to spar to bring out the best in his opponents. Which is why most of the people here enjoy the games and have supported him as the champion."

As they made their way toward the city gates, Tyla noticed the guards scrutinizing her and Danyel closely. She dropped her chin and pulled the cowl of the brown cloak tighter around her face, glancing at Danyel to see him do the same. Her eyes skated from Danyel up to Sharot, then Sharot's gaze drifted over to Makus. Makus met his mate's eyes then leaned down to Narsun. Before the guards could reach them to interact, Makus called out loudly to his son, "You should show Danyel that little shop you like so much. The one with the sweets that—"

Not waiting for his father to finish the thought, Narsun ran back to them and reached for Danyel's hand. "Oh, yeah, come on! You gotta see this!"

He pulled Danyel through the gates before the guards could question them. Sharot tugged on Tyla's arm as well and pulled her through the gates casually. "Narsun," Sharot called, "don't run too fast! Wait for us!"

They all made it through the gates without interruption. As they slowed inside, well beyond the guards, Tyla looked up at the green dragon. "Thank you," she whispered, allowing her pounding heart to ease.

"Don't thank me yet," Sharot answered, nodding to the sea of vendors and humans ahead.

Their hoofbeats resonated on the wide cobbled road inside the city. With each clop another human nearby turned at the sound. Once they realized it came from centaurs, they stopped whatever they were doing to stare at her and Danyel passing.

"I don't see many dragons," Tyla said to Sharot.

"Don't worry," she said. "I'm sure more will be along. Plus, some of these humans are also dragons."

As she said it, Tyla's eyes fell on a young girl working outside a clothing shop. A huge awning hung over the rack of dragon wrappings she hung on a line to protect the wares from the rain. Tyla studied the dragon markings of her wings at the top of her human back before she swayed and dipped her head to Sharot.

"Fair winds, Sharot!" the girl called before she hung the last of the wrappings she held. She smoothed her own brilliant blue wrappings with dark, teak-colored fingers. "Are you here for the games?"

"We are!" Sharot said.

"And your friend?" Tyla tried to avoid the shopgirl's eyes as she said it. "Has she come to watch as well?"

"Yes," Sharot slowed with Tyla. "Yalli, do you have any new wrappings in her color?" she asked, scanning the cloth hanging from the lines. "Hers are a little…well-worn. Perhaps in the new style?"

"What color would you like?" Yalli asked.

"Red," Sharot told her, "with spots of darker red."

"With the newer wrappings the spots don't stand out as much. But I'll see what we have," Yalli said and disappeared into the shop beneath the awning.

"What are you doing?" Tyla whispered to Sharot. "I don't have money and is this really the time to be shopping?"

"Calm down," Sharot said. "It's the best way to ask questions without seeming too suspicious. Yalli is a great one to ask and you could use some new wrappings anyway." She added the last with a dubius glance at her wrappings.

"I don't need new wrappings," Tyla bit back.

"Yes," Sharot twisted her snout, "you do. And we have a little money. But more importantly, you need answers, right?"

Tyla glanced down at her dragon wrappings. They were dirty and she hadn't changed into new ones for over a week, ever since the day they summoned Milah's soul wraith. She remembered seeing Eleka wrinkle her nose when she lifted her arms, but she was used to that face from her sister about all manner of things, so Tyla hadn't thought much about it. In the past, she'd always assumed she could change into her dragon form and leave the human part of her centaur smell behind. Tyla relented with a shrug.

The rain began to drip as young Yalli came back out holding three different red wrappings.

"Shall we see?" she said cheerfully.

Tyla reluctantly pulled off her borrowed cloak and changed into her dark red spotted dragon form, happy that Danyel was down the street looking at Narsun's favorite vendors, which were mostly sweet shops and human toys. She still wasn't used to parading her dragon spots around him.

As Yalli held up the different shades of red next to Tyla's scales, Sharot rolled her shoulder and curled up on the ground to make conversation. "Will you be watching the games at all? Or is your mother making you mind the shop all day?"

"Mother will be here by midday," Yalli said. "If the games are still going, I might kip over to see."

Catching on to Sharot's line of questioning, Tyla pointed at one of the random red wrappings to try it and asked, "But with your stall so close to the gates, you must get to see the challengers coming in."

Yalli chuckled. "Of course not," she said. "They're escorted to the castle well before we see them. Take off your old wrappings and lift your arms."

Tyla sat back on her haunches and lifted her front legs, grateful to take the pressure off her healing front leg. Although it felt much better, it still ached when she put pressure on it.

Tyla reached around to separate her own wrappings, which fell away a little easier than she'd expected, and unwound them, allowing the broken sword that had been tucked inside to fall into her claw. She set aside the blunted weapon and handed the dirty wrappings to Yalli, who tried and failed to hide a grimace. Yalli helped wrap the new dragon wrappings around her, stretching the silky material as it melted into her scales. The color conformed to her scales the way only majikal dragon wrappings could and stretched to fit her size as well.

"It's too long," Tyla said after more than a little wrapping. "What am I supposed to do with all this extra cloth?"

"Oh," Yalli said with a sly grin. "I'll show you."

"Yalli," Sharot said. "Narsun has been pestering me to go see the challengers while they're not fighting after hearing from his friends that they could go. Is the king allowing children to visit the challengers?"

"If he is," Yalli said, "no one knows how to get in. I haven't tried myself, but you could inquire at the castle gates. Ok, there." Yalli stepped back after completely wrapping the cloth around Tyla. "Now, try your centaur form."

Tyla changed before she could fall forward and land on her dragon wrist again. She looked down at the dark red wrappings. They were certainly cleaner and lacked the rips and tears from the branches and rocks they'd galloped through. At least they didn't smell like a human tar pit.

"We do have some of the old ones designed for centaurs to wrap only the chest, if that's really what you want," Yalli said, pointing out each detail as she said it. "But this is the new style around here. It has the same self-adhering majik so it won't fall off, and look at what the extra cloth can be used for." She stepped up to Tyla and unwrapped the first layer. "You can wrap it over your shoulders like this, or around your head or anything else, see?" She finished by wrapping the extra length of cloth around Tyla's shoulder like a mantle for an elegant effect.

"Ow," Tyla jumped when Yalli pulled the cloth around her arm.

"Oh," Yalli said, "I'm sorry. I didn't mean to hurt you."

"It's alright," Sharot said, stepping over to Tyla's side. "You can also use the cloth to do this." With deft dragon claws, Sharot wrapped the extra cloth under Tyla's arm and secured it again at her shoulder to create a supportive sling.

"Huh," Tyla sounded a little impressed, "that's actually quite useful."

Yalli beamed.

"Yalli," Sharot said, "can I have Makus settle up with you later? I don't have anything to trade with right now."

"No," Tyla said, "I don't like owing favors." She pulled out the broken piece of the ruined sword from under her old dragon wrappings. "Perhaps you could make use of the metal?"

Sharot shook her head. "No," she said. "That's far too much to exchange for one set of wrappings. She could make thousands of buttons out of that."

"Two, then," Tyla said. "Could I get a second set? The same color?"

Yalli nodded and veered back into the building.

"For my sister," Tyla explained, once Yalli had disappeared again.

"Twin?" Sharot inquired with a tilt of her head.

Tyla nodded. As much as she hated to part with any weapon, she knew the damaged tool was worse than useless. She doubted she would be allowed to carry weapons of any kind if she did compete, so the piece of sword would do her no good now. At least she had something useful to give Eleka.

"We can be on our way when she comes back," Sharot said. "I think I know who to speak with next."

17

THE KEY

"Rasco!" Narsun shouted, barreling toward another young grey dragon with an extra-large head. Tyla watched the two prance around each other excitedly in greeting before they ran off to join the crowd queuing around a fenced-off area behind the castle.

"Let me do the talking," Sharot whispered to Tyla and Danyel as they approached the blue-green dragon who appeared to be Rasco's dame. "She doesn't exactly see eye-to-eye with me on the purported misconduct of the king. But, lucky for us, she shares her ideals loudly."

"Hello, Silvi," Sharot said with a smile. "Clear skies to you!"

"And to you!" Silvi said, eyeing the group carefully. "I daresay we shall see sun today! And who do you have with you to share it?"

"This is Danyel," Sharot said, indicating her family's companions, "and Tyla. They're here to watch the games."

"Well, I certainly hope you're not going to be challengers, dears," Silvi said without a beat. "You're much too young and scrawny to last more than an instant against the champion. And he hates to hurt anyone, poor man. He really is such a dear."

"Yes," Sharot said tentatively, as her strong claws surreptitiously pulled Tyla away from the blue-green dragon. "You know Leman well, don't you?"

"We do!" Silvi said. Her eyes lingered on Danyel and Tyla's scales began to rile at how the older dragon sneered at him. "He was in the army with my Kirek. In fact, they were training together and Kirek tells me that if he hadn't been on the ground showing Leman how to take a fall, he would have been standing where Leman was at that moment and gotten the stone himself."

"Your mate was there when the champion got the stone?" Tyla asked without thinking.

"Yes," Silvi said. "He said it appeared to be thrown at him out of nowhere. Everyone says that Leman was blessed by Shurka herself. But you can come and see for yourself."

The group casually joined the growing crowd around the fenced area. The round arena fence attached to the castle along one arc of the circle. Guards stood inside the fence on either side of the giant doors leading into the stable and the castle depths, as well as outside the fence to hold back the spectators. High up over even the dragons' heads, a liberal balcony with a deep black, gilded awning jutted off the side of the castle. Lush chairs with black cushions trimmed in gold huddled from the rain under the opulent covering.

"Have you spoken to him?" Sharot asked Silvi as more spectators gathered around them. "Leman, I mean. If anyone could, it would be you. You're a noble and a friend of the champion. Narsun would love to visit the champion… or his challengers."

"Not yet," Silvi said, pushing her lip out in a small pout. "But we've sent him messages, and he's promised to visit us soon."

"What about the challengers?" Sharot persisted. "Surely their company isn't in as much demand. Their schedules can't be so overwhelmed."

"I haven't asked about the challengers. We have no interest in visiting centaurs. Besides, I assume their schedules are filled with practice and healing inside the castle," Silvi brushed aside the question. "Rasco!" she yelled over the crowd as Narsun's friend pushed aside some small humans to settle himself at the front of the fence line. "Keep your brothers with you!"

"Danyel is a healer," Tyla said quickly before the older dragon got more distracted. "Perhaps the challengers would benefit from having a centaur healer instead of a human or some other shaman."

"Hmm," Silvi glared down her snout at Tyla. "I'm sure the king is bringing in all the *best* healers to work with the challengers. I hear they are given the very best of everything in the castle. That's why so many centaurs have come to challenge. Oh, look, they must be coming!"

The crowd began to cheer, but Tyla didn't see any movement from the doors of the castle. Searching the arena and scanning the guards for any change, suddenly Danyel nudged her. She looked to see him pointing and staring up at sunbeams breaking through the clouds over their heads.

Tyla's eyes followed his and she realized as she tilted her head to the sky that no rain dripped on her face. Her heart skipped a beat. She wondered for a moment if spring had come early and her heart beat faster. Afterall, she and her friends had only about a week left until spring to get those fated keys back or the barrier between the worlds of the living and the dead would dissolve. She blinked at the magnificent sunlight as the clouds thinned, the rain ceased, and the sky glowed with radiance over the fenced arena.

The blue-green dragon took a long, deep breath next to them. "You see?" Silvi said blissfully, closing her eyes and relishing the otherworldly sunlight. "This is the other reason we come to the games. The champion shares the power of the sun with everyone. He has truly been blessed by Shurka."

As she said it, the giant castle doors opened into the arena and a burly human man marched out onto the sodden field inside the ring. He waved to the audience and the humans and dragons yelled and cheered, pounding their feet on the ground and their fists against their chests.

The champion pounded one fist against his muscular chest and held up his other arm. His chest and arms were so bulky that his legs needed to be exceptionally large and strong to hold him up, making him as tall as Tyla in her centaur form and probably three times as wide. His long black hair pulled back with a cord at the nape of his neck, and scruffy black hair adorned his chin and cheeks, stretching fully up to his ears. He held no weapons, not even a dagger, nor did he have anywhere to hide one as his only clothes were simple black breeches. He even went barefoot.

The champion looped a full circle around the arena as he waved to the crowd. Once he faced her, Tyla finally caught sight of it. Golden yellow, the shape of a droplet of water or half of a dragon's heart, and stuck fast to the right side of his upper chest. The same shape but not the same color as Jassan's and Trivnor's keys. The Sun Key.

"Tyla," Danyel whispered at her side, "are you alright?"

As the crowd cheered around them, Tyla abruptly turned to Danyel and Sharot, who eyed her with concern. Only in the back of her mind did she wonder what they might see in her eye, because she could only focus on one thing. "I have to challenge him."

"You'll do nothing of the sort," Sharot whispered harshly. "You came here for…" she checked to make sure that Silvi wasn't listening, "…other reasons." She very pointedly shot her eyes at Tyla's new—double-thick—red wrappings. She hadn't wanted to carry Eleka's new wrappings, so she had doubled them over her own.

"Yes," Tyla said, "but I have to. I know that now."

"Not yet," Danyel tried to protest. "We need more information. If you're going to challenge him—and I'm not saying you should—at least see what he's capable of first."

Tyla nodded. It was good advice. Her mother always taught her to try out an opponent for a moment before launching into the fight. Eleka would tell her the same thing.

Reluctantly, she faced the arena. After the champion paraded around the arena a few more times, the castle doors onto the king's balcony box swung wide open.

The king seemed small to Tyla as he stepped out onto the balcony and raised his hand in greeting, smaller than a grown human man normally appeared. The top of his fuzzy red-haired head might have barely reached the chins of the men around him but for the gaudy golden crown encircled by black crisscrossed swords atop it. The man stuck to the old traditions of his kingdom by wearing a soft golden cloak and tunic, the chest of which was embroidered with a black sword reaching from his shoulder to his hip. His round face was the perfect background for joviality if it didn't bear the downturned mouth and beady black eyes of a man who practiced cruelty. The illustration on his tunic come to life, at his hip he wore a pure black sword. The original version would have emanated majik, but with no hint of enchantment in this one, it was probably simply used for pomp.

As striking a man as the king might have been in all his regal attire, every eye must have been drawn to the person who appeared behind him on the balcony. While King Gormin waved to the champion and the cheers of the crowd, a black-cloaked figure drifted behind him to stand in front of the chair next to the magnificent throne. When he turned to the side briefly, Tyla caught a glimpse of dragonfly-like faerie wings; wide, iridescent and pulled through the back of his cloak, as many faeries did, to lie flat against his back. The faerie kept the hood of his cloak up and his head down, but his cleft green chin with tufts of black hair peeked out from the bottom.

Tyla's heart pounded. *It couldn't possibly be Kelraz, could it?* She scrambled through her brain trying to remember if Trivnor ever described what Kelraz looked like. Would he be here? Could he be here? He would have had plenty of time to fly to Gormirom since he didn't have to avoid wraiths. He might have even had time to either gain the king's confidence or threaten him into submission before now. But with all that time available, why wouldn't he have already taken the key from the champion instead? And if it wasn't Kelraz, was this simply another faerie who had decided to meddle in the affairs of the world outside his faerie forest? Mightn't he have already been a faerie counselor to the former king and taken on advising the new king as well?

As Tyla's mind swam through the possibilities, the doors leading from the castle stables into the arena opened again. Prying her gaze from the faerie and king, Tyla watched a white centaur with a cream-colored mane and hair shuffle into the arena. The crowd hissed and booed loudly when they saw him. Evidence of recent previous fights shimmered in the vivid scars along the centaur's chest and shoulders. His legs tilted slightly at the ankle when he applied pressure as he walked. Not a limp exactly, but a weakness in the ankle that only another centaur would notice.

"He's already injured," Danyel said, as the crowd continued to jeer at the centaur.

"Yes," Silvi sneered. "I've seen this challenger before. He must have healed well enough to think he can take the champion again. Stupid creatures."

She made no apologies to the centaurs at her side for the loud insults as the champion raised his hands for quiet.

"Who comes to challenge the Champion of Justice?" the bulky man said in a smooth bellow.

The white centaur looked around the crowd briefly before opening his mouth to answer. As soon as he did, the crowd booed even louder to drown out the centaur's voice. Even Narsun joined in with his friends with only the slightest hesitation.

The champion chuckled with irony. "Do you think that centaurs are stronger and better than humans?" he asked.

"Yes!" the centaur barked quickly before the noise rising again from the humans outside the fence could cut him off again.

"Alright," the champion nodded and grinned as he flexed his chest and arms. "Let us see, shall we?"

The centaur also held no weapons. He didn't wear a thread across his own strong chest. Bulging muscles tightened against the red strain of the previous injuries as the two men ran toward each other.

The centaur reared as the champion approached but the man seemed to recognize the tactic. He stopped and jerked to the side to avoid the deadly hooves. He dropped to his knees and sprang up underneath the centaur, connecting his massive fist to the lower belly. The centaur jolted from the contact and arched at the middle slightly, but swung his lower end into the champion, knocking him to the ground.

"That shouldn't have hurt him," Danyel said. "A single blow by a human to a centaur's lower belly. He shouldn't have even felt it."

"Leman is stronger than a normal man," Silvi scoffed. "Don't forget, he's been blessed by Shurka."

"How could I forget?" Danyel said to her with a forced smile, then inclined his head to Tyla and muttered, "Especially when she keeps reminding us."

The champion fell over in the mud onto his back, but rolled away as the centaur tried to stomp him with his back legs. The centaur backed up and continued bucking, hoping to connect with the human before the man got to his feet. Instead, the champion rolled under the centaur.

"Oh no," Tyla whispered.

The champion planted his feet against the centaur's belly and kicked both legs much the same way Tyla often used her legs to kick wraiths away from her while fighting them. The centaur flew into the air, flailing his legs the entire way. He met the height of the top of the royal box, at least one dragon length up, then flipped in the air and fell to the ground on his back.

The centaur squirmed to turn on his side. Tyla knew that if he could get to his side, he could use his arms to push himself to stand and gain his footing again, but the champion was already on top of him. From his side, the centaur tried to punch his arms, but the champion rained blows into his ribs. The deafening cracks echoed around the arena and Tyla flinched while the crowd cheered.

Eleka wouldn't have been able to watch the battle but Tyla couldn't tear her eyes away as her teeth ground together. The champion stood from kneeling on the centaur. The centaur swung his arms, trying to protect himself from the champion's new blows. He tried to pull his legs up underneath himself to stand, but he cried out in pain any time he put any weight on a leg.

"Concede." The champion breathed heavily looking down at the challenger, and the crowd quieted.

The centaur nodded his head. "I concede," he mumbled.

Danyel breathed a sigh of relief and Tyla nodded next to him. She knew full well that the centaur couldn't take any more abuse. It would kill him.

"No!" someone yelled from the crowd.

"Use the stone!" someone else called.

The champion waved to the guards by the doors. When they opened, a dozen guards came running out with a wooden pallet between them. They quickly loaded the centaur onto the litter and dragged him back into the castle.

"My friends," the champion called to the crowd and raised his arm to keep their attention. "I will have mercy on this challenger. But perhaps my next challenger will not need my mercy. Shall we meet them?"

The crowd cheered again. The champion still looked eager and energetic albeit dirty from landing in the drying mud. Tyla had no doubt he could easily handle as many challengers as were put forth throughout the day.

Waving to the guards at the door again, the champion signaled for the next challenger. When the doors opened again, a figure appeared. Hesitantly stepping out, her brown hair swinging around her shoulders, red eyes examining the audience. Eleka.

18

CHALLENGE

"No," Tyla whispered, lurching toward the arena, but Danyel's and Sharot's hands stopped her.

Eleka stepped forward, taking in the crowd, the sunshine overhead, the champion with the bright golden stone and the royal box. She wore only her dirty red dragon wrappings over her brown chest and a wide silver cuff around her back ankle.

"You won't help anyone if you're caught too," Danyel whispered in Tyla's ear.

"Won't I?" Tyla said. "At least I can fight for her."

"Would they even let you try?" Sharot said from her other side. "They won't even let the centaurs speak. We have no idea what happens within that castle so we can't assume they would allow you anything."

She added the last very low when she noticed Silvi's eyes bouncing between their conversation and the spectacle in front of her.

"She looks like you," Silvi said at last, much too loudly for Tyla's comfort. "Is she your sister?"

Tyla whipped toward Silvi, curses ready on her tongue, but Sharot grabbed her and jerked her back. "Don't say anything," she muttered under her breath so only Tyla and Danyel could hear. "She'll accuse you of coming to cause problems, then she'll raise them herself."

Silvi cleared her throat. "I thought you said you hadn't come to challenge the champion?"

"No," Danyel said, whirling on Silvi, "we haven't."

Silvi's brows creased in thought, but she shook it off and turned back to the arena. Tyla imagined the dragon's mind churning, trying to decipher if that meant they were here to support her sister or something else. When Silvi let it drop, Tyla returned to grinding her teeth toward the arena.

"Don't worry," Sharot said soothingly in Tyla's ear, "Leman doesn't kill the challenger, remember? She only needs to concede. She's smart enough to do that, right?"

Tyla nodded, slowly, while her mind raced. Yes, Eleka was smart. Very smart. She may concede quickly, but would they let her? She and Tyla both knew that the Sun Key was here, and Tyla was convinced that Kelraz was somehow mixed up in this disaster. Would he or the king simply have Eleka killed in a show of power, for their own reasons? Kelraz knew Eleka and Tyla were after the same thing he was. How long would either he or the king delay the inevitable?

"So," the champion addressed Eleka, pausing to eye her form. "Who comes to challenge the Champion of Justice?"

Eleka stood still, staring at the human. Tyla had been right in her estimate of their equal heights; he met Eleka squarely eye to eye. At first, pockets of the human audience began to boo, suppressing the ability to hear any of her words, but there was no need. Eleka didn't open her mouth as she looked past the man in front of her and continued taking in the sights around the arena.

"Perhaps," the champion said, "your pointy ears don't work as well as a human's?"

The crowd chuckled and murmured their approval.

Eleka finally opened her mouth. "I didn't come here—" she started, but the crowd cut her off with jeers. She pursed her lips in anger.

Once the crowd calmed down, the champion waved a hand at her. "Do you think centaurs are better than humans?"

Eleka kept her silence, but Tyla knew she was working out the entire problem in her brain. Centaurs were typically larger and physically stronger than humans. That couldn't be said about all of them, of course, but between an equally matched centaur and human in height, at least, the centaur would be stronger and win every time. She didn't make a move to answer, but the crowd booed and hissed anyway.

"Ah, well," the human shrugged and said dismissively, "I suppose you don't want to admit that you know I'll beat you."

Eleka's eyes snapped to the man. "I'm not here to—"

A blinding light suddenly filled the arena. Eleka was thrown into the air, her brown body flipping twice before landing hard in the drying mud.

Tyla lurched forward again, but Sharot's sharp claws caught her before she made any progress.

The crowd cheered.

"What happened?" Danyel muttered. "What did he do?"

"The stone!" Silvi cooed, her eyes widening. "He used the stone!"

Eleka lay on the ground on her side. She didn't move for a moment and neither did Tyla's heart. When Eleka's leg twitched and she took a huge gasping breath, Tyla mimicked her movements involuntarily.

Eleka kicked her legs and the champion allowed her to right herself. She searched the crowd's faces. "You won't silence—"

The crowd cut off her words with more jeering and hissing.

"But I'm not—"

Knowing what was coming next, Tyla watched as a blinding ray of sun pierced the air in front of the champion to stab into her twin.

Eleka slammed against the ground again with a rattling THUD. A lump welled in Tyla's throat. Her teeth ground together and her jaw began to ache while she jerked against Sharot's iron grip.

"Concede, child," the champion finally said with a gentle tone that Tyla didn't expect. "Before I accidentally do you more harm."

Eleka's face winced in pain when she tried to stand. She looked up at the champion in confusion, then dropped her face. "I concede."

Tyla practically ran from the crowd surrounding the arena once the guards carted Eleka back into the castle. She barely noticed the clouds closing over her head and the rain trickling down the waterproof cloth over her back while splashing through puddles in the streets.

"Tyla!" Danyel called after her. "Tyla, stop!"

She ignored him, her mind filled with her sister's face crumpled in pain. She stumbled through the cobbled streets of the massive city and only halted when she remembered the sound of Eleka's gasps. Feeling her sister's pain, she gasped too, and stopped in the middle of a wide road.

"Tyla," Danyel said, catching up to her and pulling on her arm to face him.

When he touched her, she spun on him. Her mind filled with the champion's dark bearded face and she raised a claw, imagining the champion and not Danyel standing in front of her. Suddenly Sharot jumped in front of Danyel to take the strike across her shoulder. Tyla's razor claws glanced off her scales.

Sharot roared in Tyla's face, loosing flame and forcing her to blink. Her vision cleared and she breathed again. Danyel still held a hand up to protect himself, but it wouldn't have done him any good against her claws. Her stomach dropped and her heart constricted as she realized what she might have done to him. She turned back into a centaur but couldn't force herself to speak to apologize.

"She's alive," Sharot snapped. "And if the history of these games is any predictor, she will stay that way."

"But for how long?" Tyla growled, turning from the two. They stayed a few steps behind her down the road, giving her a moment to think. In the back of her mind she wondered where her feet would take her. Back to Sharot's place? Back to the arena? The castle? The Centaur Plains?

"If she keeps trying to speak up like that," Tyla continued down the cobbles as Danyel and Sharot stepped along behind her, "they'll have to kill her. Then they'll claim that she succumbed to her injuries, I'm sure." Tyla stopped, realizing that very outcome could happen at any moment whether she was there to prevent it or not.

"Tyla," Danyel said beside her.

"I know what you're going to say," Tyla said, staring at the ground but again only seeing Eleka's pained face. "I know you think I shouldn't—"

"No," Danyel whispered harshly, "—goblins."

Tyla followed his eyes to see five goblins turning a corner toward them down the street. She immediately recognized the bright blue hair, dripping with rain, in the lead. Tyla spun her face away and pulled the extra length of dragon wrappings from around her arm to tuck under the cloak and around her face. Pinching it so it would stay around her head but off her eyes, she snapped, "Now what?"

"Trouble with goblins too?" Sharot growled. "Who *are* you?"

"Someone who can't be caught by goblins," Tyla growled back, keeping her face away from the little grey creatures.

"Please," Danyel implored, keeping his face turned as well. He wore nothing that would conceal his face so he pulled the borrowed cloak over his head and tucked his face back into it as far as possible. "We have to stay out of sight."

Sharot pursed her lips while searching the area around them. Tyla was grateful that she had abandoned the arena area and games quickly so that little Narsun was left behind with his friends and Makus.

After scanning the area, Sharot nodded. "This way," she ordered and led them around another corner away from the goblins. Only the sound of their own hooves echoed across the stones as they pushed past vendors and carts.

The three ran down the street, ducking around humans and the occasional dragon, but two human guards suddenly stepped around the corner in front of them. Danyel and Tyla ducked again as Sharot spread her wings to hide their escape before exclaiming her mock surprise at seeing the guards emerge unexpectedly.

The guards apologized for startling her and turned back the way they'd come, but the goblins pointed and shouted, "You there, centaurs, stop!"

Sharot shoved the two into an alley between buildings leading to another road lined with large homes, now drawing closer to the castle with every step. In centaur form, Tyla's head towered over the people, but her lower body bumped and jostled the carts and wares clogging the roads. Had the road been clear, or had it been nighttime, they would normally have easily outpaced the goblins and gotten away. However, the memory of the little goblin Trykirt covering the length of the House of Elders almost before she did as a dragon discouraged her from trying. As they tumbled toward the castle gates, Tyla desperately surged forward. That's where she needed to be. She had to be in there with her sister.

Two human castle guards leveled their staffs as the centaurs approached. Tyla and Danyel stopped not two dragon lengths in front of the gates. Belligerent shouts from bystanders preceded Sharot coming up behind them. More shouts repeated as the goblins came around a far corner.

"What now?" Danyel muttered, looking first toward the guards in front of them then back at Trykirt sprinting up from behind, his sword in its sheath bouncing against his back.

Tyla searched the area. They were close to the castle but still inside Gormitor city walls. Escape on wing for her alone might be possible, but she could only hope that Sharot could also get Danyel away safely. Not only that, Danyel's assessment of not being able to fly out seemed much more reasonable from this angle. The merlons and rooftops over the city walls seemed nearly impossible to climb—even as a dragon—and the guards watched everyone from every angle. Their attempted escape would draw fire. However, she knew that if she stayed, the goblins had the power to bring them all down.

They might arrest Sharot as well for helping them. Finally choosing the path of least resistance and the one she knew she could beat, she ran for the human guards at the castle gates.

She shed the borrowed cloak and wrenched the wrappings from her face and head to stand in front of the castle guards.

"I've come to challenge!" she shouted, puffing out her chest. "I've come to challenge the Champion of Justice!"

19

ACCOMMODATIONS

"So have I!" Danyel said, stumbling up beside her.

"No!" Tyla threw her good arm in front of his chest to keep herself between the humans and the centaur.

Sharot ran up behind them. "What are you doing?"

"I'm challenging!" Tyla yelled to the guards again, pushing Danyel back further. "Take me in!"

"Oh, no, you don't!" Trykirt marched up next to Tyla, his wet blue hair stuck to his forehead under the small golden obruck. "You're coming with us."

He reached out to put a hand on Tyla's flank as a gem began to glow in the obruck, but a long staff swung down between them. The goblin jerked his hand back and glared at the staff-wielding guard.

"You go' no aufori'y 'ere, goblin, and no righ' t' innerfere," the guard said. He wore the golden yellow tunic of the formerly Just Kingdom, with two small swords embroidered near his right shoulder. If Tyla remembered her human military history correctly, the emblem signified him as a lieutenant in the Just army. The other guard held his staff at the ready, but his tunic had only one sword insignia and he appeared much younger than the first; a simple staff guard taking his orders and cues from the older, more assured lieutenant. A confidence the man showed off in the face of the goblins. "You're no' the only justice in Avonoa. If fis centaur wishes t' challenge the champion, 'ats 'er right and we'll let 'er."

The goblin pulled his grey lip back over his teeth in a very dragon-like manner. "You have no idea what you're doing."

Tyla's jaw clenched at the irony of it. Their quest to find the keys and stop the barrier from being destroyed outweighed any good the goblins thought they were doing by apprehending a thief. She looked down sternly at the little goblin. "Neither do you."

The goblin glared at her, but returned his gaze to the guard. "Step aside, human. I won't warn you again."

The lieutenant lifted his staff but stepped toward the goblin. "Wot are you gonna do, 'tack me in a 'uman ci'y?"

He said it loud enough that every human within earshot stopped what they were doing. If they hadn't been watching already, they turned. If they had been watching, they took a few steps toward the spectacle, not a smile to be seen on their faces.

Trykirt slowly lowered his hand. Although the top of his head only reached the top of Tyla's leg, she was fully aware of the power in his fingers. She shivered at the thought of reliving the shock. The goblin could render her unconscious and transport her so far from Eleka that she would have to wait to become a wraith before she would see her again.

"I would like to appeal to your king," Trykirt muttered. "I do have that right, I believe."

"Affer a freat like 'at?" the lieutenant sneered. "I woo'en le' you nowhere near my king. But I'll tell you wot I will do," he said, nodding. "I'll tell 'im all abou' you. You come back t'morrow and see if 'e decides to le' you in…before I strai' out ban you from the ci'y."

The goblin bared his teeth at the man, then narrowed his eyes at Tyla. "Don't die, centaur. I want the pleasure of dragging you back to Kirlik myself."

The lieutenant moved aside, watching the goblins drift away and talk amongst themselves. The younger guard pushed open the gates onto a road leading up to the castle beyond. "I been wan'in t' be one t' allow new challengers," the lieutenant said proudly as he led Tyla and Danyel inside. "Even if 'ey are centaurs."

Tyla glanced back at Sharot outside the gates, who shook her head but didn't say anything. Once the gates banged shut again with the staff guard on the outside, Tyla watched Sharot turn without another glance back and dart down a nearby street.

"May I ask," Danyel said as the man guided them into a tunnel spacious enough for centaurs off to the side of the castle. "Why don't you like centaurs?"

"Well," the guard said, "'ey were 'orrible to us, weren' 'ey?"

"You traded with centaurs," Danyel said to keep the man talking. "Commerce and relations were strong here. At least for a time, anyway."

"Yeah," the man grumbled, "bu' centaurs were savages b'fore the dragon war. We couldn' even leave our ci'ies or villages and even 'ose would git raided and sacked for fun by centaurs."

"What?!" Danyel said. "I've never heard of centaurs raiding human villages for any reason, much less for fun."

"Well, 'ey dun i'," the man said. "Just cuz you ain' heard it b'fore, don' mean it din' 'appen. It's the reason I joined the army. In 'ere."

The man stopped at a heavy double door and banged a fist against it twice.

One of the doors cracked open. "Wha' is i'?" came a gruff voice on the other side, but Tyla recognized the gravelly sound even if she couldn't see him at first. Her heart pounded in her ears and she ground her teeth together.

The lieutenant puffed out his chest. "'ese two are come t' challenge the champion," he announced.

"Wha'?" the man on the other side said. "No one challenges the champion!" He swung the door open wider so he could step through and get a better look.

Tyla's jaw worked and her breathing quickened as the man's horrible face lit up. "You," he said in recognition, "look 'oo come crawlin'!"

"Like I said," the guard said again, undeterred by the older man's tone, "'ese two come t' challenge."

Sparse hair crawled across the ugly man's scalp, but he kept it long, Tyla assumed in hopes of hiding his otherwise freckled and lumpy head. He didn't bother with the customary guards' tunic and instead wore a dirty brown shirt, breeches and worn leather boots. Tyla wondered if he was even in the army, or perhaps he was a particularly cruel horse master that the king chose to utilize for his abhorrent strengths. He scratched the scruffy stubble on his chin and looked the two centaurs over. "I be' they 'ave," he sneered. He stepped up to Tyla, ignoring Danyel. "I knew you'd come." He smelled as bad as he looked.

Tyla's hands clenched into tight fists until pain lanced through her wrist. Her arm jerked involuntarily and the ugly man caught the movement.

"Uh-huh," he spat on the ground. "I remember a' abou' you. Don' worry," he said to the lieutenant without taking his eyes off Tyla, "I'll take 'em from 'ere."

The lieutenant stumbled backward wordlessly. Tyla had the feeling that he wanted more commendations than what he received, but he left quietly.

"Righ' fis way," the ugly man said. He opened the double doors allowing Tyla and Danyel into the dark, damp area.

As they stepped through, the odor of animal waste assaulted her senses. They entered some kind of stable with hay strewn over a long, high hallway. To the side, regular horses neighed and whickered in open stalls with tall walls on the back and sides and half doors on the front so their heads could peer over at the newcomers. Farther to the side a few sheep and goats huddled in a roomy pen together, sharing a trough and hay. She couldn't see them, but the smell of pigs somewhere further still mingled with the rest of the noxious smells.

The three continued through the stable down a main aisle and Tyla could see at the far end a set of looming double doors. They passed rows of several sets of stalls on either side and when they reached the large doors the squat little man turned around. They had arrived at two perpendicular rows with stalls leading to the left and right. More open stalls with horses snorting and nickering their restful afternoon away led off to the right; barred and fully contained stalls lingered to the left. As Tyla expected, the ugly man directed the pair to the left.

"I be' I know 'oo you wanna see," the man muttered with a grin, catching Tyla's eye. He pointed to the first stall on his left, inviting her to look.

Tyla stepped forward. Peering through the vertical bars above the half door, she eyed Eleka lying on her side in a pile of hay.

"Eleka," Tyla breathed, jumping to the stall door and gripping the bars. "Eleka, are you alright?"

Her twin didn't stir, her breathing heavy and slow.

"What did you do to her?" Danyel asked from Tyla's side. "What's wrong?"

"Nuffin'," the ugly man grunted. "The 'ealing does 'at. Don' worry," he said. "You'll see soon enuf."

Tyla felt cold metal close around her rear ankle as she stared at her sister. She shook her hoof to release it but discovered the same silver cuff attached to her leg as the one she could see on Eleka's.

"Didn' fink we would allow a dragon in the ring, did ya?" the ugly man said, grinning. Tyla raised her lips and bared her teeth at the man. "Carefu'," he muttered. "Keep the figh'in in the ring." He put his hand down at his side and lifted from a loop on his belt a long golden rod almost the length of his thigh. At the end of it, a bright yellow gem jutted to a sharp point.

"Know wha' fis does?" he said, waving the rod while pointing the gem at Tyla. "Li'l treasure shared wif us measly 'umans recen'ly. It's kinda like the champion's stone. Wanna sample?"

Tyla pursed her lips and stood up tall in defiance. She quickly assessed what she knew of that gem. Whether it worked like the keys or like the one Trykirt had used on her, it could possibly take down a fully grown dragon and she knew she wanted to stay as far as possible from it.

"No?" the ugly man said when she turned away. "'Ow 'bout you, boyo?"

He turned the weapon on Danyel, but Danyel shook his head. "Look," he said in the face of the awful man, "we've come to volunteer as challengers. What more do you want from us?"

"Meh," the man said, replacing the golden rod at his belt and letting it dangle, "I don' like draggin' your useless bodies aroun' anyway." He turned and walked a few more steps down the row. Sliding open the second stall door on his right, he waved at them to join him. "Your quar'ers, good sir."

"You can't be serious," Danyel said, inspecting the stall. Manure and moldy straw covered the floor. On the inside of the slatted wall that the open door slid against hung a bucket of brackish green water and another empty bucket with the remains of dried purple mash crusted up the sides.

"Oh, I'm dead serious," the ugly man said with a twinkle in his eye. "Now you, 'andsome, can take fis or give it t' the girl and take the nicer one down 'ere for yerself. I'll le' you choose."

Once Danyel stepped inside, the ugly man quickly slid the door shut. A lock dangled on the end of the latch and the human pushed aside his golden rod to produce a set of keys from a pocket. After making it secure, he kicked the bottom of the stall door and stomped on a bolt the width of the bottom half of his leg to drive it into the stone floor. Tyla tried to hold back the pain in her eyes as she nodded to Danyel and left him behind. She followed the man farther down the aisle past two stalls with other centaurs, neither of which were on their hooves. She tried to see if they were on the floor in the same condition as Eleka.

"'Ere's yours 'en, swee'eart," the ugly man said, sliding an extra-wide door aside for her. "Figure I migh' as well give you the royal suite seein' as you volunteered an' ev'ryfin'. Fis 'ere one is bigger an' comfier where the mares do their foalin'. But it's emp'y now and wai'in' jus' for you."

Tyla peered inside, attempting to control a gag. Instead of moldy straw on the floor, lumpy sand covered clumps of old manure. The two buckets hung in the same spot beside the sliding door as in Danyel's stall and showed just as much crust and wear.

"What do you give us for food?" Tyla said, trying to keep her voice from quivering. She did wilderness training with her father, living in the wild for several days while hunting and flying, but even the muddy crags of the mountains didn't compare to this squalor. "I was told you take good care of the challengers."

The ugly man slid the door shut with a chuckle. "Don' worry, Your Grace, you'll be fed ev'ry day," he mocked her. "And my name is Fad. I oversee the challengers."

"Fad?" she repeated, a dubious lilt in her question. "Or Thad? I can't quite understand through your crooked teeth."

"Fad, I said."

"Fad? Or Thad?"

"Fad!"

"Thad?"

"Fad!"

"Fad?"

The squat little man's face burned as he pursed his lips.

"Doesn't matter," Tyla said. "I think I'll just call you Ugly."

Ugly Fad snorted. "You're gonna be a fun one, ain' ya? I tell you wot," he said and waved his hand for her to approach the door. "I'll give you a li'l somefin' extra, you bein' new 'ere and all. Maybe you'll be the one t' free all the others!"

"Free them?"

"Yeah," Ugly Fad grinned wider, "'at's why all the challengers stay. Din' ya know? They're all figh'in for freedom. First centaur wins 'gainst the champion, frees 'em all!"

"Ah," Tyla nodded. "That's why you have repeat challengers."

"'Course!" Ugly Fad cooed. "Ya see? Since centaurs are so much be'er 'an 'umans, should be no problem a' all! Oh! An' 'ere's your li'l somefin' extra!"

Ugly Fad stuck the golden rod through the bottom slats of the stall door before Tyla could look down to see it coming. She was right in her assessment of the tool because the jolt she felt was much like the shock she'd gotten from the goblin's touch, but Ugly's little stick didn't quite match it in power. Her muscles bunched and pain ricocheted between her bones, but the disturbance quickly stopped. She took a few steps back from the door and a few deep breaths to help ease the sensation away.

Ugly didn't look completely satisfied, but he withdrew the rod and shook it at her. "'ere's more where 'at come from." He turned and stalked back down the aisle. "Enjoy your stay!"

20

VOLUNTEERS

"Danyel!" Tyla yelled through the bars of her stall door. "Can you hear me down there?"

Tyla caught a muffled shout in return. Although they were only three stalls down and across from each other, the sound was muted more than she thought it should have been. She couldn't make out any words, even listening carefully; it sounded like Danyel was on the other side of the stables, yelling into a pillow.

"I can't hear you!" she yelled louder.

"Quiet, you!" Ugly Fad poked his head around the corner he had retreated behind. "The stalls are noise padded. You can' hear each uvver but I can 'ear every word. And if I haffa listen to eever o' you yellin' all night, I'll use 'is fing and no one will ever know you were 'ere!" He dropped his golden rod to his side, then slumped back around the corner.

"You have to be quiet," a gentle voice drifted into Tyla's stall.

Tyla whipped her head around. "Who said that?"

"Over here," the voice came from the stall next to hers.

Tyla stepped to the side of the stall nearest to Eleka and Danyel. "Who are you?" she asked low. "How can I hear you?"

The wall between them stretched from her sandy floor to twice her height, although it didn't reach the raftered ceiling farther above it. Peering between the cracks of the thin slats, the white centaur she had seen challenging in the arena earlier lay stilled and appeared peaceful on the hay-strewn floor.

Up close, she could scrutinize clear evidence of how much worse his treatment in the ring had been than she thought while watching the challenge. His creamy hair and mane had been made pinkish and matted with blood and dirt. The scars across his shoulder screamed an angry red. His pink human half paled to almost the same shade of his white coat.

"I'm Myles," he said, although his chest heaved and he wheezed between words. "And you are?"

"Myles?" Tyla's mouth fell open.

"Really, your name is Myles too?" he whispered back haltingly.

"No, I'm Tyla," she forced out while she struggled with a possibility. Was he the newborn twins' lost father? How long had it been since he disappeared? "But you're Myles? From Zanna? With the new foals?"

"Yes," Myles's head lifted from the ground. "Have you seen them?"

"I met your daughter," she said.

"My daughter?" Myles's voice faltered. "She had the foals? She was still bearing when I was taken."

"Yes," she whispered. "They're all healthy and safe. The one I met…she's strong."

"They're safe," Myles mumbled and closed his eyes.

"Last I saw, anyway, and I plan to keep them that way." Tyla held back the rest of what she wanted to say. She wanted to tell him that she was going to kill the champion and take the golden key, then kill Kelraz and escape with everyone imprisoned here. But she knew Eleka would definitely stop her from saying any of that. "But first, tell me what's going on around here."

"Well, Tyla," Myles said, "the noise padding is majikal only against loud sounds, noise, or voices. If we speak in low tones, we can get messages to the others."

"Others?" she asked. "How many centaurs are here?"

"Not sure," Myles said. "I think there's still someone in the row behind me, but he hasn't made any noise for a while. Either he's still healing or there's no more need for a healer. Shay is on the other side of me, between me and the young girl. I think there's about four others."

"How long have you been here?"

"About six days."

"And is what Fad said true?" Tyla asked. "Is everyone here fighting for the centaurs' freedom?"

Myles nodded, but winced and stopped. "Yes, according to what we're told, as you were just now, that part is true. That is, a centaur who wins a challenge can set us all free. I don't believe it, but it's worth fighting for anyway. However, the punishments in the meantime are served out to everyone alike, no one is immune."

"Punishments?"

"Yes," Myles gasped and grunted. "The new centaur. The young woman who fought today. She must have been pretty unruly, because Fad came in and meted out quite a punishment to all of us."

"That's my sister, Eleka," Tyla muttered trying to keep the ache out of her voice. "She was trying to tell the humans what was really happening at these 'games'," Tyla said. "She was trying to say that the centaurs are being kidnapped and forced to fight."

"Yeah," Myles rested his head against the wall. "Yeah, that's usually what does it. Try to say or do anything the king and his humans don't like and everyone pays."

"That's why you didn't say anything while you were fighting?"

Myles nodded slowly. "We're all trying to stay alive," he said. "And at the same time, trying not to get each other killed."

She didn't want to ask, but she felt she must. "What about escape?"

"It's not for lack of trying," Myles said. "They keep us barely strong enough to put up a little bit of a fight and a show in the arena. Then they ensure that we're weak enough not to move the rest of the time. The first day in here, I broke my leg trying to kick the door down."

"Broke your leg?" Tyla yelped. "How in the world did you fight today? If it's only been a few days since then, you shouldn't even be able to walk!"

"Another cruelty of our captors," Myles said, familiarized to the pain. "Their healers are able to heal us quickly. Their methods work fast, but it takes a lot of energy on our part, and we sleep a long time after each one. Plus, the treatment is not always as thorough as you'd like. Re-injury is common. Then if a punishment is given out, we're woken and the healing is delayed."

"I saw the limp you had today," Tyla said, remembering the evidence of his story. "That was from when you first broke your leg."

"Yes," Myles whispered. "That healing took a lot out of me. I slept for two days. When I finally came to, I discovered that everyone else had been punished not only for my attempt but also for my not being able to fight again immediately."

"So they make everyone suffer collectively," Tyla said.

Myles nodded. "Every morning, they come through and ask for volunteers to fight that day. Anyone capable offers. If no one volunteers, they take whoever they want anyway. The longer the fight lasts, the more food everyone receives for the day. If Fad decides the fight was too short or you didn't do your best, everyone's punished. He says if someone tries to escape while they're out in the ring, he'll kill someone on the inside. So no, no one has tried to escape. We weren't able to explain any of this to the young woman who fought today."

"Why not?"

"For some reason they kept her separate when she was brought in," Myles said. "We didn't even know she was here until they trotted her past the end stalls to fight today. As soon as we tried to yell any advice, the noise padding stopped every word."

"Can you speak with her now?" Tyla asked, trying not to allow her hopes to jump too high. "If we whisper through the walls, can we speak with her?"

Myles sighed. "I knew you were going to ask that." Rather than standing and shifting his entire body to face the other direction, he wriggled around on the hay-strewn ground to face the wall opposite Tyla and spoke quietly with another centaur.

Tyla watched rather than heard Myles converse with someone neither of them could see. She waited impatiently, tapping her hoof quietly on the sand.

Finally, Myles turned his head back toward her side of his stall. "Shay is on the other side of me. Thank Tarka, he just woke from a strong fight yesterday. He says that the champion must have used the stone on the girl today," he whispered. "When the champion uses the stone on someone, the king usually ensures a healer is quickly available with a treatment. Then the injured centaur sleeps all night and sometimes into the next day, which means we probably won't be able to talk to her until tomorrow morning, earliest. Shay did, however, speak to the young man that came in with you. Whispers carry better than voices and he's directly across from him. Shay said his name is Danyel. Is that Danyel, the healer, from Zanna?"

"Yes," Tyla answered. "He came with me."

"I thought so," Myles muttered. "He said to tell you that he might be able to throw some of his healing supplies to others and help in that way."

"Ok, good." Tyla said. "But make sure to tell him to leave the fighting to me."

"I can't make promises for anyone," Myles said, "but I agree, it would be better to keep him out of the fights. I'll give him the message, but Fad might take any one of us to fight at any time. We don't get much choice."

Tyla lay down on the soft sand feeling some sense of relief knowing Eleka was alive. And in the same hallway nearby. She knew Eleka was safe—for the moment, at least. Danyel was safe...-ish and nearby, as well, although she couldn't hope to save either of them from having to fight. The smell of waste and mold and dust wafted into her nose, but Tyla was so exhausted from the day that she fell into a deep sleep while turning over fight tactics in her head.

"Tyla."

The voice was so soothing and gentle, it didn't disturb Tyla's sleep until it repeated a few times.

"Tyla. Tyla, wake up."

Tyla blinked herself awake, wishing she didn't have to find herself in the filth where she'd slept. "What is it?" she asked sleepily.

"It's your sister," Myles said. "Eleka. She's awake."

Tyla jumped to her feet before she was fully alert. In her haste she almost fell and that roused her enough to realize she had risked being able to fight. "She's awake? Is she ok? How badly is she hurt? Is she—"

"Now, now," Myles's gentle voice settled her. He was on his hooves now too, standing next to the wall they spoke through. His skin didn't look as mottled as it did yesterday and the angry scars from before looked several days healed now. "Calm down. I can't hear you when you shout like that."

"Oh, that's right." Tyla took a shaky breath and lowered her tone. "Is she ok?"

"Yes," Myles said. "She told us she's alright. She said she can fight if she needs to."

"No!" Tyla shouted, then lowered her voice and repeated, "No, tell her she doesn't need to fight. If I can stop any of you from fighting, I will."

"That's good of you," Myles said, "but remember, the more of us who fight, and longer, the more we eat. And we all need whatever food we can get. That means you too."

"Fine," Tyla said. "I won't try to stop you, but trust me, Danyel and Eleka should not be fighting. At all, if we can help it. We need Danyel to be healthy so he can help heal us. And Eleka's not a fighter."

Myles nodded and turned to speak with Shay on the other side of his stall.

"Wait," Tyla moved to unwrap the double-thick layers of wrappings around her, but a thought came to her before she could start. "Can you ask her something for me?"

"Of course," he said, looking back at her. "But I should warn you, we think our conversations can be overheard by our captors. We can't be certain, but there have been hints."

"Well, um," she wasn't sure how to word her question, especially if Fad were listening. She couldn't say anything about Trivnor or the keys to anyone anyway, but she had to at least find out if Eleka still had the communication obruck. If she hadn't been searched yet but Ugly Fad overheard Tyla ask about it, the obruck would swiftly be found and taken. She couldn't be too specific. "Er, would you ask her how her wrappings are holding up? Maybe ask her if the majik is wearing off?"

His brows dipped momentarily. "Alright," Myles said. Turning to the opposite wall again, he addressed Shay. After several minutes, he returned.

"She said they are heavy with mud, but still have most of their majik," Myles informed her.

Tyla nodded, her half-smile betraying her relief. Heavy. If Eleka's wrappings were heavy, that could mean they were heavy with the weight of the obruck. If they still have their majik she probably still has the majik communication circlet. Either way, if she knew her sister, the message meant that the obruck was still with her and it might be their ticket out of here. Trivnor could come and save them if they could use it to find him.

"Can you pass her something?"

Myles nodded. "I think so. So far they haven't set up any physical barriers."

Tyla unwrapped the extra layer of new red dragon wrappings that she and Sharot had bought from Yalli. She found herself shivering as she unwound them and realized how much warmer the extra layer had kept her. Knowing that her sister's single layer of wet, dirty dragon wrappings couldn't possibly be keeping her warm enough in the chilly fall season, she dusted the sand off the new ones and wished she could offer more. Holding the cloth outside the bars of her stall she waited until Myles's hand jutted from his bars too. With a gentle toss, the fresh red cloth passed into Myles's waiting fingers. "It's lovely," he said.

Tyla shook her head. "It's practical. I think she'll like them better than the muddy ones she has now."

Myles approached the wall on the other side again. Her head pressing against the bars, Tyla watched him speaking and heard a few mutters, but not enough to decipher. He passed the cloth through the bars in his door to the far side and she lost sight of it.

His mission complete, Myles turned back to Tyla. "So you're also dragons?"

"Yes," she said. "But I think these cuffs around our legs prevent us from changing. At least that's how Fad made it sound."

"You can't change?"

Tyla chided herself for not actually trying sooner before quickly attempting to start the fire in her belly that usually made her change into her dragon form.

Nothing.

She tried again, her heart aching when she realized that the fire was cold and she couldn't ignite it.

"No," she said, swallowing hard to subdue the tears she felt welling in her eyes. They had taken her dragon form from her. The loss bit into her more painfully than she could have imagined. Her parents never really put stock in the old ways of renaming her dragon form and her centaur form, but in that moment she understood why Emma's parents did it. She felt like half of her body had been ripped away.

"I'm sorry, Tyla," Myles whispered with understanding.

Tyla nodded, trying to quash the last of her self-pity. Her shoulders dropped and she stared into the rafters overhead. Eleka had the obruck, she was sure of it. Trivnor, once he was found, could get them out of here. But not before they could figure out a way to get the key from this champion and make him pay for his brutality. Until then, Tyla was determined to beat the humans at their own game. She ground her teeth until they squeaked aloud and when Ugly Fad came down the aisle asking for volunteers for the fight, Tyla's was the first hand through her stall bars.

21

THE ARENA

The sun dazzled over the arena before he spoke. "Who comes to challenge the Champion of Justice?"

"Tyla!" she barked before any boos cut her off.

Tyla glanced up into the balcony overlooking the arena while the belated jeers rang around her. The king sat under the black awning in a lush throne bedecked in gold and jewels. She could barely make out the human's bright red hair held back from his forehead by the gold and black crown. Unlike the previous day, the chair next to his was unoccupied. Guards in black tunics with swords at their belts stood next to the doors into the castle, but where was the black-robed faerie? Did he defy the king by remaining absent? Or did he have other things to attend to? Or had he been removed?

The champion pulled Tyla's attention back to the fight at hand. "And do you believe that centaurs are better than humans?" he asked.

Tyla shrugged and waited for the crowd to simmer with interest. "That depends on how you look at it."

"Really?" the champion hummed. "Enlighten us." He began circling her, appearing ready to attack should she say or do anything that might hint at the centaurs being prisoners.

"Well," Tyla stepped lightly around the circle opposite the man while trying to adopt an air of easy confidence. "Taller? Usually when the ages match. You appear to be at least ten years my senior but we stand equal."

The champion grinned and nodded, although with Tyla's sensitive centaur eyes she caught the blood rising ever so slightly in his pink cheeks.

"Faster?" she continued biding her time while testing the man's movements and mobility, noticing his feet creeping closer in their slow spiraling dance. "Centaurs are even faster than dragons on good ground. But kinder?" She looked out into the crowd and found Silvi's cold eyes. "Perhaps some more than others."

The champion chuckled. "So well spoken, you must be a poet!"

Tyla's confident smile fell, if imperceptibly, remembering the frustration of constantly being compared to her smarter and more eloquent sister. She *was* sounding like Eleka.

"Perhaps," the champion said, noticing the change in her countenance, "centaurs are better at staring at the stars and writing poems." Several loud laughs lifted from the crowd, enjoying his taunts.

Tyla's lip pulled back from her teeth slightly. He was definitely trying to get under her scales. How many times had she been mistaken for her thoughtful and intelligent sister when she had been caught stargazing? How many times had others refused to recognize her fighting ability—no matter how many times she had proved her prowess—when they only saw the same petite build as her more passive twin? How many times had everyone assumed that she depended on her dragon form to win her fights when she'd practiced her techniques nearly her whole life in centaur form?

"But fighting?" he called out so everyone heard. "And strength? Do you think centaurs are better than humans at fighting? Maybe you would prefer to fight in your dragon form?" he waved a hand at Tyla and glanced over her shoulder. The dragon wing markings on her brown back could easily be seen above her red dragon wrappings.

Tyla's face fell into a scowl. She knew she'd lost the confident smile but was ready to shift her tactic anyway. "What, this?" she flicked a hand at the champion. "This is just playtime."

She hadn't felt this cocky when she first came out. She'd planned to play along with his little game and give him a beating for it. Perhaps turning him into a wraith might make her feel better and it would certainly be easier to take the key. But with a kill the centaurs' reputation would become one of even more cruelty. She wasn't completely sure she could beat him while he still held the key, anyway. She would have to test him before she could figure out how to proceed. In the meantime, she could get in the daily practice she'd been missing out on.

The champion chuckled again, then punched his own arms. "Then let's play," he growled.

He charged.

The first time he charged, Tyla faked surprise and a slow reaction, then noticed him at the last moment and reared to punch the man in his chest. The impact should have knocked the wind out of him and sent him sprawling in the dirt half-conscious. However, the power of the key literally bounced him from the ground and didn't appear to have winded or shocked him. Tyla began to wonder how this key would play into her plans.

"Straightforward about it, eh?" He sounded as strong as ever. Tyla grew concerned for the first time. He should have been coughing and sucking air into his lungs after a punch like that. Without supernatural aid it might have broken ribs, maybe even ruptured some important internal organs that Eleka could probably name. Instead, the man ran directly at her, dodged to one side as she lifted her hooves again, and bent his knees before he used his feet to push himself into the air. He jumped higher—much higher—than she had ever seen any human jump, even her part-dragon and part-human friends. Her reflexes moved her head out of the way when he landed and threw his first blow, but his other hand landed squarely in the middle of her chest.

A thud shook her core. Nothing cracked, thank Shurka, but the vibration rendered her speechless for a moment. A few more thuds rattled her torso and sent a few shocks to her face before the champion spun away again.

"I hate to hurt someone so small," the man said when he returned to circling her. Now he was baiting her, waiting for a response. Tyla remembered that he and the king wanted a show. The champion wanted the audience and the king to see how strong he was, so he would toy with his opponents first before striking.

"Then don't shadow-fight," Tyla quipped back.

The champion shook his head with another grin. He charged again, but dodged Tyla's legs this time. She expected this move and only lifted one. She thought he would punch her in the side and she could kick him with the other leg, but his power caught her off guard.

She doubled from the blow when his fist connected to her human gut. As she bent over she expected the ground but found herself staring into the sky. Then the pain blossomed in her jawbone. Sharp blood spread over her tongue and between her teeth. He had punched her face when she bent over and the force must have thrown her. She lay on her side in the dirt as a few more thuds shuddered against her lower ribs and a crack split them. The pain stabbed her a moment later.

He again, allowed her to stumble to standing, her belly piercing, but she ignored it, unwilling to allow him the pleasure of seeing her pain. As he moved in again, she dodged, then swung around and connected to his face. She allowed one of his hands to slip inside her defenses so she could hit his face again, but his hands flew so fast that she felt several impacts to her face and chest.

When she felt another crack blossom in her chest, instead of feeling protectively for her broken ribs like she wanted to, she cupped her hands and flung them around in front of her, connecting to what she hoped was the champion's head. The man grunted and a moment later she felt the ground reverberate when he landed across the arena.

She sucked in a gasping breath, a sharp pain tearing through her ribs. She knew that at least one rib, and maybe more, were broken. She hoped the castle healers could heal her as well as Myles said they would.

"Kurta's claws," she cursed at him, every spiteful word stabbing her lungs, "you fight cloudy, don't you? Taking a shot when I'm incapacitated already? That's hardly a move that might be considered proper etiquette by anyone."

The crowd's cheers died down as he righted himself and shook his head. She wondered if she had caught him off guard with her strike this time before he could use the key to protect himself.

"All legitimate techniques," he answered her, wiping dust from his shoulder casually. "We'll have no cloudy fighting here."

"Shall we see if you've been taught this one?" Tyla decided that the man might not know some of the slightly under-hoofed shots she could pull on someone. Since he was just toeing the line of proper, she figured she would as well.

He grinned again and postured to face her in a ready stance. She aimed a blow at his head, but when he moved his arm to block hers, she grabbed it with her other hand and pulled it across his body so he couldn't use the opposite hand to block either, then drove her fist through his face.

As the man blinked in surprise at the sudden strike and her tight grip, Tyla balled her fists. Punching only with her good hand, she wailed on the man's face without mercy. She thought she probably felt every blow as much as the man did as the shockwaves shot down her arm and burst in her ribs. But she ignored them.

Her knuckles grew increasingly bloodied while she punched, but she was used to that. Yet the champion's face still didn't have a mark. She tried punching his jaw, his lip, his eye, but not a single red welt raised before he ripped his hand out of her grip and both his hands came up to protect his head. Abandoning her attempts to mar his face, she scooped her hands upward into his ribs and belly. When he doubled over to protect them, she kicked his legs and sent him sprawling in the dirt.

She lifted her front hoof to step toward him and glimpsed the key in his chest glowing brightly before she lifted nearly weightlessly, then slammed into the ground with what felt like the weight of ten dragons atop her. Arching her back, she gulped air back into her lungs, but the champion was already on top of her.

His knee connected with her lower ribs and a stabbing pressure pinned her down as his fists battered her face. She wanted to wriggle her legs under her, but every time she twisted, the stabbing pressure shook her body.

She tried to throw her hands out to block the blows to her face, but in that moment she remembered her mother's training drills not to block with her hands, and threw them over her head instead.

He pounded at her arms and they shuddered from the blows. Tyla glimpsed the king's box between her forearms for fleeting moments. The king leaned forward with a grin on his lips. The faerie's absence still evident in the empty chair.

The champion, unable to find her face tucked inside her elbows, connected one more time with her chest before relenting. He stood over and leered down. As ripples of pain like lightning shook her body, she knew he had reached her limit.

"I concede!" she muttered, throwing one of her bloodied hands toward her opponent.

The champion stood up straight and smiled down at her while he panted. The smallest dribble of blood trickled from his nose. Whether she had caught him off guard enough with a blow or he simply pretended for the audience to make it look like a fair fight, she couldn't be sure. Purple began to mottle his chest, but as she stared up at him the discoloration drained away. He wiped the blood away from his nose and no more appeared. "Did you have fun at playtime, little centaur?"

Tyla couldn't help returning his taunt. She smiled back, feeling a cut split open on her lip. "Yes," she panted, "I look forward to our next."

The champion laughed out loud as the crowd cheered and yelled for him. Tyla allowed herself to be pulled onto the litter and whisked back through the large double doors bloody, but smiling.

"Well, well, well," Ugly Fad said once Tyla had been dumped on the floor of her stall, "you gave the crowd qui'e a show." He followed her in and inspected her bloody face and hands and arms.

"I aim to entertain," Tyla's words slurred a little around her swollen lips.

"Well 'at you did," he said. "You earned a good meal for ev'ryone in 'ere. An' you earned yourself a good 'ealing! Congratulations."

He stepped out and waved a stooped old man into the stall. When Tyla pried open her puffy eyes she could see an old faerieman standing over her, his pointed ears drooping and a long white beard tickling her coat. The old faerieman adjusted his multi-colored spectacles on his nose and looked her over carefully.

"Fis 'ere is Gog," Ugly Fad said. "'e'll see to your 'ealing."

"Several broken ribs," Gog said, apparently to no one, "both horse and human."

"I'm no horse," Tyla forgot her pain as she hissed at him.

"So I've heard," the old faerie grumbled.

"We call it our 'lower half'," she said, wincing as he continued to poke and prod her.

"Don' ma'er wha' *you* call it," Ugly Fad cut in. "Looks like a 'orse's back end to me."

"Hm," Gog ignored the comments and continued assessing Tyla while she glared at Ugly Fad. "Cuts on the face and arms. Bone bruising along the human ribs, arms and face. Bleeding inside where the horse ribs are broken. Tsk-tsk. Old break on the wrist. Should I work on that as well?" Without waiting for an answer, that Ugly Fad didn't offer anyway, the faerieman pulled out a bag and shoved his hand inside. From the bag he pulled a long golden stick with a yellow gem on the end of it, much the same and almost matching the one Ugly Fad carried. Tyla half-expected him to wave it over her with some incantation fitting of his role, but instead he took the stick and began poking her with the sharp end.

He stabbed the pointed gem at the top of the stick into Tyla's upper ribs and the pain of a thousand bee stings sank into her chest then burned through. Without pausing the old faerieman continued stabbing her lower ribs too and she glanced at him between cries to make sure he hadn't switched to using a sword instead. The faerieman ignored her wails as he dragged the pointed gem along her face, all the while clutching her chin with surprisingly strong hands to keep her from moving.

She knew her bawling would be hushed by the majikal noise padding so she had no problem letting it out. Before the faerieman stopped the torture, Tyla's vision swam with Ugly Fad's grimy face grinning down at her. Pain seared through her bones, paralyzing her muscles with spasms. Finally, her head felt light while her scorching body sank as if slipping through the floor into the dirt beneath, and blackness swallowed her.

22

CONCEDE

"Tyla," came Myles's harsh whisper from the stall next to her. "Tyla, are you ok?"

"I'm fine," she croaked and cleared her throat. "What time is it?"

"Morning," Myles said, still with an edge of concern. "How do you feel?"

Tyla shook her head to clear it. Testing her muscles, she flexed and stretched her legs first, then her shoulders and arms. The pain from the previous day was mostly gone. She still felt like she'd gone a dozen rounds with their strongest warrior, having to nurse the same tingling ache in her hands and arms. As she bunched her legs under her, she found the stabbing in her ribs from the breaks had been replaced with a dull throb.

"That's amazing," she whispered, as she climbed to her hooves. The cuts on her face had disappeared, leaving the skin whole and smooth. When she applied pressure to her previously broken wrist, it stiffened and felt even stronger than Danyel's ministrations had rendered it. "How do they do it?"

"No idea," Myles said. "But you'll soon learn that it's more of a curse than a blessing. Hurry and eat."

"What? Why?"

"Voluntee' time!" Ugly Fad's voice echoed down the aisle.

"That's why," Myles whispered.

Tyla scooped some of the purple slop from her bucket. It had partially dried from sitting overnight, but she choked down a couple bites before she thrust out her hand between the stall's bars.

"Ah," Ugly Fad looked up when he saw her hand ahead of him. "Ready again so soon?"

"A warrior is always ready," Tyla mumbled around gagging the food down.

"I've 'eard 'at before," Ugly Fad chuckled as he stopped in front of her stall door. "Seems 'ey all 'ave 'igh 'opes of bein' the one t' win. They're all wrong. But 'at won't stop us from lettin' you try. As for you," Ugly Fad shook his head at Tyla and waved a hand down the hall, "you'll have t' wait your turn t' figh'. You 'ave a visi'or."

"I thought no one was allowed to visit the challengers," Tyla said without thinking. She grabbed another handful of slop from underneath that wasn't as crusty as the stuff on the top and jammed it in her mouth, not wanting the ugly human to realize that she had already been investigating them, and wanting to be ready to fight as soon as possible with food in her belly.

"I din' 'ave much choice wif 'ese ones," Ugly Fad said. He sucked his teeth and turned to lumber back down the aisle.

No one approached immediately, so Tyla hesitated while she watched Ugly Fad bang soundlessly on Danyel's stall.

"Hello, Tyla," a smooth, deep voice practically whispered up to her.

Tyla glanced up and down the hall in front of her stall, but saw no one. "Who's there?" she called tentatively, although she thought she recognized the voice.

Clicking and rattling, her stall door began to slide open by itself. Briefly considering and then rejecting the thought to sprint through the door and make a run for it, she stepped back. Not knowing whether it was Kelraz or even Trivnor on the other side, or someone else who could either hurt or help her, she wasn't going to risk everyone else's lives in a futile escape attempt.

"Hey!" Ugly Fad's voice echoed from down the hall toward Tyla's stall. He glanced down at the keys in his fist in confusion when he heard the door slide open. "You can' go in there!"

When the door slid fully aside, a small grey goblin with long blue hair stood in the entrance. The goblin took his time to look Tyla over, grin, then turn to grin at Ugly Fad. Tyla couldn't help but glance between the two men as Ugly Fad's lips pursed and his face turned the color of beet juice watching the little goblin purposefully step across the threshold of Tyla's stall. The goblin stepped inside and, lightly placing one hand on the door, slid the door shut with minimal to no effort. Tyla could hear Ugly Fad loudly protest the unexpected development outside the bars of her stall before he turned to get Danyel. Danyel watched the proceedings from his open stall door with trepidation, but grudgingly allowed himself to be led down the hall to the outside arena.

"Trykirt," Tyla acknowledged, turning her attention back to the little goblin. She noted a green stone glowing in his obruck as his hand slid the door closed and she wondered if the little goblin would be able to let himself out with it as well. She wanted to kick him, rip his obruck from his head and trap him in here while she ran for freedom, but her whole body still ached, and she couldn't abandon the others, so she settled for casually scooping more feed.

Trykirt scanned her stall critically. The water dripping from the water bucket. The trampled piles of waste kicked into the corner. The purple crusted rim of the feed bucket. Tyla purposely scooped more of the green and purple mush from the bottom and shoved it in her mouth, hoping the extra motions would give her time to gain some control over her brain before she spoke again.

"What are you doing here?" Trykirt shook his head with something close to pity in his eyes and tone.

"Looked like fun," Tyla said with a shrug. "Wanted in on it."

"You're better than this squalor," he kept his voice low. Tyla wondered whether he was aware of the majikal noise padding that would carry a soft tone.

"What, this?" Tyla scuffed the sand with her hoof. "My accommodations at home are very similar. Nice and cozy."

"You're the centaur dragon daughter of warriors," Trykirt said. So, he *had* figured out who she was. "Your parents would be livid. If they knew you were here, they would tear this place down stone by stone with their bare hands."

Tyla swallowed another mouthful. It was true, but she still wanted to hit him for saying it. She wanted to scream that yes, he was right about this horrible place and not just her, but none of the centaurs should be kept in these conditions and made to fight for the freedom they had been torn from. But more than anything, she was fighting a different battle. This was only a small skirmish in the war Kelraz waged. "This is what warriors do," she said instead. "We fight. And you have no idea how my parents would feel. They would be proud of me."

"What they're doing here is illegal," Trykirt waved a hand at the stalls around them. As Tyla followed his hand, she noted Myles's body curled at the bottom of the slats next to their shared wall. He was listening. And she assumed others must be listening as well.

Great, now he knows who Eleka and I really are, she thought. *Oh, well. Who is he going to tell unless we get everyone out of here.*

"It may be illegal in Kirlik and the whole goblin kingdom," Tyla said, "but remember, the goblin king doesn't make the laws here."

"Alright," he pressed, "but it *should* be illegal everywhere. It's barbaric. It's not right, and you know it. Anyone can see it."

"The goblins have the Just Sword," she answered. "Of course you know this isn't right or fair in any way."

"And the centaurs have the Allegiant Sword," he seethed. "That's why Grays and the others were loyal to you and let you escape from me. But if I tell the goblin king what is going on here, in the *formerly* Just Kingdom, he would march in with our entire army and free the centaurs."

"What good would that do?" Tyla snapped back. "The goblins have no authority here. You would be starting a war. Besides the fact that we would all be long dead before any of your forces got here. That would create an army of wraiths—and a triple-sided war."

"In defense of our allies," Trykirt crossed his arms, "I could send for your parents. They would lead the centaur forces to rescue you. I could free you. I could free all of you."

"And take me back to Kirlik as your prisoner?"

Trykirt glanced at the ground and sighed. "That would be the cost."

She didn't reject the choice outright. Along the way she could pass the information about the Sun Key to someone else. Maybe Eleka had already done it with the obruck. Any one of their friends might get the opportunity to track down the key if this debacle ended. She might be forced to accept help from goblins in order to save the centaurs. It might even be possible that the goblins already held Trivnor or the others captive and if she agreed to Trykirt's demands, they might all be reunited in the dungeons of Kirlik. Again.

"You know," Tyla said, trying to change the subject while she weighed her options, "that circlet on your head, the one you used to shock me, or whatever it was?"

"My obruck can do many things," Trykirt said, narrowing his eyes at Tyla.

"Yeah, but," she hemmed and something struck her when she said it. "It felt an awful lot like Fad's rod and the gem the castle healers used on me after my challenge. I bet it would be similar, yet not as powerful, as the champion's stone. I think it's all the same majik. Who do you think gave them such powerful majik?"

Trykirt seemed to consider her question a moment. His eyes bounced toward the door of her stall, then back toward the castle. "The goblins didn't give it to them, if that's what you think," he finally said.

"No? Then one can only assume that king of theirs has more power than he's willing to admit," she said to continue pointing his accusations elsewhere. Anything to distract him from *her* criminal offenses. Anything to place the blame for the situation where it deserved to be. "Your king might have more reason to invade this little kingdom than he realizes. Maybe you should focus on that."

Trykirt's eyes shifted back to Tyla as he recovered his thoughts. "And I will," he said. "But first, my king would have me deal with the problems at hand. Tyla, I can save these centaurs… if you'll hand yourself over to me. If you give me your wyrd that you'll allow me to bring you and your sister back to Kirlik for trial, I can save all of you. You know this."

Tyla leaned over and tried to delay by scraping more of the odious mush out of the bucket, but now it was empty and her fingers rubbed against rough wood. Still pretending to search the bucket, she thought hard. *What would Eleka do?* Instinctually, she didn't want to trust everything Trivnor said, but he had tried to help them, all of them, and even protect them from harm. She had given him her wyrd and she would uphold it. And the goblins didn't know it, but she was trying to help them as well. The quest their entire group had embarked on was to save all of Avonoa, not just the centaurs. If the goblins rescued them and started a war, it might save these centaurs and Danyel's settlement, but only temporarily. If Kelraz gained control of the Sun Key in the champion's possession and the other keys as well, no one in Avonoa would be safe. Ever. No, she couldn't leave here without that key. She couldn't trust her fate to anyone else. Let Myles and the others think what they will about her answer, but she didn't have any other choice.

She turned away from the empty feed bucket to stare Trykirt in the eye. "We're centaurs," she said. "We can save ourselves."

After the goblin left, Tyla thrust her arm through the bars across her stall as they dragged Danyel in, his beautiful face looking especially bloody. She needed to return to the ring immediately.

Passing Eleka's stall, her sister rested her side against the wall with her arms curled around her middle. She gave a weak smile and smoothed the new wrappings, but said nothing. However, Tyla noticed the large dark spot on one of her shoulders and her returning smile tightened.

When the champion saw her and called out the requisite greeting, "Who comes to challenge?", Tyla put on a fake pout. "Don't tell me you've already forgotten me."

"Tyla!" came a squeaky yell from the crowd.

Both Tyla and the champion searched the crowd to find Narsun bouncing up and down in the front row. Tyla met Sharot's eyes behind him. She didn't mask her concern with a smile, narrowing her eyes at both Tyla and the champion.

"You've got a fan!" the champion said, then turned to Narsun. "You don't cheer for the Champion of Justice, little dragon?"

Narsun bobbed up and down. "We all know you'll win!" he exclaimed with the excitement of a child getting attention from his hero.

The champion nodded. "Of that you can be sure!" and the crowd followed with a roar of applause.

"But I won't make it easy!" Tyla yelled right before she used her back end to bump the champion over the edge of the ring into Narsun and Rasco to raucous laughter.

As the champion righted himself and climbed back into the ring, Tyla chanced a glance into the king's box. The king leaned forward, his stubby fingers dripping in gold rings hanging over his knees, his eyes unblinking with rapt attention. The black-robed faerie had returned and sat beside him with the cowl of his cloak—and presumably his face—turned away from the fight, his own bony green fingers splayed and stiff with his palms down on the armrests.

Before she could think too much about it, the champion advanced toward her and her attention snapped back to the fight. He tried to smile but made no retort and Tyla marked his embarrassment by the pink in his cheeks.

The two danced around each other a moment more, but she could understand his fighting style better now. When the champion finally launched himself at Tyla, she leaned forward, stopping him at the shoulders with her hands. When he continued to press into her, she swiped his arms away and to the side. Under his own momentum he landed face-first in the mud.

The crowd laughed and cheered at the entertainment, but some loudly urged the champion to fight. The man sprang to his feet and glared at Tyla. "You'll pay for that, centaur," he muttered low enough so the crowd wouldn't hear him.

He ran at her again, but dodged her fists first one way then the other. He jumped into the air around one of Tyla's punches and kicked her in the shoulder. He only thumped her, so she spun at him, swinging her fist around. She connected with him before he landed; his head jerked to the side but he remained on his feet.

The champion wiped blood from his lip with the back of his arm before anyone could see it and grinned at Tyla while the cut majikally resealed itself. She reared up and tried to kick him again, but he dropped to his knees and punched into her lower belly. Asserting the power of the key, the single strike reverberated through her entire body, impacting her as badly as if she were a newborn foal.

She quickly forced air into her lungs. "Cloudy, cloudy," she forced out to the hollers of the crowd. "Can't you humans fight clear?"

Slamming her hooves to the ground, she hoped they would land on the man, but he rolled out of the way. He jumped to his feet and Tyla swung her fist back and made a weak connection to his head again before he steadied himself. Ignoring the growing ache in her ribs, she swung around wide to reach the man and punched repeatedly to attempt a stronger connection. Emboldened by the crowd's cheers and jeers at her, she continued her tirade.

When the champion brought up his fists to protect his face, she ignored them and continued punching his arms and head together. Blood dripped down the man's arms and face. Blood splattered her knuckles as the tender skin on her hands broke open again. For a moment Tyla imagined the man falling to the ground and herself being proclaimed the winner. For a moment.

Her blows slowed slightly as her eyes swung up to the king's box again. This time she saw the king's bejeweled fingers twisted into tight fists as Tyla pummeled his champion. The faerie finally turned his attention to the fight and also sat forward, his hands relaxed and his cowl and chin swiveled toward Tyla's triumph.

Finally, the champion dropped one arm and Tyla's punches slowed. She wondered if she had knocked the sense from his mind and he was giving up. She wouldn't let him concede. Retracting her fist again to strike the uncovered portion of his face, she hoped it would render him unconscious. Until the burning hit her.

The power of the key in the man's chest slammed against her body as if Tyla had been thrown into a burning lake of lava. Flying so far, she flipped one too many times and came down wrong on her back leg. The overwhelming power of the key on her body prevented her from feeling the break. Instead, cramps strangled her limb as she fell on top of it and it twisted the wrong way beneath her.

She screamed, but the champion marched toward her, grumbling, "How clear is that?"

Her mind went blank. Her vision blurred with the champion standing over her. Blood oozed from her mouth as the man punched her face. Spots floated in the darkness around her and the rough skin of his bare feet dancing against her ribs felt like she was being dragged beneath rows of swords.

She stared hard, trying to force her eyes to focus and her brain to think as the man above her finally stood still.

"Concede," he whispered.

Concede? Why would she do that? Who was she fighting again?

A warrior never concedes, she thought.

But her mother's voice in her head answered, *...except to continue the fight later.*

Yes, alright, Tyla thought, *'save yourself and your body. Recoil and return.'*

The champion swung his leg backwards at an angle toward her head.

"I concede!" Tyla yelled as a wave of scorching heat shook her from her leg to her face. "I concede," she whispered as the pain subsided again. She had been right.

Although much more powerful, the Sun Key was the same as Fad's rod, the healing rod and Trykirt's gem. Now she had to figure out what to do about it.

23

THE FAERIE

She woke screaming. Pain lanced from her shoulder to her hooves and fingers, sharp and hot like a scalding ember slowly burning through her bones. Instinctually Tyla tried to turn into her dragon form knowing that the burning pain would only feel like a small tickle, but she couldn't change and the searing heat continued. Sucking in a breath as the assault subsided, she blinked her eyes. Ugly Fad's crooked teeth glared down at her in the flickering light of a torch as he withdrew his long golden weapon from between the stall door slats.

"Sorry t' interrup' your 'ealing sleep, luv," he said without a drop of concern coloring his smile. "You've go' annuver visi'or."

"It's like a goblin crossroads in here," she grumbled, trying to close her eyes, but the healing sleep threatened to take over again.

"On your fee', girl," Ugly Fad grunted at her, "or I'll wake you up again."

Tyla murmured and grimaced. Her healing wasn't complete, like Ugly Fad said, but she couldn't begrudge being woken for anything she might need to do. Missing out on anything was intolerable, even if she needed to heal.

"You didn't tell me you could do that with that stick of yours," she said, struggling to her feet. "If you had, I would have requested that you wake me *every* morning so I could volunteer."

"Not to worry, princess," Ugly Fad said. "I'll keep i' in mind. But I don' fink you'll have to worry 'bout i' much longer." He swung his head to the side. "She's all your'n."

A figure stepped from the darkness next to her stall door to enter the tiny circle of light from the torch. "You wan' the torch?" Ugly Fad mumbled, offering the small flame.

"No," the figure whispered. The voice was steady, somewhat soothing, and like that of most adult faeries, almost musical in nature, juxtaposing with the dank environment. "My eyes will adjust and once hers do, I'm sure Tyla will be able to see better than any of us."

Ugly Fad grimaced and pulled the torch back to himself. "I'll be down the end o' the 'all if you need me."

"You will not." The hooded person snapped their head toward Ugly Fad. "You will go back into the castle and not listen to a word said here. Do I make myself clear?"

"Now, look 'ere," Ugly Fad began to puff up, "I'm in charge of 'ese monsters—"

"—and I'm in charge of the others." The person whispered, but the words cut through Ugly Fad's bluster, draining the man's face of all its splotchy color. His mouth hung loose like the skin on his face and neck before he snapped it shut and shuffled off, taking the torch topped with the small circle of light.

"Princess?" the hooded stranger asked, turning their attention back to Tyla. "So, he knows who you are?"

"Just something stupid that he must have overheard," Tyla said, but the realization snapped in her brain. Myles was right. Ugly Fad heard every word said within the stalls. He must have overheard the conversation with Trykirt and surmised that Tyla was someone important to the centaurs.

Remembering Myles, she glanced at the edge of the wall she shared with him, but Myles's head was on the other side of his stall.

Good, she thought, *I don't need to be worrying about what he might overhear too.*

"I'm no princess," she said, dropping her voice, while trying to deflect the idea from the stranger. Her eyes began to adjust quickly as the stranger slid forward.

"No, no," the figure acknowledged. Tyla could make out dark and light shades of facial hair on the stranger's chin. "Not directly, I grant you. But if something horrible were to happen to your uncle and his family, you would be in line to lead the centaurs, would you not?"

Tyla didn't say anything. Her mind was still slow, so she used it to keep her tongue. Who was this person? She had her suspicions, but couldn't be sure, not yet. Hiding her connection to her uncle and her whole family was the only way she knew to keep them from the current danger that she and Eleka found themselves in, although their ruse might not last much longer.

"Who are you?" she snapped.

"A faerie," the smooth voice whispered again. He raised his gaze to her and swept the cowl from his head. His green skin shown darker than most faeries' above the slope of a black beard stretching down his jaw. A sliver of silver in his beard matched the one in his hair hanging slightly off to one side of and framing his face. His face was long and his eyes wide and held a certain amount of wisdom. Almost thoughtful, but not kindly. "I counsel with the king."

"I've seen you," Tyla said, shifting the weight off her back right hoof as the ache began to spread up her leg. "On the balcony. What are you doing here?"

"I was going to ask you the same thing," the faerie said. "I came here to consult with the king concerning these games. I hear you volunteered."

Tyla squinted her eyes at the faerie. "I was under the impression that the faeries claimed they would stay out of everyone else's business. I believe the word used was that they would 'diminish'."

The faerieman allowed his lips to curl up at the edges. "Yes," he said, his voice soothing and sickly sweet, "that is what was said. You've a decent education, I see. But not every faerie feels the need to harbor themselves in the forest."

"What do you want with me?" Tyla asked.

"What would you say if I told you that I could help you?"

Tyla tilted her head and a spike of pain shot through her neck so she quickly righted it. "How?" she asked suspiciously, snapping to cover the wince.

"You don't seem surprised by my offer," the faerie said.

Tyla shrugged, slowly and gently because of the pain, but she hoped it displayed an air of indifference. "Already been offered help from the goblins," she said. "See how well that went? I'm still here."

"But you also don't seem offended by the idea," he went on. "Almost every individual in Avonoa would be disgusted by the thought of even speaking to a faerie, much less accepting help from one. In fact, some faeries feel that way about their own kind. Just getting in to see the king here was quite the undertaking. I might have expected you to refuse to speak to me and yet you seem comfortable enough. Even curious. Do you have any faerie friends?"

Tyla's throat tightened as if someone wrapped their hands around it. "I'm no faerie lover," she croaked, although she didn't feel as much malice saying the words as she would have two weeks ago. While she didn't love Jassan, certainly not the way Emma seemed to, she had to admit that toward the end of their time together his presence no longer bothered her. Over the time she had known him she grew to tease him more with good-natured humor than from hostility. She could mock him with friendly rivalry rather than spite. She had grown to rely on him, trust him and even call him a friend. He *was* her friend. Now she was as concerned for his safety as much as the safety of any of her other friends and she hated to admit it to herself, but she couldn't wait to mock his stupid freckles again.

"No?" the faerie said. "That's not what I've heard. I understand that before you got here you ran around with goblins and faeries and even humans too."

Tyla peered into his eyes and she could see flecks of silver and other colors in the blackness. "Where did you hear that?"

The faerie grinned, but looked down as if seeing something far off in his mind, before he looked back up and shrugged, "Those goblins that were here had some fantastic stories. Tell me, did you really steal a gem from the goblin king?"

Tyla's face began to burn. Her heart thudded against her ribs. "No."

"I figured you would say as much," the faerie chuckled. "I don't care if you did or not. I only wanted to offer you my help to escape this place, remember?"

"And what can you do for me that the goblins can't?"

"Quite a bit, actually."

"The goblins offered to raise an army to get us out," Tyla said. "I don't think the faeries would rise up to save us, so what are you offering?"

The faerie leaned in so close Tyla felt his breath on her nose. "An army of the dead and the living world," he hissed.

Tyla had always been taught to stand her ground and face things bravely, but blood drained from her cheeks and she took a step back. "W-what?" she stammered.

"You heard me," he said. "I can give you whatever you want. I can give you your friends' lives. All of them. Even Jassan's."

Tyla's knees shook and she went numb. "Kelraz?"

"So, he did tell you about me."

Tyla's brain swirled. What did this mean? If Kelraz was already here, consulting with the king, was he biding his time until he took the key? Had he already gotten the keys from the others? She swiftly searched for his hands, but he kept them tightly concealed beneath the sleeves of his robes.

"What do you want?" she forced out. Perhaps if she kept him talking she might figure out what to do, or at least catch a glimpse of any other keys he might be holding.

"Like I said," he grinned perfect white teeth at her, "I want to help you escape."

That statement made no sense to Tyla but seemed to shake loose her fear. "Why?" She peered at him again.

He huffed. "Your friends are dead. There's no reason for any more loss."

Tyla's breath shook. Her brain hurt and felt filled to the brim. The information couldn't get in and just spilled over the sides. "They're what?"

His voice was low. "Dead," Kelraz said. "They're all dead."

"But you wanted to trade," Tyla mumbled, remembering her conversation with the faerie wraith. What had it said? What did this faerie say? She couldn't trust this faerie; she couldn't trust any faerie. Could she?

Kelraz shook his head. "It's too late for that," he said. "I'm here to bargain for *your* life now."

"What are you talking about?" She fought to understand. Her friends? What friends? Who were they? How many? What were their names? "Didn't you just say you could give me their lives?" *Yes! Success!* Her mind had formed a question. An important question. That much awareness had entered her brain, but nothing else. What was he saying now?

"I control souls, Tyla," he whispered so low that she barely heard him and struggled to focus her mind on his words. "I can give you their souls and they will exist alongside you for the rest of your days in this world. Normal and natural, exactly the way you remember them. They will be themselves and unspoiled. Or, I can send you to be with them in the World of Souls. I will leave you be, all of you happy and together in the next world. Which would you prefer? Either way, you'll be reunited."

Tyla knew she couldn't trust him. *Can't trust a faerie,* her mind stressed. Slowly, like pouring water into an overfull cup, some of the less important things shifted and made room for what she needed to think about.

"What do you want me to do?" That was an important question too. Suddenly, her thoughts sprang to her friends. The human one, the girl. *What was her name?* Her head hurt but she came up with it. *Yeah, Emma.* Was she dead? He could be lying, right? And her brother, the little one. *Burk? Yes.* He might be dead too. She couldn't be sure of any of it.

The names and faces of all her friends, including Jassan, poured into her mind. They couldn't be dead. They couldn't. The quest they all endured together. The keys.

Trivnor. The World of Souls. The truth returned, all tumbling back into her mind.

"Are you listening to me?"

Tyla met Kelraz's eyes. He had been talking, but she hadn't heard a word of it as she remembered her friends and the faeries that she *did* trust. Refusing to hear any more lies about her friends, like upending the cup in her mind, she stared into Kelraz's face to focus on his words.

"Leave," he said. "Walk away."

Tyla blinked. Everything coming into clear focus again. Kelraz. Trivnor. The keys. Her friends. Their quest to find the keys. Save the world. Both worlds. "Walk away?"

"Walk away," Kelraz repeated. "There's nothing for you here. I'll see that the king releases you and the other centaurs. You can leave this place behind and never think about it again."

Tyla pried her eyes from Kelraz and mulled over her suspicion. What would he gain by getting her to leave? Then she remembered it. The Sun Key.

Tyla tilted her head to the side and let the question form in her mind as she stared back at Kelraz. "Why don't you have it yet?" she asked, once the reality of the situation became clear. "Why haven't you just taken it?"

Kelraz's lips tightened and his nostrils flared. "The key?" he cleared his throat and shrugged a shoulder, seeming to gain control of himself again. "I guess Trivnor hasn't told you everything."

"What hasn't he told us?" Tyla said, narrowing her eyes at him.

"Did he tell you what happens when spring begins?"

"Yes," Tyla answered, unsure. "The barrier breaks down. So what happens if no one has all the keys before the barrier dissolves?"

Kelraz shook his head. "Nothing for *me*," he said. "I have time on my side. I *want* to break down the barrier, remember? It only serves me. So, I'm allowing the king and all the rest of you to enjoy your little games until *I* decide you're done. Then I'll take the key and control of everything. If you and your sister leave now and let this play out here, none of it will affect you. You'll both be safe. The centaurs will all go home and none of you will need worry about me or the keys ever again. Just walk away, Tyla."

"And if I don't?" she asked. She knew the answer, but she wanted to hear him say it.

"Then I'll have the champion put you and your sister to death," he said, "and you'll both be in my power."

Her voice caught. She struggled with her breathing not wanting Kelraz to hear her fear through her voice. She steadied herself enough to cough. "How…?" Clearing her throat, she forced the words out. "How would we let you know if we accept?"

"That's easy," he said, stepping back from the door. "You will concede to the champion in front of the king and in front of the crowd before the fight starts. If you do that, I'll know that you are taking up my offer. Tell the champion that you concede that humans are better than centaurs, et cetera, et cetera, and I'll convince the king to let you go free. But…you only have two days to make your choice. By sunrise the day after tomorrow, you concede to the champion or I'll have him kill you both."

24

MESSAGES

"Your sister has a message," Myles whispered quickly as soon as Tyla woke.

Tyla jumped up from the floor, growing accustomed to the routine of waking in pain and hurriedly snatching at food before Ugly Fad came through for volunteers. The whispered messages came into her stall just as quickly.

"What is it?" she whispered back before she shoved a handful of dark orange glop into her mouth.

"We have to be careful," Myles said in a hushed tone. "They're listening."

"Is that the message?" Tyla said, pausing to snap at him. "I already know that!"

"Volunteers!" came Ugly Fad's cry down the aisle. "Challengers!"

"No," Myles said quickly. "That's not it. She told us to repeat this exactly as she said it, word for word. She said to tell you, 'My will is a tree when I use my mind, I give to fleas when we are all restrained, this sacred plea when we need to be free.' That's it."

Tyla paused, confusion wrinkling her brow. "What the *spit* does that mean?" she muttered, although something tickled at the edges of her memory.

Ugly Fad stopped at her stall. "I know, you challenge, swee'eart," He shook his head and nodded toward Eleka's and Danyel's stalls. "You'll wai' today. King wan's to see your sister an' 'at boy of yourn firs'."

"What? No!" Tyla recognized the malevolent grin on Ugly Fad's face. "She's no fighter. I'll fight for her. And him!"

"Oh, don' worry," he said. "You'll ge' your figh' la'er awrigh'. King wants to have some fun wif the crowd. See if 'ey can tell the diff'rence 'tween you two!" He chuckled to himself and trudged down the aisle past her. Stopping in front of Danyel's stall, he turned to wink at her as he pulled his golden rod from his belt.

Tyla kicked her stall door in anger but it only produced another chuckle from Ugly Fad and a painful shockwave up her leg. Danyel held his arm close to his chest after fighting the day before and limped from the stall now. She could see the angry red scars crisscrossing his handsome face when he turned it toward her, but Tyla felt his gentle eyes rest on her and imagined his kind smile. Tears burned and she desperately wanted to turn away but couldn't force herself to stop looking as the horrible human prodded Danyel down the hall and out the doors to the arena.

Once Danyel disappeared into the brilliant sunshine and the doors slammed shut behind him, Tyla sat down by the wall adjoining Myles's stall. "What else did she say?" She urged him through the slats to tell her more.

"Nothing," he said. "That was the whole message."

"What? That's it?" she asked. "Are you sure? Could you have gotten any of it wrong?"

"No," Myles said. "Shay and I both practiced each part before I passed it to you. It's correct."

"Urgh," she grumbled. "Leave it to Eleka to tell me so much without telling me anything. Perhaps she means—"

"No!" Myles whispered harshly, so loud that his voice was slightly muffled by the noise padding spell. "You can't tell me what it means. Like I said, they're listening. They hear every word. That's why she can only say so much."

"How can they hear us? We're muffled."

"No idea," Myles said, "other than majik, obviously. All I know is that whenever we've talked about escaping, the humans hint that they know by using the same phrases that we used. We have to assume that they hear everything. Only our thoughts are safe."

Thoughts! Her mind! Of course, Tyla's mind jumped to the answer. *Eleka has been using the obruck! She must be communicating with the others. But that means they ARE alive! That slimy green liar! At least I know for sure now who I can't trust.*

'*When*', she thought, *she used that word three times. Obviously it's a riddle. Something she has had time to code. But I'm not nearly as smart as her.*

"Myles," she whispered. "Give it to me again."

As Myles repeated the message a few more times, Tyla attempted to pick it apart.

'When'. She's using that to separate the phrases. 'My will is a tree'. Why did that sound familiar? Didn't Trivnor say that to us once? Was it when Jassan turned into a tree? Or was it something about the keys? Maybe it's a rhyming connection?

The message was obviously two in one. Eleka was telling her something about the keys and something about their friends. 'We are all restrained' meant that everyone had either been captured, or worse. She wouldn't have to code that for anyone to hear, and if they were dead, that message would have been clear too. Tyla hadn't taken that news very well when Kelraz gave it to her, but she thought she could take it from Eleka, if it were true. So they must be alive, but prisoners of someone somewhere.

At least Kelraz is spending his torture on us and not them, Tyla thought as tears burned her eyes again.

"He's coming back in," Myles's urgent voice ripped her out of her confusion and sorrow.

Springing to her feet, Tyla clung to the bars of her stall door as the humans dragged Danyel inside through the double doors and down the hall, stopping at his door. She couldn't see them unload him, but once the guards had left, Tyla was struck by the utter lack of sound coming from his stall. Through the cracks in the front of his stall door she could tell that he lay very still. Maybe too still.

The champion doesn't kill. The champion doesn't kill. The champion doesn't kill, she chanted in her head. But that mantra ceased abruptly when she realized that Kelraz had no such compunctions. He would kill them all. Tomorrow.

"Myles," she forced the words out, "tell me again."

"You're next!" Ugly Fad cut off anything Myles might have replied. The human held his golden rod pointing at Myles as he pulled the stall door open. "Ge' a move."

"No!" Tyla exclaimed, but the majikal padding around her stall didn't allow any sound to reach either the human or centaur. Ugly Fad turned to walk away, but he turned back when Tyla pounded on the doors of her stall.

The rotund human shuffled over to her as two other humans led Myles away. He tapped his rod on her front wall. "You should get some beau'y rest while you can, li'l princess. A li'l nappy-nap will 'elp you 'eal a li'l more and you'll be figh'in fi'. Then maybe you can be *free.*" He winked at her and made his way back down the hall with a grin and an unmistakable skip in his step.

Tyla felt sick and shook her head in disgust. The ugly little human probably knew that she was slated to die tomorrow, as publicly and humiliatingly as possible.

'We need to be free', of course we need to be free! But Shurta's tangles and Khurta's claws, how? Tyla crumpled into the sand at her feet. *I give to fleas' makes perfect sense because she's giving* me *nothing but riddles.* Absent-mindedly Tyla dug at the sand next to the wall as she thought. *'This sacred plea'. Is she pleading with me? The king? Kelraz? Our friends? Maybe she's asking them for help? The only person that could help us at all only wants the key and he already proclaimed that he'd get it over our*

dead bodies. Oh, wait! Without thinking, she tried to smack herself in the head, but she could only lift her arm halfway before it twitched in pain so she let it fall back to her side. *The message is about the key, of course! So many words rhyme with 'key'. But she doesn't have the key and the one person here who does is waiting for the command to kill us with it.* She had dredged so much of the sand while she'd been deep in thought that her fingertips scraped the cold hard stone underneath her where the wall met the floor.

The first part of the message is something about the key, she decided, *and the words that follow each 'when' must be about their friends. So the second message is clear, 'when I use my mind, we are all restrained, we need to be free.' But what is she trying to tell me about the key?*

As she stewed, the muffled sounds of Myles's moans approaching and him being dragged back into his stall assaulted her ears. Squeezing her eyes shut, she refused to watch, but couldn't block out the muffled screams as his "healing" began.

Eleka will probably be next, she thought. *I have to think like her to get this riddle. What would she do about the key? Try to take it from the champion, of course. But she's not strong enough. And really, neither am I.*

Her mind reeled and her thoughts spun as her fingers found more sand to sift. Closing her eyes, Tyla envisioned ripping the key out of the champion's chest and his blood draining through her fingers just like the sand falling from her hand.

"Your turn, dearie," Ugly Fad appeared at her stall door. "Your sister's been ou' and the king go' a big kick ou' o' them all calling 'Tyla! Tyla!'. You were righ', though, she ain' no figh'er."

"What? Already?" Tyla shot to her feet and met him at the door, shaking drowsiness from her eyes. She must have been so deep in thought that she had dozed off after the lengthy interruption to her own healing. And Eleka had already gone out?

"Ah," he smiled, "you took my advice and go' some sleep. Good for you, luv. No need to worry abou' 'ese uvver jabs. No need to climb trees or give 'em fleas or anyfin' like 'at."

More proof that Myles had been correct. Ugly Fad and anyone else who worked with him, heard everything they'd said to each other. But the question remained, how much of it had gotten back to Kelraz and how quickly? She needed to play it out properly. "Oh Ugly, I'm sure we already have your fleas," Tyla mocked but grimaced when he quickly prodded her with the rod, giving her a short burst of shock, then shoved her down the hall and out the arena doors.

"TYLA!" the crowd yelled in unison as she limped into the arena.

Kelraz would be lurking overhead, hoping, but not necessarily expecting, her to concede. She still had another day to do that.

"Seems I don't have to ask who comes to challenge me?" the champion said, still fresh after the fights he'd already won that day.

Squinting into the radiant sunshine, she ignored the champion and stared blatantly up into the king's box. This time the short, red-headed king with the stubby bejeweled fingers sat straight up in his golden throne. Kelraz's hood was thrown back as he leaned toward the king. Tyla could see his dark green lips muttering to the human and he flicked a green finger down in her direction.

What was he telling the king? Was he whispering the meaning of the coded message? No, he didn't want to tell the king that much. Could he be whispering that the king should let Tyla go? Only if she concedes, but even then Kelraz would have a hard time persuading him to do that. He would more likely be up there convincing the king to have her killed. Would he mention any deal he'd offered her? No, there *was* no deal. He wouldn't do anything he'd told Tyla he would do. Would he be offering to help the king kill her? Probably.

"Tylaaa!" The squeaky call could be heard over the din of the rest of the spectators.

Hearing her name yelled innocently from the crowd made both her and the champion turn their heads toward the sound. Narsun perched in the front row again. He happily waved a claw toward her and Tyla forced a tight smile, but everyone around Narsun booed and hissed and soon his little claw fell back to the ground.

The champion stepped toward the edge of the arena where Narsun sat. Tyla hid a real smile when Leman kept his face toward her this time. Pride swelled a little in her when she realized he had learned to be cautious of her tricks. She wouldn't be bumping him over the edge anymore, but he would also be watching her very closely. She stayed still and glanced up at the king and Kelraz, glowering over the proceedings. Their faces also followed

Narsun's voice, and Kelraz whispered in the king's ear again.

"Let's ask the little one this next question," the champion said loudly and turned to Narsun. "What do you say, young dragon, do you think centaurs are stronger than humans?"

"Definitely not against you!" Narsun squealed in excitement for the hero. "But Tyla puts up the best fights!"

"She does," the champion nodded in agreement, "doesn't she? Shall we see how she fares today?"

Tyla's eyes drifted back to the king's box and saw Kelraz pull away from the king's side. But instead of turning his attention to the fight, he lowered his chin toward his chest then to his other side, looking away from the king in thought, as if listening to someone speaking next to him. But besides the two guards at the doors behind them, no one other than Kelraz and the king were in the box. Was Kelraz watching something? Did he hear something? Or was his mind focused on something no one else could see?

Her mind snapped back to the present when the champion thudded his fist against her head. With her ears ringing, she turned to him.

"What did you do that for?!" she yelled at him.

"What do you think?!" He shouted his retort at her and grinned. "You aren't yourself today. Is she? Perhaps we accidentally brought your sister out again." He waited for the cheers and laughter to die down. "I think the crowd wants to see the fire of a centaur!" he yelled and the crowd cheered again.

"Do they?" she answered. "Probably because they know they won't see any fire from a human!"

Jeers and hisses filled the arena, but Tyla also couldn't miss hearing a few hoorays and laughter bubble up. She wondered if she was slowly winning the crowd over with her tenacity, but she knew they would never entirely be hers. And certainly not in time.

"Aha!" the champion called. "There's my good enemy!"

He raced toward her and she deflected him; not nearly as quick as she would have liked, but she learned to make him run around her—a trick her mother constantly tried to drill into her, but she had never mastered it… until now.

"You know," Tyla said after she kicked him away again and he took a moment to breathe, "I believe you've taught me more about fighting than even my own mother ever taught me." She decided that their pettifog and banter could help her spirits, if nothing else. Plus, the audience might at least question the morality of such games if she died in front of them after proving her mettle. If nothing else, their laughter might distract the champion and give her short reprieves.

The champion smiled. "You don't say," he said. "Did she teach you to defend this?"

He ran at her and attempted some strange move she'd never seen anyone do. Jumping into the air, he spun wildly in front of her with legs and arms thrashing. Instead of waiting for him to finish his acrobatics, she reared and punched him out of the air.

He let out a yell as he sailed across the arena and sprawled in the dirt.

"No," Tyla said, "but you just did."

The crowd cheered and laughed.

The champion jumped from the ground. Without a word he sprinted at her. Jumping into the air again, this time he didn't spin or flail. He brought both of his hands together in a joined fist over his head. Tyla instinctively brought her arm up to block the heavy blow. But when it came down she received the all-too-familiar shock of agony up her arm and heard the loud crack when it broke. Again. At least it was her left arm this time and not her more capable right arm, which had finally regained its strength.

She cried out as the crowd roared their approval of the champion. Grinding her teeth, she willed the pain of her freshly broken arm out of her mind.

After several more blows shook her ribs and face, Tyla staggered. Her legs barely holding her, she knew they might buckle soon. Blinking away blood from her eyes, she barely caught sight of the champion jumping toward her again.

Luckily, he was getting as lazy as she was depleted. This was, she knew, his fourth or fifth fight today. She slapped aside his hand and struck her forehead against his nose. They both staggered, and her eyes swelled and dripped with blood. Her fist wouldn't tighten or grip his arm with her broken arm, so before he fell away from her, she wrapped it around his back. She used her good hand to punch him in the face again and again and again.

The champion's free hand tried to wave away her blows as his eyes rolled back into his head. Just as it appeared he would black out and fall, his eyes snapped open. He struggled to get his legs under him before sinking to the ground on his knees.

Tyla tried to push him to knock him over, but he grabbed her good arm. Suddenly pulling her into him, he grasped her shoulder and slung himself onto her back, as if mounting a common horse.

Tyla panicked. Red tinged her vision and her heart pounded like an entire settlement of centaurs galloping over her chest. "How dare you?!" she wailed, rage overpowering any sense of strategy or decorum. It was the one situation a centaur couldn't and wouldn't allow. She would not submit to his twisted forced sense of power over her. Bucking her back legs, she reared but the champion clung to her waist.

As she came down, her back leg cracked again and she crumpled to the ground. The champion landed on top of her with both his feet digging into her back. He grabbed her with one hand by the hair on top of her head and punched her with the other in the back of it.

Her vision filled with black spots. Her head pulsed and throbbed with each blow. It felt like her brain would ooze out through her bloody, watery eyes at any moment.

Finally, he stopped and let her fall to the ground. As the crowd hooted, the champion stood over her. Lifting her head from the ground by her hair again, he brought her ear close to his mouth.

"Listen carefully," he rumbled threateningly, "no one is coming for you. No army is on the horizon, no one is rising, no preparations are being made. No goblins. No centaurs. No one is coming. They won't even allow the goblins to send or receive messages in here. Listen to me—you don't have any keys to free yourselves and you never will. And tomorrow, instead of being freed, the king has declared that you will have an accident in the ring. Unfortunately, tomorrow will be the first time we lose a challenger in these games… publicly. Tomorrow… you die."

Tyla couldn't hear the cheers and praise for the champion before the world around her turned black.

She felt the hard wooden litter. The tangy scent of blood mingled with must from the planks wafted into her nostrils. Was that her blood or someone else's? She felt water pouring over her eyes. Was she crying? She didn't feel emotional.

My mind is a tree.

Her stomach churned. Was she hungry? She felt sand under her fingers and her body being rolled into it. The roiling in her middle burbled up her throat.

I have to restrain fleas.

Gog's sagging pink skin and white hair fluttered over her while he muttered to himself. The stabbing pain from his stick of torture cleared Tyla's mind for a minute.

I can't stand against that stupid key and that stupid champion who doesn't even know what he's got, she thought through the pain while she screamed. *Shurta's tangles! How am I going to win? How can I get that key? How can I beat him?*

25

GAMES

That night Tyla woke screaming again. Her eyes wandered the dark stables, but she couldn't see anything take shape as her vision focused and unfocused repeatedly. Mumbling and groaning, she finally found the source of her pain.

"I'm sorry to wake you," Kelraz said. "It must hurt very much."

The faerie stood over her, close enough that his long black robe brushed her lower belly. Normally, she thought in the back of her mind, that might tickle but instead felt like small blades tracing her soft skin into ribbons. She hurt in so many places she didn't know where to put her hands for self-comfort, so they shook in front of her.

Perhaps Ugly Fad hadn't been able to wake her on his own. Or perhaps Kelraz didn't want to bother with threatening him to do so. Either way, the faerie stood over her with the golden rod in his hand and the door to her stall closed behind him. Ugly Fad was nowhere to be seen—or smelled.

"Tyla," Kelraz knelt next to her. Black hair brushed his emerald cheeks. His dark eyes expressed something close to compassion. "It doesn't need to be this way," he whispered. "You've become entangled in issues you can't even conceive. Trivnor should never have involved any of you. You've thought the same thing, admit it." He practically purred.

"He n-needed our help," Tyla mumbled, wishing her voice wouldn't shake. But she wished her hands wouldn't either and she didn't have the strength to stop either of them.

"No," Kelraz said. "He should have handled it himself and not put any of you in danger."

"Danger?" Tyla said. "Are we in danger?"

"Only if you oppose me," Kelraz said through a tight smile.

She shouldn't ask it. Eleka wouldn't have asked it, but she spit it out anyway. "W-was your village in d-danger when you destroyed it?"

Kelraz's teeth ground. "No," he said when he composed himself, "but it was a village of fools. You don't need to be one too."

"What would you d-do?" she asked, clenching her good fist as pain shot through her broken arm again. "With the keys?"

Kelraz stood. "I would do what I was born to do…rule."

"That's why we're in d-danger," Tyla said without thinking.

"And Trivnor?" Kelraz said. "Where is he? Is he here to save you?"

"I thought you said he was dead," Tyla mumbled.

"He's as good as," he answered.

"And my friends?"

"I'm sorry, they're all gone."

"Then I have nothing else to lose."

"On the contrary," Kelraz twisted to glance out the bars in her stall door. "Your sister. The other centaur, Danyel, is it? And what was the name of that little dragon who cheered you on today? Narsun?"

Tyla shook violently, wanting to wring those names from his evil green mouth. She wanted to spring up and trample his face with her hooves.

"Concede tomorrow," Kelraz murmured. "Walk away and save the ones left."

"Do you have the other keys?" Tyla asked, willing her sense of realization to overcome her pain.

Kelraz hesitated almost imperceptibly. "I know where they are," he said, attempting to cover his pause. "Two of them are on their way to me as we speak."

"Trivnor's key?"

"Yes," Kelraz answered quickly. "You can't win, Tyla. If you're fighting for him because you think he's the good faerie, you're fooling yourself. He wants the power just as much as I do. Maybe more."

"But he wants to stop y-you," Tyla protested. The edges of her vision started closing in with darkness again.

Kelraz bent over her. "He *can't* stop me," he hissed, "and he won't. He's only using you to get himself closer to what he and I both want. When you can't take him any farther, he'll dump you and use whoever else he can trick into helping him next. He won't save you."

Tyla laid her head back against the cool sand of the floor. Before she passed out again, she forced out two words. "I know."

"Tyla," Myles's urgent whisper stabbed through the hazy fog in her mind. "Tyla, you have to wake up."

"I volunteer," she mumbled sleepily, blinking through the pain.

"Fad's already been by," Myles said.

"What?" Tyla felt white-hot pokers stabbing into her ribs and limbs. Even feeling like she'd already been through her fight, she pushed herself to her feet.

"Don't worry," Myles said. "He said he'd be returning for you anyway. But I have to pass another message to you from Eleka before he comes back."

"No one is coming," Tyla said through her fog, "the champion told me so in my fight yesterday."

"Maybe, maybe not," Myles said, "but she told me to tell you, you must win for her."

"I know I have to win, but I can't," Tyla grumbled as pain shot up her legs and she held onto the feed bucket to help herself clamber to her hooves. "Don't give me any more mysterious messages. I have no idea what she's trying to tell me. I can't win. I can't do it! Have you told her that?!"

Salty wetness stung her eyes as spasms compressed her chest and ribs. Unable to resist anything anymore, she allowed heavy tears to fall. She couldn't do it. She was going to die today. No one was coming to rescue them. She would die. Then Eleka would die. Then Danyel would die. They would all turn into wraiths and probably be allowed to beat each other for the amusement of the humans.

"This has been hardest on you of all of us," Myles whispered.

Tyla shook her head. She had always been warned not to indulge in self-pity. "No," she said, wiping the tears with the dirty back of her arm. There wasn't an area of her limbs that didn't hurt when touched. Her arm cramped when she moved it so she let it fall and allowed the tears to wash over her face. "No," she said. "You were captured and you've been here longer. It was foolish to come here willingly. It was foolish to think I could beat the champion when others better than me couldn't."

"Tyla," Myles said, gently, "Eleka saying 'you must win *for* her' means she believes that you *can* win."

Tyla choked against her tears and chuckled ironically. "Win for her? I've been *trying* to win for her! I've been trying to win for all of us. But I can't. Not anymore. I'm going to die today."

"No," Myles whispered encouragingly, "you won't die today. You'll continue. You can concede then return and try again. Perhaps you should take a day off from volunteering. Perhaps…"

"You don't understand," Tyla said. "I have been told that I *will* die today."

Myles didn't answer. He had no more ways to reassure her. But she had one more thing to say. "Myles," she whispered, "tell Eleka I'm sorry. Tell her I love her and I'm sorry I couldn't save her. I'm sorry I couldn't win for her."

True to his word, Ugly Fad came to collect Tyla whether she volunteered or not. "I'm goin' to miss your li'l quips," he said as she limped from her stall. He didn't even bother to pull out his golden rod to threaten her.

Tyla couldn't answer. He didn't deserve an answer anyway. He would lead her to her death and she clopped along beside him sedately. The aisle to the double doors had never seemed so long. Passing Danyel's stall, she caught a glimpse of him through the bars. It felt so long since she'd savored his comforting presence. He whispered something that Tyla couldn't hear. Then he yelled and pounded his fist against the stall door. The door shook but the sounds and his words were muffled enough to be indiscernible. She mustered a weak smile and looked back as long as she could see him. It was all she could manage as a goodbye.

Passing Eleka's stall, Tyla observed her sister lying still on the dirty hay. She walked slowly enough that she could see her sister's chest slowly rise and fall. She was sleeping. Possibly sleeping off another healing. Had she gone out before her again?

"Did you take Eleka out today?" she asked Ugly Fad as they waited in front of the double doors before the guards opened them from the other side. "Did she fight?"

Ugly Fad tossed his head toward Eleka. "Your twin? Nah, no' today. She don' figh', like you said. Nah, she's sleepin' offa 'ealing from a good long questionin' the faerie gave her. I hear mos' people would prefer t' face the champion 'an 'at faerie."

"He questioned her? What did he want?"

"'Ow should I know?" he said. "I jus' do as I'm told. Like you."

Tyla tried for one last glimpse into Eleka's stall, but the doors opened at that moment and Ugly Fad motioned for her to step through them into the sunlight of the arena.

Stumbling out into the unnatural sunshine beaming into the arena, Tyla felt her eyes drift up to the king's box as usual, but her eyes quickly snapped to three dragons sitting beneath it, surrounded by guards with their swords drawn.

The little grey dragon glanced nervously between the guards around them and his sires' stern faces. Unlike Narsun, Sharot and Makus stood with their backs rigid, glowering at Tyla. The guards surrounding them kept their eyes sharply on the dragons.

Tyla pried her eyes away from the family who had helped her and been nothing but kind to her and Danyel. She gaped up at Kelraz, his eyes lowered to the dragons as well, and glared at him until his eyes met hers.

'Walk away,' he mouthed to her. He motioned with his green hand toward the family of dragons.

Tyla's eyes drifted back down to them. She met Sharot's eye. The green dragon nodded then lifted her front wing joint claw to drape her wing over Narsun. The young dragon must have realized the tension around him, so he snuggled close to his dame's chest and settled without opening his mouth.

Keys. 'Free'. 'Tree' and 'fleas'. Tyla closed her eyes and thought frantically to herself, her mind skipping to anything in Eleka's messages that rhymed or would be of help. *Win for her. Of course I'm trying to win for her. I'm trying to win for everyone. Narsun. Kira. Danyel. Myles. What else does she want from me?*

She felt the false sunshine warming her skin and it helped her to think.

'My will is a tree'. I'm not a tree and neither is my will. A tree is slow and stupid. I'm the opposite. …Aargh, stupid cryptic Eleka and her codes and hints —it's opposite! The last word. Free! My will is free!

Tyla's eyes popped open. Of course! Eleka had been passing a message about the others, yes, but also the spell to release the key! That was the second part to the code!

Riddles. Riddles. She's using riddles to tell me what to do. Tyla's brain worked faster than ever. As the champion asked who came to challenge him, she ignored his questions.

Win for her? Win for her? I've been trying to win for her. But I can't win, I'm not strong enough against his key. I'm not fast enough. I'm not even smart enough to figure out her riddles.

Tyla's head jerked up to face the champion. He squinted at her and grinned. "Could this centaur finally be realizing that she's not as good as a human?" he shouted to the cheers of the crowd.

Not win FOR her. Win AS her. The light clicked on in her head as quickly as most of her bones snapped in her fights. Eleka wasn't telling her to use strength to win the fight for her, she wanted Tyla to win the way *she* would, with her mind, defying the king and Kelraz with her messages.

"Too bad you've realized it too late!" the champion yelled as he rushed at her.

"STOP!" Tyla yelled, holding up her hand. Shocked by her sudden command, he skidded to a halt. She glanced up at the king's box. Kelraz sat still next to the king, tilting his head.

He's curious. Good, she thought. *I'll keep him guessing.*

"Ah," he said, "finally coming out of your stupor?" The champion smiled. A genuine smile. He almost looked relieved. Tyla thought it possible that he didn't really want to kill her. Perhaps under his bombast he had morals and wanted these games to end before they went too far. The image in her head of her claws ripping the key from his chest dimmed. Then another image of her winning for Eleka replaced it.

"Yes," Tyla took a deep breath. "And I *have* come to challenge you."

The crowd cheered. Were their cheers louder than normal? The champion shook his head ever so slightly at the unexpected incongruence. Almost believing she saw disappointment and a plea in his eye, she ignored it. Tyla glanced back up at Kelraz sitting next to the king. Both of them leaned forward, their attention rapt on the two beings facing off in the arena.

"I do believe centaurs are better at fighting than humans," Tyla said loud enough for everyone to hear and their voices quieted. "I do believe any centaur could beat you in a fair fight, Leman." She sneered his real name, purposefully omitting his pretended title. It had the effect she desired. The crowd cheered and crowed and howled and hooted, but Tyla didn't revel in it, she swung her eyes up to the king's box. The king kept his eyes trained on the two opponents, but Kelraz jumped to his feet. With one swift movement, he pushed past the king and his guards and disappeared through the dark doorway into the castle. Tyla smiled and turned back to Leman.

"Yes," the champion nodded, but his smile wavered, "that's why we're here."

He pulled back one of his meaty fists, but Tyla stepped to the side so it wouldn't land. "No," she said. "I think you've proven only that your blessing from Shurka can beat any centaur. And what that means is that Shurka can best both of us."

The champion scowled at her, showing his first real sign of anger since her opening challenge. His eyes darted questioningly up to the king's box. Tyla followed his gaze and saw the king waving on the champion as if encouraging him to handle the issue. Tyla suppressed a smile.

"I propose a new contest," she bellowed to the crowd. "I believe that centaurs are better fighters than humans because we are both stronger AND smarter than humans. I propose a contest of the mind. A game of riddles!"

26

RIDDLES

The crowd roared their approval. The champion's tight smile betrayed his concern. Of course Eleka was *much* better at riddles than she was. But she prayed silently to Kurta that she would outsmart the champion in Eleka's stead. That's all she needed.

"I agree to your proposal," the champion said. When the crowd cheered and yelled, he waved his hands for quiet. "However, these good people have come here to see a fight and a fight I shall give them. I propose the game thus. Four questions each."

"Four claws does a dragon make," Tyla recited the old fledgling saying.

Leman nodded in acknowledgment. "If the opponent answers a question wrong, the one putting forth the question is allowed to give one blow…undefended. And if they get it right…the same the other way."

"So, if I answer correctly, I land a blow?" she clarified. "But if I'm wrong, you land a blow?"

Leman nodded slowly. Tyla hesitated. She knew she would answer some of the questions incorrectly. She would never get all of them right. The champion could use his undefended strike to his advantage, eventually killing her and claiming it an accident. But she'd come this far and didn't see a way around his counterproposal that wouldn't invite something worse from the king's box.

"Agreed," she said.

"Who shall go first?" Leman smiled.

Tyla forced a small bow. "The Champion of Justice should decide, of course."

Leman bowed back. "Ask your question."

With all the commotion Tyla hadn't thought this far and Eleka's riddle still tumbled through her head, so she asked the first question that came to her mind. "I cannot talk but always reply when I am spoken to. What am I?"

The champion's brows creased only briefly. Then he grinned. "An echo."

Oh spit, her mind rattled before his fist landed and her head rang. She stumbled to the side from the strike, but managed to keep her hooves under her.

That was an easy one but he still had to think about it. Now I need to make sense of Eleka's message.. 'I use my mind', 'we are all restrained', 'we need to be'... 'a tree'?

The crowd hooted and cheered the winner. Tyla nodded and waved for Leman to ask his question.

"A man goes out for a walk in the storms of fall with nothing to protect from the rain. He has no hat or hood or shade. But by the end of his walk there isn't a single wet hair on his head. Why doesn't he have wet hair?"

Tyla pawed nervously at the ground. She didn't know this one. She had never heard it before. Probably because it was a human hair riddle and she didn't know many humans. Or rather most of the humans she knew were also dragons. She thought for a moment but came up with nothing. Did the man use a tree to protect him? She glanced up at the king and Kelraz's empty chair. The king reclined casually on his throne with an amused smile on his face.

Tyla looked over the king's head. *The awning? No. No shade. Why isn't his hair wet? Eleka would know this. Eleka would try to trick me with it. The man wouldn't have any hair.* "Aha!" she yelled. "The man is bald!"

The champion's face fell and he took a step back.

"Undefended, right?" Tyla said, stepping closer.

Having been broken and healed numerous times in the past few days, her wrists couldn't take much more abuse, so she swung her whole upper torso, folded her fist into her chest and struck the man across the jaw with her elbow.

As the champion fought to regain his balance, Tyla took a moment to rehearse Eleka's message and find a new one for Leman. *'My will is free', 'I give to fleas', 'this sacred plea'. I give to the key this sacred plea?* That sounded almost correct, but she needed a question for the champion quickly.

"Alright!" she said loudly. "Lighter than what I'm made of, more of me is hidden than is seen." She had never actually seen one of these, nor had she ever traveled to a place where she could, but she and Eleka had learned about them from her father, and it was her father's riddle.

The champion chuckled a moment but his smile wavered. He searched the crowd, the sky and the king. "Um…"

As he took time to think, Tyla stepped closer to him. Her smile grew and her wide eyes brightened. She just might get another free strike. She raised her front leg in anticipation.

"Um…a soul?"

Tyla shook her head emphatically. "An iceberg."

"Yes!" Tyla and Leman turned toward the happy little cry as Narsun shrank back into his mother's side. Then they turned to the king, who waved his bejeweled hand at Tyla to take her blow. She didn't have the strength to push off her back legs like she wanted to, so she settled with pounding her hoof into the man's gut. With a solid connection, the man doubled.

"Ask your next question," she directed. "If you can."

Leman took a minute to breathe and eventually stood up straight to look at Tyla. She recognized the anger and maybe even, she thought, a little hurt in his eyes.

"The more you take, the more you leave behind," the man said, his tone almost daring her to get it right.

'My will is free', she thought quickly while he waited for her response. *'I give to fleas', 'this sacred plea'. Well, we're not giving anything to fleas. This might be the spell to give the key to someone else, so it could be 'I give to thee'. And we're talking about the keys, so 'this sacred plea' could be 'this sacred key'!*

Tyla needed to answer Leman's riddle so she scuffed the ground with her hoof to buy time before she answered. She knew she was getting close. *The more I take? What can I take? Blows? A beating? Apparently not. But this whole process is taking too much time. We have less than three days before the end of fall and the beginning of spring. If we're too late—*

"Time," Tyla answered quickly. But something else struck her deep in her mind. The key. She had to take the key now, and Eleka had instructed her how to do it in her message.

The champion shook his head with a delighted, evil gleam in his eye. "Footsteps!" He laughed heartily at her miss.

"But," Tyla held up her hand, her mind spinning between Leman's and Eleka's riddles, "'time' could be the answer too!"

Still chuckling, the champion looked questioningly to the king again and Tyla followed his eyes. The king leaned forward in his throne and shook his head.

Tyla braced herself, but the champion punched her in the shoulder so hard that she flew up and away the entire height and length of a dragon. She slid along the ground when she landed and almost passed through the fence that enclosed the arena.

Blinking into the brilliant blinding sunshine, her eyes watered while her lungs begged for air. She couldn't breathe. Slamming a fist into her human stomach, she forced herself to take a long, rattling breath. She knew she was down, but she was still alive and conscious.

Coughing, she used her weak left wrist to push herself up and gradually got her hooves under her. Every cough rattled her body with prickly shockwaves. She forced herself to take even breaths. She couldn't absorb another hit. But if she didn't get back in the game, the champion wouldn't allow her to live.

'My will is free, I give to thee, this sacred key'. Alright Tyla, her mind insisted, *you got Eleka's key riddle, now what?*

She knew the outcome would be the same whether she gave the champion hard or easy questions, and whether she won this contest or not. She pulled something from her memory, not really caring how difficult it was. "I'm found in the sea and on land but I can't walk or swim. I travel by foot but I'm toe-less. No matter where I go, I'm never far from home."

Leman scrunched his brow. She didn't think it was a difficult riddle, but perhaps this human was even more dense than she realized. After all, he only ever—in the arena, anyway—relied on his brute strength and Shurka's supernatural gift.

"Um…" the champion scratched at his chin.

Tyla crept closer, putting her broken left hand behind his back in a friendly manner. If she got another strike, she would try to do as much damage as possible and she needed her good hand to do it.

"Uh…is it…" Leman looked up at Tyla's oversized eyes. "Is it water?"

Tyla grinned. "A snail." And drove her elbow into his ribs. She didn't feel the satisfying crunch of bones breaking, but she smiled when he gasped for breath. The crowd gasped along with him.

The champion coughed a little with his hands on his knees, then stood up straight to face her.

"Oh, do you need a moment to catch your breath?" Tyla taunted, hoping to keep him mentally off-balance. But she knew she couldn't win. Even if she won this contest of riddles, the king wouldn't free any of the centaurs he held in the castle. She would die after she answered her last question, whether she won or not. He would use that key and silence her forever.

My will is free, I give to thee, this sacred key.

The champion grinned but he narrowed his eyes. "I'm going to miss you," he whispered. Then cleared his throat. "Only one color but not one size. Stuck at the bottom, yet easily flies. Present in sun, but not in rain. Doing no harm and feeling no pain."

Tyla rolled her eyes. She had obviously overestimated this human's intelligence. Trotting away as if in thought, she easily recalled only a week ago when her sister gave her the same riddle.

Trying to hide her pleasure before turning to look over her shoulder, she answered, "A shadow," then quickly threw her back leg into his face. Luckily his soft head had enough give to protect her leg from breaking again, but the jolt did lurch up into her haunches.

Strategy, she thought. *Brains, that's exactly how Eleka would win.*

She allowed a smile to tickle her lips but quickly wiped it away. She willed herself not to look up at the king's box, but from the corner of her eye she could see a black figure come back out of the castle doors to the balcony and sit down next to the king. Her heart pounded. This would be much harder with Kelraz present, but she no longer had a choice. Quickly, she estimated how far the faerie would have to fly from the box to reach her and how long it might take. It would be close, especially with how slow Leman seemed to be in the head. His slow brain and slow tongue might give Kelraz the advantage.

Casually walking to the edge of the arena in front of the crowd farthest from the king's box she waved Leman toward her with her good arm. "How about a different kind of riddle for my last one?" she called out. "We'll need the crowd's help for this."

The crowd murmured with excitement as the champion came closer. Fighting the screaming pain in her bad shoulder and arm, Tyla lifted her left hand to welcome her opponent and waved the right one to the crowd. "Can you help us," she called out again, "with a tongue twister?"

The crowd cheered and clapped and yelled their approval.

"A what?" Leman asked. "I'm not twisting anything."

"No, no," Tyla grinned at his dim-wittedness. "Young centaurs are taught tongue twisters—you might call them tongue teasers or mouth riddles." She kept her voice raised so the audience would understand the game. "I say something and you have to repeat what you heard three times, quickly, immediately after I say it. The crowd can make sure you say it correctly. What do you think?"

She turned to the crowd and received raucous applause. They also seemed ready for something different. She turned back to the champion smiling. He couldn't turn her down now.

"Alright," he said. "Let's hear it."

Tyla placed her hand on Leman's shoulder, just above the key in his chest. "Are you ready?" she said.

He nodded, but turned his head away from the crowd to face her ear. In a low whisper that only she could hear he said, "I'll still blast you to pieces when this is all over. Even if you win, it won't save your life."

Tyla forced a false grin as if he'd said something pleasant and took a deep breath. No matter what he had said to her thus far, she was glad she had another means of gaining the key without hurting the simple-minded human.

Before she could lose her nerve, she faced the crowd with the king and Kelraz on the balcony at her back, leaned in close to Leman and quickly rattled off, "My will is free, I give to thee, this sacred key."

Several things happened around her at once but Tyla focused on the golden key glowing brighter and stronger in the champion's chest, hoping she'd said the right words and counting on Leman to repeat them and not just blast her instead.

The champion clamped his eyes shut, focusing on repeating every word correctly. "My will is free, I give to thee, this sacred key…"

Behind her, she heard a guttural scream "NO!" from the direction of the king's box. Still facing Leman, she barely spotted in her peripheral vision the black robe flying down from the king's box, emanating the musical hum of faerie wings. As much as she wanted to check

Kelraz's progress, she couldn't rip her eyes away from Leman and the key.

"… My will is free, I give to thee, this sacred key…" he repeated a second time.

Dark figures appeared in the sky through the rain surrounding the castle and beyond, flying over the city walls toward the arena. The crowd of onlookers noticed them as well and a rumble ran through the people.

The brilliant sunshine overhead dissipated and rain descended on the arena and spectators. Many heads turned up in confusion.

"…My will is free, I give to thee, this sacred key."

The golden key lifted free from the champion's chest and hovered a talon's length above his smooth pink skin. Tyla's breath caught in her throat. With her hand on his shoulder, Tyla allowed her arm to swipe her hand down at the key just as Kelraz's hand met hers. They crashed together and slammed against the ground past Leman.

"NO!" Kelraz screamed in her face as he jerked at her hand.

Tyla squirmed, but in her defeated state Kelraz easily pinned her to the ground. Her vision blurred but she didn't know if it was from the rain in her face or the fact that her head hit the ground so hard. The faerie grabbed her broken arm and slammed it into the soil as rain poured around them. Tyla screamed before she blinked to clear her vision and she and Kelraz both turned their heads to look at her hand. Painstakingly, she allowed her fingers to peel open. Embedded in the middle of her palm glowed the golden Sun Key.

27

INCURSION

Leman stood bewildered and shrunken in the rain nearby as Tyla struggled in the mud with Kelraz. She tried to push him off, but the faerie was too strong. He pressed his knee into her lower belly and she howled. He wasn't strong enough to rebreak her ribs, but he came close when he cracked some. His wings quickly lifted him and he circled behind Tyla bringing her arm with him. Placing a knee in her human shoulder, he turned her and pressed her face to the ground. Mud slithered into her mouth and nostrils and rain poured over her in torrents.

She tried to turn and push at the faerie, but he pressed harder, cracking more ribs and compressing her entire body. Tyla tried to worm her hooves under her but at the angle Kelraz held her, she couldn't twist far enough to stand. She twisted her face up to him looming over her, pulling a dagger from under his rain-soaked black robe.

"I'll take it myself," he muttered.

As the dagger lifted over her, Tyla looked at the Sun Key in her palm. She had to be able to use this to her advantage. But whether she used it or not wouldn't matter because Kelraz already knew exactly where it was, so the most important thing now was keeping it from him. He must not have been able to take it from Leman without incurring the wrath of the king and the rest of the humans and probably even being attacked by the champion himself. It was up to her now to keep it away from Kelraz. But how could she use it? What could she do with it?

She had once asked Jassan what it felt like when he used the unique power of his key. He said that he felt a pinch in his chest when he thought about using the Moon Key, and then he could transform into anything he could imagine. But with her body so bruised and broken she knew she would never pinpoint a single pinch in her chest or anywhere else.

However, Trivnor said that when he wanted to use his key it felt like his stomach was turning or twisting. Hearing two different stories had made her and Eleka wonder if the feeling inside was different for every person and every key, with only the gatekeeper able to discern and use each key in perfect harmony. In any case, eyeing the glittering dagger poised above her heart, she knew she needed the power of the Sun Key she held in her hand at this moment more than ever.

Her teeth ground as she wished she could change into her dragon form and use her claws to dig into the faerieman's face and chest and rip his little dagger and arm from his puny faerie shoulder. Imagining the burning in her chest hotter than ever, she felt the same sensation as when the little old faerie healed her and prayed to Shurka that she would be able to change into a dragon. The dagger flew toward her chest. Tyla screamed and slammed her palm with the key against the ground. Her wrist snapped away from the ground and several cracks tremored up her arm as her arm broke and folded back against itself unnaturally.

She wailed and waited for the dagger to strike. Instead, the weight of the faerie slid from her shoulder. A rumble of thunder tore through the rain and a sound like a mountain falling from the Rock Clouds and crashing to the ground shuddered the world.

She held her eyes closed a moment against the coming attack, then slowly blinked them open when the dagger *didn't* strike home. No dagger protruded from her chest. No new wounds opened anywhere. Easing herself into a sitting position with her non-mangled arm, she surveyed the arena. Leman, Kelraz, the guards, all the people who had gathered to watch the games, Sharot and her family, even the king and his guards lay quiet and still, their eyes closed, littering the ground in and around the arena.

She slowly wriggled and got her hooves under her. Rain poured around her in sheets. Turning a slow, limping circle, she gawked at the king's box, which had disintegrated and fallen to the ground in shattered chunks of stone and gilded cloth. The double doors between the arena into the castle stable and centaur stalls were gone. A massive gaping hole in their place led to scattered pieces of wood and stone where the stalls had been. She could see through to the other side of the stables, beyond the rest of the animals' shelters, where another enormous hole yawned into the front courtyard of the castle… and the way to freedom.

"Eleka," Tyla mumbled, staggering toward the stable. The wreckage of the stable walls had been blasted past the centaur stalls. Tyla cradled her arm against her chest as she picked her way into the rubble.

She lifted the remnants of a stall door to find Danyel, lying on his side. Nicks and bruises covered most of his face and chest, but he breathed shallowly.

Tyla leaned over him and placed her shattered hand with the key in it on his chest. If anyone could heal her or any of the centaurs still living, it was Danyel. She needed him. She needed him healed and capable.

The heat in her chest from when she wished and prayed to turn into a dragon hadn't left. A warmth glowed in her broken hand and Danyel took a deep breath before his eyes popped open.

"Tyla?"

Tyla yanked her hand away from him to cradle it back against her own chest. In the back of her mind, she noticed a subtle easing of pain in her hand and wondered if it had anything to do with Danyel. "Danyel?"

"What happened?" he looked up at her and asked.

"I'm not entirely sure," she said honestly, "but we need to get out of here, as quickly as possible."

Danyel clambered up to stand next to her and surveyed the scene. "What did you do?"

Tyla shook her head. "I don't know. Please don't ask."

The two centaurs' heads snapped to the side when the sound of a groan drifted to them, then another.

"Tyla."

She heard her name whispered over the sound of the building rumbling around them.

"This thing is going to come down," Danyel said, waving dust away as he inspected the trembling rafters over their heads. "Go get her. We have to get everyone out of here."

Tyla limped through the wreckage to where Eleka lay covered in mud and hay and wood. Half sobbing and half laughing, she dug her twin out of the rubble with her barely functional hand.

"What happened?" Eleka asked as she grew alert and pushed herself to her feet amidst the carnage. As Tyla helped her sister stand, Eleka grabbed the hand that held the Sun Key and pulled it toward herself. Tyla yelped but wasn't strong enough to stop her. Eleka's eyes gazed at the key as she whispered, "What did you do?"

"Talk later," Tyla answered curtly, pulling her hand back to her chest. She remembered the trick Sharot had shown her with the extra long wrappings around her chest. Unwrapping the outside layer, she slung it over her broken arm and attached it to her chest.

Centaurs, guards and animals around them began to stir with moans and groans and neighs and snorts, but she continued searching the carnage. The rubble appeared to begin shifting on its own with prisoners and guards alike trying to dig themselves out of the heaps.

Danyel pulled stones off one of the centaurs. "Myles!" Tyla exclaimed and stumbled through the rubble to help.

"Tyla, we need to go," Eleka urged, keeping her face turned toward the arena outside, where humans who had been in the crowd began to rouse.

Tyla didn't respond and helped pull Myles to his feet. Danyel grabbed his healer's pack from the remains of his stall and moved to another stall to help other centaurs.

"You," came a gravelly voice from further inside the blasted stable space. Ugly Fad pushed slats of wood from himself. Blood slicked the side of his face as he stood to face Tyla. "You'll never ge' ou' of 'ere alive. I'll see to tha'. I don't care wot creature you turn into."

He reached to his side and pulled from its loop his long golden rod with the sharp yellow gem on the end. Tyla stepped toward him.

"Tyla, no," Eleka said, pulling at her shoulder. "We need to go. Now."

Tyla pushed her sister's hands away. "Help the others," she ordered under her breath as she brushed past.

Tyla stood in front of Ugly Fad, who waved his weapon in her face.

"Well, Ugly," she said. "It's been fun. But I think I won this game." She lifted her palm to reveal the golden key shining down at him.

"Never," he hissed.

Ugly Fad's face shrank into a pinched grimace. His lips pulled back in a grimy snarl as he stabbed the golden rod toward Tyla. Without the confines of a stall or shackles or hobbles to hinder her, she easily side-stepped the jab.

Grabbing the shaft of the rod just above Ugly Fad's hand with her good hand, she firmly twisted it up and out of his grip. Her muscles remembered the move her mother drilled her on and flipped the rod in her grip, stabbing the pointed gem back into Ugly Fad's chest. The man went rigid and wailed. His knees buckled and he fell to the ground in a sizzling heap.

"Sorry I didn't have time to make you suffer like I promised," she muttered, standing over him. Her face spread into a satisfied smile until she watched a short, balding wraith rising from Ugly Fad's body.

Tyla's eyes widened. "Now we have to go!" she yelled.

All the captive centaurs had wrestled themselves out from under the rubble and stumbled to the opening opposite the arena. Tyla scampered down the row toward them with Ugly Fad's wraith at her tail. The path through the wreckage led to the castle entrance and beyond that, the main gates and their escape.

Tyla met up with Eleka, still in the remains of the stable, and looked together back toward the growing sounds in the arena where Kelraz, Leman, the king, the spectators and all the guards clambered to their feet. Beyond the arena they could see the dark cloud of approaching wraiths growing larger in the sky.

"Stop them!" Kelraz yelled, pointing at the centaurs.

"Go!" Tyla directed Danyel and Myles and the rest of the centaurs, pushing them toward their freedom.

They didn't hesitate. Having shaken off most of the rubble from the blast, the centaurs moved faster through the still rumbling castle. They hobbled through the remains of the stalls, but Kelraz and the guards were already climbing over the stable rubble as well. As she and Eleka stayed back and pushed the rest of the centaurs through the entrance doors, several wraiths flew in behind them through the gaping hole from the arena with Ugly Fad's gnarled and twisted wraith in the lead.

Tyla wanted to scream but any sound caught in her throat. She lifted both hands in front of her as if she could stop the oncoming swarm with her will alone. Then she remembered. She didn't have her will alone. She had a blessing from the goddess of the sun, Shurka.

Pulling her arm from her makeshift sling, she pointed her palm at the rushing enemies, then braced it with her right hand. She thought of the power the champion had used—the heat and force the key exerted against her—and directed it toward her attackers.

The key had every effect she hoped for. The burning in her chest surged above any other sensation in her body, but instead of feeling the painful sear of Ugly Fad's healing rod or punishments, this intense heat was comforting like sitting in the sun on a warm summer day. Her body skittered back a step as the power of the sun slammed the oncoming horde back out of the far opening on the opposite side of the stable. Only when they all lay on the ground motionless, even the wraiths, did Tyla wrap her arm against her chest again. Turning, she followed her sister through the stable doors and beyond the castle gates to freedom.

Tyla blasted the gates leading from the king's castle to the city of Gormitor with the power from the key and the broken and bruised centaurs stumbled through the cobbled streets, pushing past onlookers who stared in the direction of the castle.

"Where are all those centaurs going?"

"Are the games over?"

"Did they come from the castle?"

"Did one of them win?"

The clamor grew as they fled past bewildered humans gawking between them and the castle. Tyla and Eleka glanced behind themselves hoping not to see any wraiths or guards in chase, but soon could no longer see the castle as they fled past buildings and vendors in the city.

"What do we do now?" Tyla felt so relieved being able to ask her sister for support. They slowed to watch the other centaurs help each other push aside all the humans to escape.

"Get these centaurs home," Eleka answered. "Heal everyone, then we head south. Emma, Gizi and Dasha need help."

"If we can get out of the city," Tyla said as she spotted Danyel supporting Myles and the two stumbling together through the streets. "Danyel can heal them when they reach Zanna and send everyone home from there. You and I need to—"

"No, Tyla," Eleka leaned closer to Tyla's ear so no one else would hear. "Haven't you figured it out yet? The yellow stones that they used to heal us—"

"—and punish us—"

"Yes, and punish us," Eleka continued, "those stones also hold the power of the sun—the sun can both harm and heal."

"What are you saying?" Tyla pushed past a vendor without thinking to wade after the others. She had her own theories about the stones that had been used on her, but she wanted to hear it from Eleka before she would believe them.

"I think Kelraz taught the king how to put the dual power of the sun into those stones," she said, following. "One stone to hurt, the other to heal. That means you can do both with the key."

"I can heal with the key?" Tyla asked, searching out Danyel in the crowd of centaurs and humans again. Danyel happened to glance back at her and she saw him give her the smallest smile. She remembered putting her hand with the key on his chest and wishing he would wake up, and he did.

"I think so," Eleka said. "But anyone you heal might become extremely tired like we did. The sun can sap your energy too."

"True enough," Tyla mused, remembering slipping into unconsciousness repeatedly after healing.

"But if you don't heal too much—"

"—if I'm careful—"

"—you could heal *everyone*," Eleka finished.

She put so much emphasis on the last word that Tyla glanced over at her sister. Eleka gave her a knowing nod. *Everyone.* The word echoed in her mind as the realization hit her. The power of the Sun Key could heal Jassan's unhealable injuries. Tyla could use the key to heal

Emma's father, all the centaurs in the Zanna hospital. Everyone.

The healing images sank into her head as the centaurs stumbled closer to the gates of Gormitor, their last barrier to freedom. Human guards opened the gates and centaurs streamed through them ahead of her and Eleka. It was ridiculously obvious to her that most of the humans, even the king's own guards, had no idea that the king had been keeping the centaurs captive. Tyla had never been so happy that a king kept secrets from his people.

"Where to now?" Danyel yelled back at the twins.

"Zanna!" Eleka waved him on. "Keep going!"

The road to Zanna from Gormitor led directly past Sharot's little village and through the trees beyond that marked the last of the Kingdom of Gormirom. As the centaurs stumbled down the path, dozens of wraiths of every form descended on them from the trees to the south, screeching and bellowing their fury.

"No!" Tyla shouted. Fleeing the horrifying monsters, the centaurs scattered from the road and across a field toward Sharot's village.

Tyla lifted her broken arm and pointed the key toward the wraiths. Bracing it with her good hand, she blasted the power of the sun toward them. Several fell in their tracks—not dead, but still and quiet. Blasting the ones behind, she took out several more, but neglected to support her wrist again and felt it snap.

Screaming, Tyla pulled the fresh break to her chest. "I can't do it!" she cried. "I can't keep using it with my broken arm!"

Eleka pressed her hands against Tyla's cheeks and opened her large eyes wider as she drew her sister close. "Tyla," Eleka's voice was soft and even. Her face filled Tyla's vision so she couldn't see the wraiths behind her. "Heal yourself."

"But I need to help everyone else," she muttered, her voice shaking.

"What has mother always told us?"

Tyla remembered again her mother's admonishment to save herself and her body. "We can't help anyone if we don't take care of ourselves first," they recited the phrase together.

"Heal yourself," Eleka said again.

"What if I become to tired?"

"You won't," Eleka insisted. "The power of Shurka flows through you. It won't overpower you."

Tyla nodded, although unsure how to do it. She stared down at her broken arm held by her good hand. The warmth in her chest spread and she thought of her wrist and arm being healthy and whole. She imagined her legs strong again. She thought about her broken ribs knit back together and her breathing easing. She coerced her mind to clear, her spine to straighten, and imagined her muscles flexing and contracting strong and firm.

Blinking away the diminishing throbs of discomfort, she brought her focus back to Eleka, who smiled at her.

"Ok," Eleka said, taking a deep breath. "*Now* you can help everyone else."

28

OFFENSIVE

Tyla ran beside Eleka across the field and slipped between two small buildings at the edge of Sharot's village. Sharot's home, the one she shared with traveling dragons, sat on the far side of the little cluster of buildings in the distance, easy to spot being larger than most of the others. In front of them within the village, wraiths poured through the rain, eagerly searching for hiding centaurs and anyone else they could find. Humans escaped into their homes and buildings, but those caught outside quickly joined the growing ranks of wraiths.

Tyla and Eleka rounded a corner and saw Danyel supporting Myles against a wall while he kicked a human wraith away from them. Tyla lifted her left hand with the key and forced the power of the sun into the wraith Danyel was fighting then into another coming around a different corner. Both wraiths fell away to lie still in the mud. Her fully healed arm and mind buzzed with power.

"How did you take it from the champion?" Myles choked when Tyla and Eleka joined them under the eaves of a little home.

"Um," Tyla glanced at Eleka, but returned her gaze to Myles, "very carefully and with great skill," she finally said. "I won it the way Eleka would have."

"However you did it," Danyel said, glancing between her and the unconscious wraiths, "we need to use it to get the centaurs home safely. Maybe if you lead the way into the trees, then we can escape from the humans and you can make a path for us through—"

"She can't," Eleka interrupted. "She can't use it too much. It would, um, it would alert the humans and they could follow us." She turned to Tyla. "Isn't that right?"

"Yes," Tyla said, not hesitating to support her smarter sister's explanation. "It's like a beacon, after all. Then humans and wraiths and everyone else would be chasing us. But I'll try to make a path."

Two more faerie wraiths flew around the corner and headed for them, so Tyla quickly used the key to pound them against another home. Once they were motionless, the four centaurs ran toward the far side of the village. Tyla knocked four more dragon wraiths from the sky as they gained a clear view of the forest beyond the village.

Roaring and screaming echoed through the trees. The four centaurs stopped short as more dripping black creatures billowed from the road to the south, descending upon the centaurs now galloping toward the forest cover.

Tyla used the key to blast four more wraiths. Five. Six. Seven.

"I can't keep this up forever!" Tyla yelled.

"There's too many of them!" Danyel called.

Suddenly a roar echoed over all the others through the trees in front of them. Tyla's heart dropped when three dragon shapes lifted above the treetops. But her eyes widened and her heart sang when she recognized the brilliant blue of Vanora with two other dragons. The next moment, out of the trees sprang dozens of centaurs, every one of them armed with ropes and crossbows.

With Vanora in the lead, the dragons glid down upon five dragon wraiths. Tyla used the key to drop one of them out of the way. With rope dangling from their claws, the dragons immediately entangled the monsters. Vanora lifted to hover and the Zanna centaurs whooped and hollered to attract the wraiths' attention, then shot their majikal ropes through them and whipped the ends to wrap the ropes around each one.

As the Zanna centaurs attacked the wraiths, the freed centaurs slipped quickly into the trees. Other smaller and younger centaurs, who had been concealed withing, pulled them into the forest darkness to disappear inside.

Tyla struck down one of the dragon wraiths before it overpowered Vanora. Once the other dragons had the dragon wraiths under control, Vanora swooped down to settle next to Tyla and Eleka.

"Thank Shurka, it's good to see you!" Danyel rejoiced when the blue dragon landed.

"Father!" the youthful call erupted across the field from the trees. When Tyla located the voice's owner, she recognized the little Zanna centaur girl who had come to fetch Danyel to help feed Myles's newborn centaur foals.

Myles pulled his head up and his arm away from Danyel's support. "Mazzi?" he mumbled, then louder, "Mazzi!" He stumbled and tripped his way across the field. When a faerie wraith swooped down to try to snag him, Tyla pummeled it with the key. Finally, Myles tumbled into his daughter's waiting arms.

Little Kira's mother stood next to their older daughter with a crossbow in her hands and a coil of rope over her shoulder. If Tyla had to guess, she assumed she must have left the babies in May's care and joined most of the rest of the settlement coming to help. Myles briefly embraced his mate, then turned his head to Tyla. Mazzi and her mother followed his gaze. When Myles placed a hand on his chest and nodded to Tyla his family did the same. After she nodded back at them, the reunited family turned and fled into the forest.

A dripping black faerie wraith tried to reach the escaping group, but once they were out of sight its attention turned to Tyla and the others. Vanora stomped on it as it swept toward them and pinned it down with her claw.

"We need to go," she growled, flinging the creature away over three rooftops.

"It's alright," Danyel said. "Tyla has the champion's stone. She can use it to blast our way to Zanna."

Tyla and Eleka stared at each other. "I can't, though," Tyla said. "I have to stop using it and find another way to escape."

"Why can't you use it?" Vanora snapped her head around to Tyla and didn't see the human wraith running at her from behind. Tyla zapped the wraith and Vanora took a moment to look it over before adding, "Because a lot more of those are coming."

"Uh," Tyla started, but she had no idea how to answer. So she turned to Eleka for help.

"Using it, uh, draws more wraiths to it," Eleka said.

"But the wraiths weren't drawn in when the champion used it," Danyel said, eyeing Tyla and the key in her hand.

Tyla's stomach twisted at Danyel's pained face. She knew that he knew she wasn't telling them the whole truth and her heart hurt lying to him, even only if by omission. "It didn't work that way for him," was all she could force out while she tried to hide her hand.

Vanora stood by, glaring at the twins.

"It's complicated," Eleka finally said. "But what we need to do now is find somewhere to hide and figure out how to get out of here."

"Vanora!" a voice whispered loudly.

Their heads turned at the sound and Tyla recognized Sharot standing in the doorway of her home. She waved a claw for them to join her inside.

Scanning around them, Vanora spread her wings to cover their movement and the three centaurs trotted toward the dragon home. They heard a scream and turned toward the sound. Two small humans huddled between a wall and the backside of a centaur standing in front of them. The centaur thumped its hooves against a faerie wraith as the wraith tried to lift into the air. Tyla began running toward them just as another human ran out from the other side of the building with a length of rope in their hands.

"Will this do?!" the human yelled to the centaur.

"Yes!" the centaur yelled back. "I'll pin its arms and you tie it down!"

The centaur threw himself into the wraith and slung his arms around the monster. The human looped the rope and threw it around the wraith. The centaur pulled back on the rope to tighten the loop and the centaur and human wrapped the wraith entirely, containing the threat.

"They're working together," Danyel said from Tyla's side.

"That can only mean good things," Vanora said, urging the three on.

They witnessed the aftermath of the battle as they scampered through the rain under Vanora's protective wings toward Sharot's doorway.

A centaur and a human helped each other wrap a long blanket around a human wraith's head. "This is no longer the person you knew," the centaur said solemnly. "You'll have to find somewhere to keep these creatures away from everyone else."

Another female centaur was helping three humans hobble and blind a centaur wraith. "He died a long time ago," the centaur said. "I've accepted that."

One of the humans put her hand on the centaur's arm. "I'm sorry," she whispered up to her.

"Things are going to change," Vanora said low in Tyla's ear.

Vanora ran ahead, Tyla assumed to guard their retreat, and reached Sharot's home first. With Danyel and Eleka ahead of her, Tyla followed. A dark shape came out from behind a corner to their left, but when Tyla snapped her head around in alarm, she saw the grey dragon elder from Zanna, Sylam.

"Watch out!" he yelled, pointing a claw at the group.

Before Tyla turned, a swirl of writhing smoke twisted around Eleka, lifting her and then carrying her before tackling her to the ground several dragon lengths away. The centaur wraith screamed and wailed as it clawed and pounded on Eleka. Tyla's breath caught in her throat. She tumbled toward the creature, trying to change into her dragon form, but the cold metal cuff still attached to her leg restricted her and she felt only coldness in her belly. Eleka screamed. Vanora and Sylam appeared on top of the writhing forms and ripped the wraith from Eleka. They pinned the wraith to the ground as another centaur joined them with ropes and Sylam and the centaur set to bind the wraith.

Tyla stumbled forward, her eyes locked on Eleka.

"Get her inside!" Vanora yelled.

Tyla scooped Eleka by the arms, her fingers sliding on blood and rain. She tried to pull her up to stand, but her leg wobbled at the wrong angle and Eleka screamed again. Danyel joined Tyla on Eleka's other side and they finally dragged her together through the entrance to Sharot's and Makus's home.

Laying her down on the warmed stone floor, Tyla quickly assessed the damage. Eleka cried as Tyla's hands moved over her. Blood covered her from fresh, deep gouges digging into her face, neck, shoulder and chest. Tyla pulled the extra cloth from Eleka's wrappings to wipe the blood away from the skin around her lacerations.

As Tyla tended her injuries, Eleka grew quiet. Gentle moans escaped as Tyla watched black speckles spread over the seeping wounds. Eleka's breathing shook and quickened.

"Tyla," Danyel said. "You have to heal her. Tyla!"

Danyel tugged on Tyla's shoulder to seize her attention. But Tyla shook her head to refuse him; the only vision in her mind was of Eleka telling her she shouldn't use the key. "I'm not supposed to use it. More wraiths will come."

Danyel shook his head. "Tyla," he said, his lowered voice gentle but urgent, "I can't heal this. I saw you heal yourself. You have the power. You have to do it."

Tyla searched the room and saw Sharot, Makus and Narsun cowering against a wall. Vanora sat in front of the heavy cloth over the doorway, guarding the entrance. Danyel stood over her and Eleka. She couldn't let Eleka die. But if she used the key, Kelraz would send more wraiths to find her and who would be hurt or killed next? She couldn't protect them all, heal them all, and flee at the same time. She must heal Eleka, but she had to do it carefully.

"If I heal her with the stone," Tyla said, her eyes bouncing between Danyel and Vanora, "more will come."

"I'll hold them off," Vanora said, crouching in an attack stance. "Do what you must."

"I'll hold them off too," Sharot said. "We're already planning to go back to the Island Ruck after what happened here today. I'll help you fight your way out."

"But how will we get away?" Tyla said, touching the metal cuff still attached to her leg. "I can't fly."

"I have an idea," Danyel said suddenly. He turned to Makus. "Do you have a long strip of dark-colored cloth? Something I can wrap around myself?"

Makus thought for a moment, then his lips twitched into a grin. He nodded and slipped down the stone stairs into the earthen caves below.

Danyel turned back to Tyla. "You're going to have to trust us," he said. "Well, Vanora, in particular."

Vanora narrowed her eyes at him. "What are you planning?"

"Well…" Danyel grinned at her. Makus clomped quickly back up the stairs and handed Danyel a length of brown cloth. He thanked the dragon and Makus rejoined Narsun, wrapping his wing around the little dragon. "I think," Danyel said, throwing the cloth around his chest and over his head with a flourish, "that it's my turn to play dragon."

"Ok," Tyla sat next to Eleka, who moaned and seeped blood onto the warm stone floor of Sharot's home. Black speckles spread over the raw flesh on Eleka's face and chest. Tyla's leg pulled up next to her sister and Danyel and Vanora stood over them. "I heal her, burn this thing off my leg and we hoof it, right?"

"Right!" Vanora and Danyel said together.

"You'll take care of her," Tyla said in warning, trying to give Vanora the same stern look she'd seen from her mother so many times before.

"You have my wyrd," Vanora said. "I'll die for her."

"Let's hope you don't have to," Danyel said. Pulling the ends of the brown cloth, he swathed it around his chest and over his head before tucking them into the folds he'd created. "Does it look ok?"

"You look horrible," Tyla said, shaking her head. She cast her eyes over to Sharot, standing by the doorway and next to Vanora. "I'm sorry," she said. "I'm sorry I brought your family into any of this."

Sharot pursed her lips. "Sometimes life has to get worse before it can get better," she said. "We'll weather this storm."

Tyla tipped her head to thank Sharot and Makus, then looked at Danyel and Vanora. "Ready?"

They both nodded.

Tyla took a deep breath and held it as she placed her hand with the key on Eleka's arm below one of the gashes which continued to seep blood and ooze black spots across it. Warmth intensified in her chest and spread through her as she imagined Eleka's wounds healing, the black corruption disappearing and the skin closing.

Everybody watched the gashes remake themselves as Tyla thought about each one. Blood that had seeped out remained on Eleka's skin, but the skin sealed itself and became whole and unblemished. Her leg and arm snapped into place and the broken skin and hide pressed together over their wounds. Eleka gasped several times as the healing took place, then finally drew in a long, deep breath. With the healing completed, Eleka's eyelids fluttered closed, her breathing evened and her head lolled to the side.

"She'll probably be out for a while," Tyla said, pulling her hand away.

Everyone froze at the sounds of a screech and a roar outside.

"Quickly," Vanora hissed. "The other."

Tyla nodded and pressed the key against the band around her leg. Recalling the warmth in her chest, she pushed searing, white-hot power into the metal. The cuff warmed under her hand, and heat penetrated through it to her leg. As the metal grew hotter it scalded her ankle.

She groaned through clenched teeth as the pain grew worse, wishing the job done but wondering if she needed to continue.

"Tyla!" Danyel screamed, yanking her hand away from her leg.

The heat in her chest eased as Danyel moved her hand away, but the cuff stayed in place. The metal where she had placed the key glowed the color of daisy petals. Danyel reached down and grasped the cuff on either side of the burnished color and snapped the ring apart.

Once it fell away, Tyla roared! She never loved her dragon form so much as she did in that moment—spots and all. Dragon fire burned hot in her belly and she smiled as she held up her claw with the key embedded in her pad. She sprang to her feet as more roaring reached them from outside the entrance.

"Go!" Vanora shouted to the others, running back toward Eleka.

"Go!" Sharot yelled, pushing Makus and Narsun to the door. Vanora scooped up a drowsy Eleka before they all bolted through the opening. Several dark shapes smashed against a building outside.

"Come on!" Danyel called. Tyla wrapped her claws around Danyel's belly while Vanora did the same with Eleka.

"Be careful with her!" Tyla yelled. "I'm trusting you!" Her voice followed Vanora, with a limp Eleka in her grip, as they flew out the door.

29

MISGUIDED

"Where are they?" Tyla grumbled, pacing the length between two huge boulders overlooking the same gorge where, on the other side, Eleka had been kidnapped by humans. "They're taking too long."

"They'll be here," Danyel said. "It took us a while to get here too."

Tyla wrung her hands and stared into the trees. She and Danyel had flown in the opposite direction of Vanora, who carried Eleka. Danyel hung limp in Tyla's claw to make it look like she was carrying an unconscious Eleka. Under the rainy night sky, no one watching would have been able to tell which pair might have been Tyla and Eleka, although neither of them were. Wraiths followed both pairs, but she had hoped that more of them would have followed her and Danyel.

"It won't be safe for you," Tyla worried for Danyel and the rest of the centaurs. "When you and Vanora fly away, any wraiths to see you might follow you as well as us. You might lead them back to Zanna."

"I can always come with you," Danyel said suggestively, a small grin playing on his lips. Tyla knew he only partially meant it. By now she could tell that he would choose to accompany her on her journey even if it meant mortal danger every moment. But he also knew what her answer would be.

"I'm sorry, you can't," was all she could muster as an answer.

"I know," Danyel said, scuffing his hoof in the mud. "I don't know *why,* so I'll just keep asking."

Tyla shook her head, looking into the trees around them. "It wouldn't be safe," she repeated. "What we're doing, no one will be safe with us. We never should have involved any of you."

She paced as she thought back to the argument she and Eleka had only days ago about whether to seek protection in villages or settlements. She regretted now that she had insisted on it and ever considered asking someone to take them in. She should have listened to Eleka and found somewhere to hide well away from any settlement. Then none of this would ever have happened to the centaurs *or* the humans.

"If you hadn't," Danyel countered, his face following her trot back the other way again, "you wouldn't have stopped those atrocious games and you wouldn't have saved dozens of centaurs."

"The humans at Gormitor would still be free of wraiths, though. Sharot and her family would be safe in their home too. Even the centaurs in Zanna would have learned to stay out of the forests and been safe."

Danyel stopped her with a hand on her arm, swinging her around to face him. "Would we, though? I have a feeling that things wouldn't have stayed safe and quiet for anyone."

She couldn't answer him. Pursing her lips, she turned away. She hated his eyes gazing on her as if she were the most beautiful flower and the sharpest blade rolled together in one. She felt like neither of those things.

"Eleka and I have to leave when she gets here," she said finally, "for everyone's sake."

Danyel's hand slid from her arm when they both heard footsteps pound through the trees behind them.

"Get back," Tyla hissed, waving Danyel to one of the boulders.

She ran to the other, which hovered over a drop the length of two dragons down toward the raging river below them. As she peered around the edge of the boulder, she saw Vanora, limping through the trees with Eleka on her back.

"Vanora," Tyla breathed with relief. "Where have you been?"

Vanora pulled Eleka from her back and Danyel eased the still-sleeping centaur to the ground.

"We had to double back a few times," Vanora panted. "I got here as fast as I could, but the way was cut off by dozens of wraiths."

"Did the other centaurs make it back to Zanna?" Tyla asked, inspecting her sister.

"Yes," Vanora lay down on the muddy ground. "Most of the wraiths followed us or tried to cut us off from going south for some reason."

"I know why they did," Tyla said. She stopped short of explaining that somehow Kelraz knew her friends were in the southern part of Avonoa. He wanted to keep the twins from rejoining them at all costs. He couldn't have them reunite and find more keys.

Tyla pushed Eleka's hair away from her face, then stood to face Vanora and Danyel. "You two should go," she said. "But be careful. And if I can ask one last favor of you, please try to keep them away from us as long as possible."

Vanora nodded, but added, "what about the goblins?"

"Goblins?"

"The same ones from Zanna," Vanora answered. "I saw them pressing this way too. They move quickly for such small creatures."

Tyla groaned. "I almost forgot about them. How are they finding us?"

"I'm sure they're just following the most commotion," Vanora waved at her.

"Are you sure I can't come with you?" Danyel asked. "I could try to intervene with the goblins."

"The best use you can be to us now," Tyla said, "is as a distraction. For both goblins and wraiths. I'm sorry."

Danyel nodded, but held his tongue.

"It's alright," Vanora said, standing next to Danyel. "We'll do our best to steer everyone away from you. Fair winds, my friend."

Tyla slowly lifted her eyes to Danyel's face. The pain in it twisted her heart. She suddenly realized what it must feel like for a male dragon's heart to break for someone. Hers felt like it was splitting in two.

"Be careful," she said, and stepped away. "Fair winds."

"Fair winds, Tyla," Danyel said. He allowed Vanora to urge him through the forest and trotted to keep up with her. After they disappeared into the darkness, his voice echoed back to her when he shouted, "I'll see you again!"

When they were gone, Tyla quietly muttered back, "I hope so."

Tyla bent over her sister's face and held her breath as Eleka's eyes blinked open. She reached her claw to wipe away the water on her cheeks, unsure if it had come from the sky or from her own eyes.

"What happened?" Eleka croaked, struggling to become alert. "Where are we?"

"'What happened?'" Tyla asked, clearing her throat so her voice wouldn't catch. "Well, I saved you…again. 'Where are we?'" She drew herself up to stand tall. "Let's see. We have a key, and not just any key!" She waited for Eleka to look up at her before she waved her padded palm with the Sun Key embedded in it and watched Eleka's eyes grow wide. "We have to find Emma and Gizi and Dasha. We have to find Jassan, Trivnor, Lokna and Burk. We have to get that band off you." She pointed a claw at the metal cuff around Eleka's leg. "And once we do all that, wraiths will descend on us and try to kill us and drag our souls back to Kelraz. That's about where we are."

"I meant where in *Avonoa* are we?"

"Oh, I figured you already knew that." Tyla pointed and said, "farther north than I would like. Somewhere in the northern part of Gormirom. I had to carry you here to avoid some wraiths. You're welcome. Again."

Eleka blinked up at her sister. "You're healed?"

Tyla lifted her front leg with the key in her pad. "Still. Yes."

"And everyone else—Vanora, Myles?"

"Better off than we are, I imagine."

"Danyel?"

"Gone." Tyla gazed into the dripping sky. "With any luck he and Vanora made it back to Zanna and are holding off any wraiths."

"I'm sorry, Ty."

"Me too," Tyla said, scratching her neck with one claw. "But if I were you I'd be more sorry for *us* right now. We have to find Dasha and the rest and get all these keys back to Trivnor, and we only have two days to do it."

"So we melt this thing off me and claw it to the south to find the others?" Eleka said tapping the metal band on her leg.

"That's about it," Tyla said. "I wanted to wait until you were conscious again to use the key so I didn't have to carry you the entire way."

"Smart," Eleka said.

"Yeah," Tyla said, "I'm learning to think like you."

"Terrifying."

"That's what I thought."

A roar sounded in the distance and the two girls' heads swiveled toward it.

"Alright," Eleka said, stretching her leg out to Tyla. "We need to go."

Tyla reached out with her claw and placed it on Eleka's leg. "It's not going to feel great," she warned before she started.

"What? Ow! Ow! Ow!" she yelped as the key burned through the metal against her leg.

A louder roar sounded. Closer.

"Hurry! Ow!" Eleka yelped again.

Tyla pulled her hand away from the band. It glowed like a white-hot ember. Wrapping her claws around either side of the brilliant color, she twisted it and the metal snapped and fell away from Eleka's leg.

Another roar and a louder screech. Much too close.

"Change!" Tyla yelled and Eleka jumped up beside her in her own dark red striped dragon form.

Tyla charged toward an opening in the trees and spread her wings with her sister on her tail. The red pair lifted into the drizzling rain above the trees. More dark shapes materialized on the horizon. Her centaur dragon eyes could make out three different shapes in the sky and more against the dark ground, coming fast.

"This way!" Eleka called as she flew ahead of her.

"But that's the wrong way," Tyla yelled back. "You're going north. Emma is to the south!"

Both girls swung their heads, searching the trees around them. More wraiths lifted into the air to the west from Gormirom. To the east, wraiths popped out of the treetops. Under them the forest moved as shadows dripped between the branches. To the south, several faerie wraiths and an immense dragon wraith lifted into the sky. To the southwest, a small group of grey-skinned goblins pointed to the dragons in the sky and ran even faster than they should toward them over the hilltops.

Both dragons' eyes met. At the same time, they both yelled. "North!"

THE END

The adventure will continue in

THE GIANTS OF TORTHOTH

DRAGONS OF AVONOA

BOOK THREE

Note to Readers!

I hope you are enjoying the adventure in Avonoa as much as I enjoyed creating it! Although I love to write and create these stories, being an independent author is hard. I don't have teams of people ghost-writing, editing, formatting and marketing for me. I do it all on my own, so my only support comes from readers like you! Thank you for supporting me and my craft.

Another way you can support a lowly indie author like myself is to leave me a review. Feel free to use the link and/or QR code below to let others know how much you enjoyed the story! You can also pick up one of my other publications, the Avonoa series, or People of the Storm!

You can also sign up for my newsletter to be the first to hear about sales, signing events and new books! Sign up at avonoa.com, hrbcollotzi.com, or peopleofthestorm.com.

Or follow me on social media…
Facebook @hrbcollotzi
Instagram @hrbcolloti